Mary and the Giant

Books by Philip K. Dick

THE BEST OF PHILIP K. DICK
THE BOOK OF PHILIP K. DICK
CLANS OF THE ALPHANE MOON
THE COLLECTED STORIES OF PHILIP K. DICK
CONFESSIONS OF A CRAP ARTIST
THE COSMIC PUPPETS
COUNTER-CLOCK WORLD
THE CRACK IN SPACE
DEUS IRAE (*with Roger Zelazny*)
THE DIVINE INVASION
DO ANDROIDS DREAM OF ELECTRIC SHEEP?
DR. BLOODMONEY
DR. FUTURITY
EYE IN THE SKY
FLOW MY TEARS, THE POLICEMAN SAID
GALACTIC POT-HEALER
THE GAME-PLAYERS OF TITAN
THE GANYMEDE TAKEOVER (*with Ray Nelson*)
THE GOLDEN MAN
A HANDFUL OF DARKNESS
HUMPTY DUMPTY IN OAKLAND
I HOPE I SHALL ARRIVE SOON
IN MILTON LUMKY TERRITORY
THE MAN IN THE HIGH CASTLE
THE MAN WHO JAPED
THE MAN WHOSE TEETH WERE ALL EXACTLY ALIKE
MARTIAN TIME-SLIP
A MAZE OF DEATH
NOW WAIT FOR LAST YEAR
OUR FRIENDS FROM FROLIX 8
THE PENULTIMATE TRUTH
THE PRESERVING MACHINE
PUTTERING ABOUT IN A SMALL LAND
RADIO FREE ALBEMUTH
ROBOTS, ANDROIDS, AND MECHANICAL ODDITIES
A SCANNER DARKLY
THE SIMULACRA
SOLAR LOTTERY
THE THREE STIGMATA OF PALMER ELDRITCH
TIME OUT OF JOINT
THE TRANSMIGRATION OF TIMOTHY ARCHER
UBIK
UBIK (*screenplay*)
THE UNTELEPORTED MAN
VALIS
THE VARIABLE MAN
VULCAN'S HAMMER
WE CAN BUILD YOU
THE WORLD JONES MADE
THE ZAP GUN

PHILIP K.
DICK

Mary and the Giant

• • • • • • • • •

ARBOR HOUSE New York

 Published in the
United States of America by Arbor House Publishing Company
and in Canada by Fitzhenry & Whiteside, Ltd.

Manufactured in the United States of America

10 9 8 7 6 5 4 3 2

Library of Congress Cataloging-in-Publication Data.

Dick, Philip K.
Mary and the giant.

I. Title.
PS3554.I3M3 1987 813'.54 86-26502
ISBN 0-87795-850-5

For information about the Philip K. Dick Society, write to:
PKDS, Box 611, Glen Ellen, CA 95442

Design by Laura Hough

Mary and the Giant

1

To the right of the hurrying car, beyond the shoulder of the highway, stood a gathering of cows. Not far beyond rested more brown shapes, half-hidden by the shadow of a barn. On the side of the barn an old Coca-Cola sign was vaguely visible.

Joseph Schilling, seated in the back of the car, reached into his watch pocket and brought out his gold watch. With an expert dig of his nail he lifted the lid and read the time. It was two-forty in the afternoon, the hot, midsummer California afternoon.

"How much farther?" he inquired, with a stir of dissatisfaction. He was weary of the motion of the car and the flow of farmlands outside the windows.

Hunched over the steering wheel, Max grunted without turning his head. "Ten, maybe fifteen minutes."

"You know what I'm talking about?"

"You're talking about that town you marked on the map. It's ten or fifteen minutes ahead. I saw a mileage sign back a ways; at that last bridge."

More cows came into sight, and with them more dry fields. The far-off mountain haze had, during the last few hours, settled gradually into the depths of the valleys. Wherever Joseph Schilling looked the haze lay dully spread out, obscuring the baked hills and pastures, the assorted fruit orchards, the occasional calcimined farm buildings. And, directly ahead, the beginnings of the town: two billboards and a fresh egg stand. He was glad to see the town arrive.

"We've never been through here," he said. "Have we?"

"The closest we've come is Los Gatos, on that vacation you took back in '49."

"Nothing can be done more than once," Schilling said. "New things must be found. As Heraclitus would say, the river is always different."

"It all looks alike to me. All this farm country." Max pointed to a herd of sheep collected under an oak tree. "That's those sheep again . . . we've been passing them all day."

From his inside coat pocket Schilling got out a black leather notebook, a fountain pen, and a folded map of California. He was a large man, in his late fifties; his hands, as he gripped the map, were massive and yellowed, the skin grained, fingers knobby, nails thick to the point of opaqueness. He wore a rough tweed suit, vest, somber wool tie; his shoes were black leather, English-made, dusty with highway grime.

"Yes, we'll stop," he decided, putting away his notebook and pen. "I want to spend an hour getting a look around. There's always the possibility this one might do. How would you like that?"

"Fine."

"What's the town called?"

"Thigh Junction."

Schilling smiled. "Don't be funny."

"You have the map—look it up." Grumpily, Max admitted, "Pacific Park. Set in the heart of rich California. Only two days of rain a year. Owns its own ice plant."

Now the town proper was emerging on both sides of the highway. Fruit stands, a Standard station, one isolated grocery store with cars parked in the dirt plot alongside it. From the highway wandered narrow, bumpy roads. Houses came into sight as the Dodge pulled over into the slower lane.

"So they call this a town," Max said. Gunning the engine, he swung the car into a right turn. "Down here? Over here? Make up your mind."

"Drive through the business section."

The business section was divided into two parts. One part, oriented around the highway and its passing traffic, seemed to be mostly drive-ins and filling stations and roadside taverns. The second part was the hub of the town; and it was into that area the Dodge now moved. Joseph Schilling, his arm resting on the sill of the open window, gazed out, watchful and absorbed, gratified by the presence of people and stores, gratified that the open country was temporarily past.

"Not bad," Max admitted, as a bakery, a pottery and notion shop, a modern creamery, and then a flower shop went by. Next came a book shop—Spanish adobe in style—and after that a procession of California ranch-style homes. Presently the homes fell behind; a gas station appeared and they were back on the state highway.

"Stop here," Schilling instructed.

It was a simple white building with a painted sign that flapped in the afternoon wind. A Negro had already risen from a canvas deck chair, put down his magazine, and was coming over. He wore a starched uniform with the word *Bill* stitched across it.

"Bill's Car Wash," Max said as he put on the parking brake. "Let's get out; I have to take a leak."

Stiffly, with fatigue, Joseph Schilling opened the car door and stepped onto the asphalt. In getting out he was obliged to crowd past the packages and boxes that filled the back of the car; a pasteboard carton bounced onto the running board and he bent laboriously to catch it. Meanwhile, the Negro had approached Max and was greeting him.

"Right away. Put it right through, sir. Already call' my assistant; he over getting a Coke."

Joseph Schilling, exercising his legs and rubbing his hands, began walking around. The air smelled good; hot as it was it lacked the stuffy closeness of the car. He got out a cigar, clipped off the end, and lit up. He was breathing dark blue smoke here and there when the Negro approached.

"He working on it right now," the Negro said. The Dodge, pushed bodily into the wash, had half-disappeared into the billows of soap and hot water.

"Don't you do it?" Schilling asked. "Oh, I see; you're the engineer."

"I'm in charge. I own the car wash."

The door of the men's room was open; inside, Max was gratefully urinating and muttering.

"How far is San Francisco from here?" Schilling asked the Negro.

"Oh, fifty miles, sir."

"Too far to commute."

"Oh, they commute, some of them. But this no suburb; this a complete town." He indicated the hills. "A lot of retired people, they come here because of the climate. They settle; they stay." He tapped his chest. "Nice dry air."

Clouds of high school students roamed along the sidewalks, across the lawn of the fire station, gathering at the windows of the drive-in on the far side of the street. One pretty little girl in a red sweater held Schilling's attention as she stood sipping from a pasteboard cup, her eyes large and vacant, her black hair fluttering. He watched until she noticed him and ducked defensively away.

"Are those all high school children?" he asked Bill. "Some of them look older."

"They high school students," the Negro assured him with civic authority. "It just three o'clock."

"The sun," Schilling said, making a small joke. "You have sun most of the year . . . it ripens everything faster."

"Yes, crops here all year round. Apricots, walnuts, pears, rice. It nice here."

"Is it? You like it?"

"Very much." The Negro nodded. "During the war I live down in Los Angeles. I work in a airplane factory. I ride to work on the bus." He grimaced. "Shee-oot."

"And now you're in business for yourself."

"I got tired. I live a lot of different places and then I come here. All during the war I save for the car wash. It make me feel good. Living here make me feel good. I can sort of rest."

"You're accepted here?"

"There a colored section. But that good enough; that about all you can expect. At least nobody ever say I can't come and live. You know."

"I know," Schilling said, deep in thought.

"So it better here."

"Yes," Schilling agreed. "It is. Much better."

Across the street the girl had finished her soft drink; crumpling the cup, she dropped it into the gutter and then strolled off with friends. Joseph Schilling was looking after her when Max emerged from the men's room, blinking in the sunlight and buttoning his trousers.

"Hey, hey," Max said warningly, seeing the expression on his face. "I know that look."

With a guilty start, Schilling said, "That's an exceptionally lovely girl."

"But none of your business."

Returning to the Negro, Schilling said, "What's a good place to walk? Up toward the hills?"

"There a couple of parks. One of them just down there; you could walk over. It small, but it shady." He pointed the direction, glad to be helpful, glad to be of service to the large, well-dressed white gentleman.

The large, well-dressed white gentleman looked about him, his cigar between his fingers. His eyes moved in such a way that the Negro knew he was seeing past the car wash and the Foster's Freeze drive-in; he was seeing out over the town. He was seeing the residential section of estates and mansions. He was seeing the slum section, the tumbledown hotel and cigar store. He was seeing the fire station and high school and modern shops. In his eyes it was all there, as if he had caught hold of it just by looking at it.

And it seemed to the Negro that the white gentleman had traveled a long way to reach this one town. He had not come from nearby; he had not even come from the East. Perhaps he had come all across the world; perhaps he had always been coming, moving along, from place to place. It was his cigar: it smelled foreign. It wasn't made in America; it came from outside. The white gentleman stood there, giving off a foreign smell, from his cigar, his tired tweed suit, his English shoes, his French cuffs made of gold and linen. Probably his silver cigar cutter came from Sweden. Probably he drank Spanish sherry. He was a man of and from the world.

When he came, when he drove his big black Dodge up onto the lot, it was not merely himself that he brought. He was much bigger than that. He was so immense that he towered over everything, even as he stood bending and listening, even as he stood smoking his cigar. The Negro had never seen a face so far up; it was so far that it had no look, no expression. It had neither kindness nor meanness; it was simply a face, an endless face high above him, with its smoking, billowing cigar, spreading out the whole world around him and his assistant. Bringing the whole outside universe into the little California town of Pacific Park.

Leisurely, Joseph Schilling walked along the gravel path, his hands in his pockets, enjoying the activity around him. At a pond children were feeding bread to a plump duck. In the center of the park was a bandstand, deserted. Old men sat here and there, and young, full-breasted mothers. The trees were pepper and eucalyptus, and they were extremely shady.

"Bums," Max said, trailing behind him and wiping his perspiring face with a pocket handkerchief. "Where are we going?"

"Nowhere," Schilling said.

"You're going to talk to somebody. You're going to sit down and talk to one of these bums. You'll talk to anybody—you talked to that coon."

"I've fairly well made up my mind," Schilling said.

"You have? About what?"

"We'll locate here."

"Why?" Max demanded. "Because of this park? There's one like it in every town up and down—"

"Because of this town. Here there's everything I want."

"Such as girls with big knockers."

They had reached the edge of the park. Stepping from the curb, Schilling crossed the street. "You can go find yourself a beer, if you prefer."

"Where are you going?" Max asked suspiciously.

Ahead of them was a row of modern stores. In the center of the block was a real estate office. GREB AND POTTER, the sign read. "I'm going in there," Schilling said.

"Think it over."

"I've thought it over."

"You can't open your store here; you won't make any money in a town like this."

"Maybe not," Schilling said absently. "But—" He smiled. "I can sit in the park and feed bread to the duck."

"I'll meet you back at the car wash," Max said, and shambled resignedly off toward the bar.

Joseph Schilling paused a moment, and then entered the real estate office. The single large room was dark and cool. A long counter blocked off one side; behind it, at a desk, sat a tall young man.

"Yes, sir?" the young man said, making no move to rise. "What can I do for you?"

"You handle business rentals?"

"Yes, we do."

Joseph Schilling moved to the end of the counter and regarded a wall map of Santa Clara County. "Let me see your listings." From between his fingers appeared the white edge of his business card. "I'm Joseph R. Schilling."

The young man had risen to his feet. "I'm Jack Greb. Glad to meet you, Mr. Schilling." He extended his hand warily. "Business property? You're looking for a long-term lease on a retail outlet?" From under the counter he got a thick, stave-bound book and laid it open before him.

"Without fixtures," Schilling said.

"You're a merchant? You have a California Retail Sales License?"

"I'm in the music business." Presently he added, "I used to be in the publishing end; now I've decided to try my hand at record retailing. It's been a sort of dream of mine—to have my own shop."

"We already have a record shop," Greb said. "Hank's Music Bar."

"This will be a different type of thing. This will be music for connoisseurs."

"Classical music, you mean."

"That's what I mean."

Wetting his thumb, Greb began spiritedly turning the stiff yellow pages of his listings book. "I think we have just the place for you. Nice little store, very modern and clean. Tilted front, fluorescent lighting, built only a couple of years ago. Over on Pine Street, right in the heart of the business section. Used to be a gift shop. Man and his wife, nice middle-aged couple. He sold out when she died. Died of stomach cancer, as I understand."

"I'd like to see the place," Joseph Schilling said.

Greb smiled slyly back across the counter at him. "And I'd like to show it to you."

2

At the edge of the concrete loading platform of California Readymade Furniture an express truck was taking on stacks of chrome chairs. A second truck, a P.I.E. van, waited to take its place.

In faded blue jeans and a cloth apron, the shipping clerk was lethargically hammering together a chrome dinner table. Sixteen bolts held the plastic top in place; seven bolts kept the hollow metal legs from wobbling loose.

"Shit," the shipping clerk said.

He wondered if anybody else in the world was assembling chrome furniture. He thought over all the things people could be imagined doing. In his mind appeared the image of the beach at Santa Cruz, the image of girls in bathing suits, bottles of beer, motel cabins, radios playing soft jazz. The pain was too much. Abruptly he descended on the welder, who, having slid up his mask, was searching for more tables.

"This is shit," the shipping clerk said. "You know it?"

The welder grinned, nodded, and waited.

"You done?" the shipping clerk demanded. "You want another table? Who the hell would have one of these tables in his house? I wouldn't give them toilet space."

One gleaming leg slipped from his fingers and fell to the concrete. Cursing, the shipping clerk kicked it into the litter under his bench, among the bits of rope and brown paper. He was bending to pluck it back out when Miss Mary Anne Reynolds appeared with more order sheets ready for his attention.

"You shouldn't have done that," she said, knowing how clearly he could be heard in the office.

"The hell with it," the shipping clerk said, as he got down a fresh leg. "Hold this, will you?"

Mary Anne put down her papers and held the leg while he bolted it onto the chair frame. The smell of his unhappiness reached her, and it was a thin smell, acrid, like sweat that had soured. She felt sorry for him, but his stupidity annoyed her. He had been like this a year and a half ago, when she started.

"Quit," she told him. "Why keep a job you don't like?"

"Shut up," the shipping clerk said.

Mary Anne let go of the completed table and watched the welder fuse the legs in place. She enjoyed the sputter of sparks: it was like a Fourth of July display. She had asked the welder to let her try the torch, but he always grinned and said no.

"They don't like your work," she said to the clerk. "Mr. Bolden told his wife that unless your work picks up, he isn't going to keep you on."

"I wish I was back in the army," the clerk said.

There was no use talking to him. Mary Anne, with a swirl of her skirts, left the work area and returned to the office.

At his desk was elderly Tom Bolden, the owner of California Readymade; and, at the adding machine, was his wife. "How's he coming?" Bolden asked, presently aware that the girl had returned. "Sitting around loafing, as usual?"

"Working very hard," she said loyally, seating herself before her typewriter. She didn't like the shipping clerk but she refused to involve herself in his downfall.

"You have that Hales letter?" Bolden said. "I want to sign it before I leave."

"Where are you going?" his wife asked.

"Up to San Francisco. Dohrmann's says there's defects in the last load."

She found the letter and passed it to the old man to sign. It was a faultless page she had done, but she felt no pride; chrome furniture and typing and the problems of a department store blurred meaninglessly into the clatter of Edna Bolden's adding machine. She reached within the material of her blouse and adjusted her bra strap. The day was hot and empty, as always.

"Should be back by seven," Tom Bolden was saying.

"Be careful of the traffic." That was Mrs. Bolden, who was holding the office door open for him.

"Maybe I'll bring back a new shipping clerk." He had almost left; in the girl's ears his voice receded. "Ever seen out there? Filthy as a pigsty. Rubbish everywhere. I'm taking the panel truck."

"Go up El Camino," Mary Anne said.

"Whatsat?" Bolden halted, cocking his head.

"El Camino. It's slower but a lot safer."

Muttering, Bolden slammed the door. She heard the panel truck start up and move off into traffic . . . it didn't really matter. She began examining her shorthand notes. The noise of the power saws filtered through the walls into the office; and there was a series of taps as the shipping clerk pounded at his chrome tables.

"He's right," she said. "Jake, I mean."

"Who in the world is Jake?" Mrs. Bolden asked.

"The shipping clerk." They didn't even know his name. He was a pounding machine . . . a faulty pounding machine. "There has to be litter around a shipping bench. How can you wrap without litter?"

"It's not for you to decide." Mrs. Bolden put down her adding-machine tape and turned toward her. "Mary, you're old enough to know better—talking this way, as if you're in charge."

"I know. I was hired to take dictation, not to tell you how to run your business." She had heard it before, a number of times. "Right?"

"You can't work in the business world and behave this way,"

Mrs. Bolden said. "You've got to learn that. You simply must have respect for those above you."

Mary Anne listened to the words, and wondered what they meant. They seemed to be important to Mrs. Bolden; the heavyset old woman had become upset. It amused her a little, because it was so silly, so unimportant.

"Don't you want to know things?" she asked curiously. Apparently they didn't. "The men found a rat in the fabric shed. Maybe rats have been eating the fabric rolls. Wouldn't you want to find out? I should think you'd want somebody to tell you."

"Of course we want to find out."

"I don't see the difference."

There was an interval of silence. "Mary Anne," the older woman said finally, "both Tom and I think the world of you. Your work is excellent—you're bright and you're quick to learn. But you must face reality."

"What reality is that?"

"Your job!"

Mary Anne smiled, a slow, meditative glimmer. She felt light-headed, filled with a buzzing sound. "That reminds me."

"Reminds you of what?"

"I think I'll pick up my brown gabardine coat from the cleaner." With deliberation, she examined her wristwatch; she was conscious of Edna Bolden's outrage, but the old woman was wasting her time. "Can I leave early this afternoon? The cleaner closes at five."

"I wish I could reach you," Mrs. Bolden said. She was troubled by the girl, and her distress showed. Mary Anne could not be appealed to; the usual promises and threats meant nothing. They fell on closed ears.

"I'm sorry," Mary Anne said. "But it's so stupid and mixed up. There's Jake out there hating his job—if he doesn't like his job he should quit. And your husband wants to fire him because his work is sloppy." She gazed up intently at Mrs. Bolden, distressing her even more. "Why doesn't somebody do something? It was like this a year and a half ago. What's the matter with everybody?"

"Just do your work," Mrs. Bolden said. "Would you do that? Would you turn around and finish your letters?"

"You didn't answer me." Mary Anne continued to scrutinize her, without compassion. "I asked if I could leave early."

"Finish your work and then we'll discuss it."

Mary Anne considered a moment and then turned back to her desk. It would take fifteen minutes to get to the cleaners, if she walked from the factory directly into town. She would have to leave at four-thirty to be sure of arriving in time.

As far as she was concerned the matter was settled. She had settled it herself.

In the tired brilliance of late afternoon she walked along Empory Avenue, a small, rather thin girl with short-cropped brown hair, walking very straight-backed, head up, her brown coat slung carelessly over her arm. She walked because she hated to ride on buses, and because, on foot, she could stop when and wherever she wished.

Traffic in two streams moved along the street. Merchants were beginning to emerge and roll up their awnings; the stores of Pacific Park were shutting for the day.

To her right were the stucco buildings that made up Pacific Park High School. Three years ago, in 1950, she had graduated from that school. Cooking, civics, and American history; that was what they had taught her. She had been able to use the cooking. In 1951 she had got her first job: receptionist at the Ace Loan Company on Pine Street. In late 1951, bored, she had quit and gone to work for Tom Bolden.

Some job that was—typing letters to department stores about chrome kitchen chairs. And the chairs weren't very well built, either; she had tried them out.

She was twenty years old, and she had lived in Pacific Park all her life. She did not dislike the town; it seemed too frail to survive dislike. It, and its people, played odd little games, and the games were taken seriously, as were the games of her childhood: rules that could not be broken, rituals that involved life and death. And she, with curiosity, asking why this rule, why that custom, and playing anyhow . . . until boredom came, and, after it, a wondering contempt that left her cut off and alone.

At the Rexall drugstore she halted a moment and inspected the rack of paperbound books. Bypassing the novels—they were too full of nonsense—she selected a volume entitled *Thirty Days to a More Powerful Vocabulary*. That, and a copy of the Pacific Park *Leader,* cost her thirty-seven cents.

She was coming out of the drugstore when two shapes encountered her. "Hi," one said, a young man, well-dressed. A salesman from Frug's Menswear; his companion was unknown to her. "Seen Gordon today? He's looking for you."

"I'll telephone him," she said, starting away. She disliked the odor of flowers that hung over Eddie Tate. Some men's cologne smelled all right; Tweany's was like the smell of wood. But not this . . . she had no respect for this.

"Whatcha reading?" Tate asked, peering. "One of those sexy books?"

She appraised him in her fashion: calmly, with no intention to do harm, merely wanting to know. "I wish I was sure about you."

"What do you mean?" Tate said uneasily.

"One day I saw you standing around the Greyhound terminal with a couple of sailors. Are you a fairy?"

"My cousin!"

"Gordon isn't a fairy. But he's too stupid to tell the difference; he thinks you've got class." Her eyes widened; the sight of poor Eddie Tate's dismay amused her. "You know how you smell? You smell like a woman."

The man's companion, interested in a girl who would speak so, waited close by, listening.

"Is Gordon at the gas station?" she asked Tate.

"I—wouldn't know."

"Weren't you hanging around there today?" She didn't let him go; she had the creature stuck.

"I was by for a minute. He said maybe he'd drop over to your house tonight. He said he came around Wednesday and you weren't home."

Tate's voice diminished as she, collecting her coat, started off, not looking back at either of them. Not caring, really, about either of them. She was thinking about home. Discouragement set in, and she felt her pleasure, the lift that fairy-baiting gave her, fade.

The front door was unlocked; her mother was in the kitchen fixing dinner. Noise clanged in the six units of the building: television sets and kids playing.

She entered, and faced her father.

In his easy chair Ed Reynolds sat waiting, muscular and small, with gray hair like strands of wire. His fingers gripped the chair and he half-rose, gurgling and blinking rapidly; a beer can fell to the floor and then he swept newspaper and ashtray aside. He wore his black leather jacket and beneath it his undershirt, his cotton undershirt, stained with sweat and dirt. Smears of grease crossed his face, his neck; by the chair were his heavy work boots, lumpy with grease.

"Hello," she said, startled as always to see him, as if she had never seen him before.

"Just getting home?" His eyes glowed and his protruding Adam's apple wallowed in brisk little quivers of skin and bristling hair. As she walked toward her bedroom he came after, close on her heels, treading in his sticky socks across the carpet.

"Don't," she said.

"Don't what? Why you just getting home?" He pursued her. "Stop off with some of your nigger friends?"

She closed the bedroom door after her and stood. On the other side his breathing sounded: a low rattle, like something caught in a metal pipe. Not turning her back to the door, she changed to a white shirt and levis. When she came out he had returned to his chair. Before him the TV set radiated.

Entering the kitchen, she said rapidly to her mother: "Did Gordon call?" She avoided the sight of her father.

"Not today." Mrs. Rose Reynolds bent to inspect the casserole steaming in the oven. "Go set the table. Be some help." Back and forth, scurrying between the stove and sink. She was thin, too, like her daughter; here was the same sharp face, eyes that moved constantly, and, around the mouth, the same lines of worry. But from her grandfather—now dead, now buried in Forest Slope Chapel Cemetery in San Jose—Mary Anne had got her directness, the aloof boldness; and her mother lacked that.

Mary Anne examined the contents of pots and said: "I think I'm going to quit my job."

"Oh, good Lord," her mother said, tearing at a package of frozen peas. "You would, wouldn't you?"

"It's my job."

"You realize Ed won't be working a full week for the rest of the year. If it wasn't for his seniority—"

"They'll always make pipe. They won't lay him off." She didn't care; she wished him no good luck. Seating herself at the table she opened the *Leader* to the editorial page. "Want to hear what morons people are? Here's a letter from somebody in Los Gatos saying that Malenkov is the Antichrist, and God will send angels to destroy him." She turned to the medical column. " 'Should I be concerned about a painless sore on the inside of my lip that doesn't seem to heal?' He probably has cancer."

"You can't quit your job."

"I'm not Jake," she said. "Don't make me a Jake."

"Who's Jake?"

"He's been there five years." She found the help-wanted columns and smoothed the newspaper flat. "Of course, I can always marry Gordon and sit home sewing while he fixes flat tires. Little soldier in a uniform. So obedient. Wave a flag, Jake. Gordon."

"Dinner's ready," her mother said. "Go tell Ed."

"Tell him yourself. I'm busy." Absorbed in the help-wanted

columns she reached about for a pair of scissors. The ad looked good, and it was the first time it had appeared.

> Young woman wanted for retail selling. Must be able to meet public and be personable in dress and appearance. Knowledge of music valuable but not essential. Joseph R. Schilling MA3-6041 9 A.M to 5 P.M.

"Go get him," her mother was repeating. "I told you; can't you help me a little? Can't you be of some use?"

"Lay off," Mary Anne said nervously. She cut out the ad and carried it to her purse. "Get up, Ed," she said to her father. "Come on, wake up."

He sat there in his chair, and the sight halted her with dread. Beer had leaked on the rug, an ugly stain that grew as she watched. She didn't want to go close to him; at the doorway she stopped.

"Help me up," he said.

"No." She felt sick; she couldn't imagine touching him. Suddenly she shouted: "Ed, get up! Come on!"

"Listen to her," he said. His eyes were bright, alert, fixed on her. "She calls me Ed. Why can't she call me Dad? Aren't I her father?"

She began to laugh, then, not wanting to but not able to keep from it. "God," she said, and choked.

"Show your father some respect." He was on his feet and moving toward her. "You hear me? Young lady. Listen to me."

"Keep your goddamn hands off me," she said, and rushed back into the kitchen, by her mother; at the cupboard she took out plates. "If you touch me I'll leave. Don't let him touch me," she said to her mother. Trembling, she began setting the table. "You don't want him to touch me, do you?"

"Leave her alone," Rose Reynolds said.

"Is he drunk?" Mary Anne demanded. "How can a man get drunk on beer? Is it cheaper?"

And then, once more, he had hold of her. He had caught her by the hair. The game, the old, terrible game.

Again Mary Anne felt his fingers against her neck, the very strong little hand at the base of her skull. His knuckles dug into her skin and smeared her; she felt the stain grow and spread and seep. She cried out, but it was hopeless; now the rancid beer-breath billowed into her face and he was twisting her around to face him. She, still holding plates, heard the crackle of his leather jacket, the stirring of his body. She closed her eyes and thought of different things: good things and quiet things, things that smelled nice, things distant and peaceful.

When she opened her eyes he had gone; he was sitting down at the table. "Hey," he said, as his wife approached with the casserole, "she's getting nice little tits on her."

Rose Reynolds said nothing.

"She's growing up," he said, and pushed back his sleeves to eat.

3

"Gordon," she said. But it wasn't David Gordon. It was his mother who opened the door, looking out into the night darkness and smiling vaguely at the girl standing on the porch.

"Why, Mary Anne," Mrs. Gordon said. "How nice."

"Is Dave home?" She had, in jeans and cloth coat, left her own house as soon as dinner was over. The sense of escape was strong in her, and she had the ad in her purse.

"Have you had dinner?" Mrs. Gordon asked. Warm dinner smell drifted out. "I'll go upstairs to his room and see if he's still in."

"Thanks," she said, breathing her impatience, hoping he was home because it made things more convenient; she could go to the Wren alone, but it was better to have somebody along.

"Don't you want to come inside, dear?" It seemed natural that her son's fiancée should come in; the woman held the door open, but Mary Anne stayed where she was.

"No," she said. She had no time; she was hunted down by the need to act. Damn it, she thought, the car's gone. The Gordons' garage was empty, so Dave was out. Well, that was that.

"Who's there?" Arnold Gordon's hospitable voice sounded, as he materialized with his newspaper and pipe, slippers on his feet. "Mary, come on in here; what's the matter with you, standing out there?"

Backing down the steps she said: "Dave isn't home, is he? It doesn't matter; I just wanted to find out."

"Aren't you coming in? Just the old folks, Mary. Look—how about ice cream and cake, and we can chat?"

"We haven't seen you in so long," Mrs. Gordon added.

"Good-bye," Mary Anne said. Dear, she thought, how wonderfully my new egg dicer works. You must take it when you and David set up housekeeping. Any date yet? Have some more ice cream.

"Dave's at the Junior Chamber of Commerce meeting," Arnold said, emerging on the porch. "How've you been, Mary? How's the folks?"

"Fine," she said, closing the gate after her. "If he wants me I'm at the Wren. He'll know."

Hands in the pockets of her coat, she started walking in the direction of the Lazy Wren.

The bar was smoky with the confusion of drinking people. She pushed among the tables, past the individuals clustered around the bandstand, and to the piano.

At the piano was Paul Nitz, the intermission pianist. Slumped over, he gazed off into space, a lean, shaggy-blond young man with a dead cigarette between his lips, his long fingers tapping at the keys. Lost in his trance, he smiled up at the girl.

"I thought I heard," he murmured, "Buddy Bolden say." Into the texture of his music he wove a hint of the old Dixie tune. The thread, elaborated and diminished, was lost in the dominant theme: the bop tune "Sleep."

Assembled at the piano were a very few admirers, listening to Nitz ramble. Eyes half-shut, he nodded to one of them; the listener's face responded, and the two men nodded sagely together.

"Yes," Nitz said, "I thought I heard him as clearly as I see you now. News for you, Mary?"

"What?" she said, leaning against the piano.

"Nose is running."

"It's cold outside," she said, brushing her nose with the edge of her hand. "Is he going to sing, soon?"

"Cold," Nitz echoed. He ceased playing and, from around the piano, his few admirers drifted off. The real group waited at the bandstand, and they were more patient. "You don't care," he said to the girl. "You won't be here. Minors. The world's full of minors. Do you care if I'm playing? Do you come and listen to me?"

"Sure, Paul," she said, liking him.

"I'm a hole. I'm a faintly audible hole."

"That's right," she said, sitting down on the bench beside him. "And sometimes you aren't even audible."

"I'm a musical silence. Between moments of greatness."

She felt a little calmer, and looked around the bar, measuring the people, listening. "Good group tonight."

Nitz passed her the remains of his unlit reefer. "You want this? Take it; be delinquent. Go to hell in a bucket."

She dropped the cigarette to the floor. "I want to ask your advice." Since she was here, anyhow.

Getting to his feet, Nitz said: "Not now. I have to go to the bathroom." He started unsteadily off. "I'll be back."

Now she sat alone, picking without enthusiasm at the keys of the piano and wishing Paul would return. He was, at least, a benign presence; she could consult him because he made no demands on her. Withdrawn into his private obsessions, he ambled between the Wren and his one-room apartment, reading Western novels and constructing bop tunes on his piano.

"Where's your pal?" he said, plodding back and settling himself beside her. "That kid, the one with the clothes."

"Gordon. At the Junior Chamber of Commerce meeting."

"Did you know that I was once a member of the First Baptist Church of Chickalah, Arkansas?"

Mary Anne was not interested in the past; burrowing in her purse she produced the ad she had cut from the *Leader*. "Look," she said, pushing it to Nitz. "What do you think?"

He examined the ad at great length and then returned it to her. "I already have a job."

"Not you. *Me*." Restlessly, she put the ad away and closed her purse. It was, of course, the new record shop on Pine Street; she had noticed the remodeling. But she couldn't go there until tomorrow, and the strain was wearing her down.

"I was a member in good standing," Nitz said. "Then I turned against God. It happened all of a sudden; one day I was saved and then—" He shrugged fatalistically. "Suddenly I was moved to get up and denounce Jesus. It was the strangest thing. Four other church members followed me to the altar. For a while I traveled around Arkansas converting people away from religion. I used to follow those Billy Sunday caravans. I was sort of a Blue-Monday Nitz."

"I'm going over there," Mary Anne said. "Tomorrow morning, before anybody else does. They'll have to call, but I know where it is. I'd be good on a job like that."

"Sure," Nitz agreed.

"I'd have a chance to talk to people . . . instead of sitting in an office typing letters. A record store's a nice place; something's always going on. Something's always happening."

"It's lucky for you," Nitz said, "that Eaton stepped out." Taft Eaton was the owner of the Wren.

"I'm not afraid of him." A Negro was crossing the room, and she sat suddenly very upright on the piano bench. And she forgot Nitz beside her, because there he was.

He was a large man, with blue-black skin, very shiny, and—she imagined—very smooth. He stooped, a slump of his muscular body; that was an unbending of his personality, and she, watching him, could feel it flowing across and reaching her even where she sat. His hair glowed oilily, thick, rippled; important hair, elaborately attended to. He nodded to several couples; he inclined his head toward the people waiting at the bandstand, and then he passed on, massive in his dignity.

"There he is," Nitz said.

She nodded.

"That's Carleton B. Tweany," Nitz said. "He sings."

"He's big," she said, and watched fixedly. "Jesus," she said. "Look at him." It made her ache to see him, to imagine him. "He could lift a truck."

It had been a week, now; she had first spotted him on the sixth, the day his stand at the Wren opened. He had, they said, come down from the East Bay, from a club in El Cerrito. In this interval she had measured him, gauged him, absorbed from a distance as much as possible.

"Still want to meet him?" Nitz asked.

"Yes," she said, and shuddered.

"You're sure hopped tonight."

She poked Nitz with her elbow, urgently. "Ask him if he'll come over. Come on—*please*."

He was approaching the piano. He identified Nitz, and then his great dark eyes took in the sight of her; she felt him noticing her and becoming aware of her. Again she shuddered, as if she were rising through cold water. She closed her eyes for an instant—and when she looked again he was gone. He had started on, his hand around his drink.

"Hey," Nitz said, without conviction. "Sit."

Tweany halted. "I got to go make a phone call."

"One second, man."

"No, I got to go call." There was weary importance in his voice. "You know I have matters on my mind."

To Mary Anne, Nitz said: "Golf with the President."

She started to her feet, resting the palms of her hands on the piano top, leaning forward. "Sit down."

He contemplated her. "Problems," he said, and at last found an empty chair at a nearby table; dragging it over with one scoop of his hand, he sat beside her. She settled slowly back, aware of his closeness, aware, in a kind of controlled hunger, that he had stopped because of her. So the coming here had not been wasted, after all. She had got him; for a little, at least.

"What problems?" Nitz inquired.

The magnitude of Tweany's preoccupation increased. "I'm on the third floor. The hot water heater's up there, the one for the whole building." Studying his manicured nails, he said, "The bottom rusted through and sprang a leak. It's leaking water down on the gas jets and on my floor." Indignation entered his voice. "It'll ruin my furnishings."

"Did you call the landlady?"

"Naturally." Tweany scowled. "A plumber was supposed to show up. The usual runaround." He lapsed into moody silence.

"Her name's Mary Anne Reynolds," Nitz said, indicating the girl.

"How do you do, Miss Reynolds," Tweany said, with a formal nod.

Mary Anne said, "Your singing is real cool."

The man's dark eyebrows moved. "Oh? Thank you."

"I come here every chance I get."

"Thank you. Yes, I believe I've noticed you. Several nights, in fact." Tweany stirred. "I have to go phone. I can't have my sofa ruined."

"Imported Tasmanian mohair," Nitz murmured. "The extinct, primitive, fuzzy-haired mo."

Tweany was on his feet. "Glad to have met you, Miss Reynolds. I hope I'll see you again." He departed in the direction of the phone booth.

"The *green* fuzzy-haired mo," Nitz added.

"What's the matter with you?" Mary Anne demanded, annoyed by Nitz's singsong of dissent. "I read about a hot water heater that exploded and killed a whole bunch of children."

"You read that in an ad, a Prudential ad. Seven danger signs of cancer. Why didn't I insure my roof?" Nitz yawned. "Use aluminum pipe . . . deters garden pests."

Mary Anne looked after Tweany, but she could no longer see him; the haze had swallowed him up. She wondered how it felt to know somebody like him, to have such a big man nearby.

"You're wrong," Nitz said.

She started. "What?"

"About him. I can tell the way you're looking . . . there you go again. Another plan."

"What plan?"

"Always. You in your coat, and your hands in your pockets. Standing around somewhere, with that worried, plotting look on your face. Waiting for somebody to show. What's the trouble, Mary? You're smart enough; you can take care of yourself. You don't need brave Sir Noodlehead to protect you."

"He's got poise," she said. She was still watching; he was bound to reappear. "I respect that. Poise and bearing."

"What's your father like?"

She shrugged. "None of your business."

"*My* father," Nitz said, "used to sing me good-night songs."

"So," she said. "Fine."

"They do that," Nitz murmured. "Mum, mum, mum," he trailed off sleepily. "Oh, I see my coffin comin', mamo. Whump, whoo-whoo." He tapped on the piano with a coin. "Now play it. Yah."

Mary Anne wondered how Nitz could be sleepy when there were so many things to worry about. Nitz seemed somehow to expect the world to take care of itself. She envied him. She wished, suddenly, that she could let go for a moment, relax long enough to have comforting illusions.

In her mind appeared the remnant of a long-ago rhythm, a terrifying lullaby. She had never forgotten it.

. . . *If I should die before I wake . . .*

"Don't you believe in God?" she said to Nitz.

He opened one eye. "I believe in everything. In God, in the United States, in power steering."

"You're not much help."

In the corner of the bar Carleton Tweany had reappeared. He was chatting with groups of patrons; tolerant, superior, he moved from table to table.

"Pay no attention to him," Nitz mumbled. "He'll go away."

The shape of Carleton Tweany neared, and again she tensed herself. Nitz radiated disapproval, but she was far above caring; she had made up her mind. Now, in a quick single motion, she was on her feet. "Mr. Tweany," she said, and apparently her feeling was there in her voice, because he paused.

"Yes, Miss Mary Anne?" he said.

She was suddenly nervous. "How's—your hot water heater?"

"I don't know."

"What did the landlady say? Didn't you call her?"

"I called, yes. But I couldn't get hold of her."

Breathlessly, afraid he would start on, she demanded: "Well, what are you going to do?"

The man's lips twitched, and, gradually, his eyes filmed behind shadow. Turning to Paul Nitz, who was still slumped at the piano bench, he said: "Is she always like this?"

"Most of the time. Mary lives in a universe of leaky pots."

She flushed. "I'm thinking of the people downstairs," she said defensively.

"What people?" Tweany asked.

"You're on the top floor, aren't you?" She hadn't lost him yet, but he was beginning to slide away. "It'll drip down on them—it'll ruin their walls and ceilings."

Tweany started off. "They can sue the landlady," he said, dismissing the subject.

"How long before you're through singing?" Mary Anne asked, hurrying after him.

"Two hours." He grinned with superiority.

"Two hours! Maybe they'll be dead by then." She had a vision of chaos; erupting geysers of water, splintered boards, and, behind everything else, the sound of fire. "You better go over right now. You can sing later. It isn't fair to those other people. Maybe there're children downstairs. Are there?"

Tweany's amusement faded to exasperation; it did not please him to be bossed. "Thank you for your interest."

"Come on." She had decided.

He gaped at her with dense vacantness. "What's that, Miss Mary Anne?"

"Come on!" She caught hold of his sleeve and tugged him toward the door. "Where's your car?"

Tweany was indignant. "I'm perfectly capable of handling the situation."

"In the lot? Is your car in the lot?"

"I don't have a car," he admitted sulkily; his cream and yellow Buick convertible had recently been repossessed.

"How far is it?"

"Not far. Three or four blocks."

"We'll walk." She was determined to keep within physical reach of him; and, in this urgency, she had swallowed his problem whole.

"You're coming along?" he was asking.

"Certainly." She started off.

Tweany reluctantly followed. "Your interest is not necessary." He seemed to expand behind her, to become even taller and more upright. He was a troubled commonwealth. He was an empire plagued at its borders. But she had stirred him into action; she had, in her need of him, prodded him into awareness of her.

Holding the street door open, she said: "Stop wasting time. We'll be back; you can sing later."

4

The two of them trudged through the closed-up slum business district, neither having much to say. Presently dark stores gave way to houses and apartment buildings. The houses were old.

"This is the colored section," Tweany said.

Mary Anne nodded. Her emotion had waned; now she felt tired.

"I live in the colored section," Tweany said.

"No kidding."

He glanced curiously at her. "Don't you ever take it easy, Miss Mary Anne?"

"I'll take it easy," she said. "When I'm good and ready."

He laughed loudly. "I never met anybody like you." Now that they had left the Wren some of his formality was eroding. An expansiveness replaced it; roaming along the deserted evening sidewalk, Tweany began to enjoy himself.

"You love music, don't you?" he said.

She shrugged. "Sure."

"There has been some conflict between I and Nitz. He prefers to play the usual line of popular jazz. As you've probably noticed, it's my desire to bring in a more refined musical form."

Mary Anne listened without really hearing the man's words. His deep voice reassured her; it dissipated some of her uneasiness, and that was enough.

The presence of Negroes had always lulled her. In the Negro world there seemed more warmth, and less of the struggle she had known at home. She had always been able to talk to Negroes; they were like herself. They, too, were on the outside, in a separate world of their own.

"You can't go a lot of places either," she said aloud.

"What's that?"

"But you have so much ability. How does it feel to be able to sing? I wish I could do something like that." She remembered the ad tucked away in her purse, and her restlessness increased. "Did you study somewhere? Some school?"

"At the conservatory," Tweany said. "My ability was noted at an early age."

"Did you belong to the Baptist Church, too?"

Tweany laughed tolerantly. "No, of course not."

"Where were you born?"

"Here in California. I've made California my permanent home. California is a rich state . . . it has boundless possibilities." To certify his point, he indicated his coat sleeve. "This suit was tailored for me personally. Designed and fitted by an expert firm in Los Angeles." His fingers strolled over his silk hand-painted necktie. "Clothes are important."

"Why?"

"People can tell you have taste. Clothes are the first thing people notice. As a woman you must be aware of that."

"I suppose so." But she didn't care; clothes, to her, were a civic duty interwoven with cleanliness and posture.

"It's a nice evening," Tweany observed. He had got around to the street side of her, a gesture of gentlemanly alertness. "We have excellent weather here in California."

"Have you been in other states?"

"Of course."

Mary Anne said: "I wish I could travel."

"When you've seen the various big cities you'll know one fundamental thing. They're all alike."

She accepted his words, but the longing was untouched. "I'd like to go somewhere, to some better place." That was the most she could summon; the idea was no clearer. "What would be a better place? Name a real nice place, where the people are nice."

"New York has its charms."

"Are people nice, there?"

"New York has some of the finest museums and opera houses in the world. The people are cultured."

"I see."

Guiding the girl from the pavement, Tweany said: "This is it. My house." His expansiveness soured as the old house loomed up before them. "Not much to look at, but . . . good music lacks commercial appeal. A person has to choose between riches and artistic integrity."

A dark outside staircase led from the yard to the third floor. Mary Anne felt her way through the gloom; ahead of her was Tweany and to her left was the house itself. A rain barrel glided by; it was filled with soaked and decomposing newspapers. Next came a line of rusting oil drums, and then the steps. Under her feet the wood groaned and gave; she clung to the banister and stayed close behind Tweany.

The apartment was a blur of shadows as Tweany led her down the hall to the kitchen. She gazed around her in wonder; she was seeing a vast clutter of furniture and shapes, nothing distinct, nothing she could properly make out. And then the light was on.

"Excuse things," Tweany murmured. He left her standing in the kitchen as he prowled, tomcat-wise, from room to room. His possessions seemed to be safe: nobody had stolen his shirts; nobody had ruffled his drapes; nobody had drunk his whiskey.

In the kitchen a slight pool of water shone; the linoleum was damp with evidence of the catastrophe. But the heater had been repaired and the mess mopped up.

"Fine," Tweany said. "They did a good job."

Subdued, aware now that her alarm had been wasted, Mary

Anne padded here and there, examining bookcases, peering out of windows. The apartment was very high up; she could see across town. Along the horizon ran a series of clear yellow lights.

"What's those lights?" she asked Tweany.

He was indifferent. "A road, maybe."

Mary Anne breathed in the faintly musty scent of the apartment. "You have an interesting place. I've never seen a place like this. I'm still living at home with my parents. This gives me a lot of ideas for my own pad . . . you know?"

Lighting a cigarette, Tweany said: "Well, I was right."

"I guess the plumber came."

"Nothing was the matter after all."

"I'm sorry," she said, feeling uncertain of herself. "I was thinking about the people downstairs. I read an ad, once. An insurance company ad about a hot water heater that exploded."

"Might as well take off your coat, now that you're here."

She did so, pushing it over the arm of a chair. "I guess I got you away from the Wren for nothing." Hands in the back pockets of her jeans, she returned to the window.

"Beer?"

"Okay." She nodded. "Thanks."

"Eastern beer." Tweany filled a glass for her. "Sit down."

She sat, holding the glass awkwardly. It was cold and damp with drops of collected moisture.

"You don't even know if there *are* any people downstairs," Tweany said. He had made a point and he intended to develop it. "What makes you think there's somebody downstairs?"

Staring at the floor Mary Anne murmured: "I don't know. I just thought about it."

Tweany settled himself on the edge of a heaped table; he was now located well above her, in a position of authority. The girl seemed quite small in comparison to him, and quite young. In her jeans and cotton shirt she might have been a teenager.

"How old are you?" Tweany demanded.

Her lips barely moved. "Twenty."

"You're just a little girl."

It was so. She felt like a little girl, too; she could sense his eyes fastened mockingly on her. She was, she realized, about to undergo the ordeal of a lecture. She was going to be reprimanded.

"You got to grow up," Tweany said. "You got a lot of things to learn."

Mary Anne roused herself. "For cripe's sake, don't I know it? I *want* to learn things."

"You live here in town?"

"Naturally," she said, with bitterness.

"You go to school?"

"No. I work in a lousy broken-down chrome furniture factory."

"Doing what?"

"Stenographer."

"Do you like it?"

"No."

Tweany contemplated her. "Do you have talent?"

"What do you mean?"

"You should do something creative."

"I just want to go somewhere where I can be with people and they won't let me down."

Tweany went over and turned on the radio. The sound of Sarah Vaughan drifted out and into the living room. "You've been dealt some hard knocks," he said, returning to his vantage point.

"I don't know. I haven't had it so bad." She sipped her beer. "Why does eastern beer cost more than western?"

"Because it's finer."

"I thought maybe it was the freight cost."

"Did you?" His great contemptuous grin reappeared.

"See, I've never had a chance to find things out. Where do you find out things like that?"

"A lifetime of broad experience. A cultivated taste is acquired gradually over the years. To some people eastern beer and western beer taste exactly alike."

Mary Anne didn't like beer of any kind. Dutifully she sipped at her glass, wishing, in a wan sort of way, that she was older, that she had seen more and done more. She was aware of her ordinariness in comparison with Carleton Tweany.

"How does it feel to be a singer?" she asked.

"In art," Tweany told her, "there's a spiritual satisfaction that goes beyond material success. The American society is only interested in money. It's shallow."

"Sing something for me," Mary Anne said suddenly. "I mean," she murmured, "I like to hear you."

"Such as?" He raised an eyebrow.

"Sing 'Water Boy.' " She smiled at him. "I like that . . . you sang it at the Wren, one night."

"It's a favorite of yours, then?"

"We sang it once in grammar school assembly, years ago."

Her thoughts eddied back to her earlier life, when she, in scotch-plaid skirt and middy blouse, had trooped as part of an obedient line from one classroom to another. Crayon drawings, current events, air raid drills during the war . . .

"That was better," she decided. "During the war. Why isn't it like that now?"

"What war?"

"With the Nazis and the Japs. Were you in that?"

"I served in the Pacific."

"Doing what?" She was instantly curious.

"Hospital attendant."

"Is it fun to work in a hospital? How'd you get to do it?"

"I signed up." His activity in the war had never ranked high in his own estimation; he had come out as he had gone in: a private earning twenty-one dollars a month.

"How do you get to be a nurse?" she asked.

"You take courses, like anything else."

Mary Anne's face glowed. "It must be wonderful to be able to devote your life to something real and important. A cause—like nursing."

Distastefully, Tweany said: "Bathing old, dried-up men. There's no fun in that."

Mary Anne's interest waned. "No," she agreed, sharing his aversion. "I wouldn't like that. But it wouldn't be that all the time, would it? Mostly it would be healing people."

"What was so fine about the war?" Tweany said. "You never seen a war, young lady. You never seen a man get killed. I've seen that. War's an awful business."

She didn't mean that, of course. She meant the unanimity that had arisen during the war, the evaporation of internal hostility. "My grandfather died in 1940," she said aloud. "He used to keep a map of the war, a big wall map. He stuck pins in it."

"Yes," Tweany agreed, unmoved.

But she was greatly moved, because Grandfather Reynolds had been a vast and important person to her; he had taken care of her. "He used to explain to me about Munich and the Czechs," she said. "He loved the Czechs. Then he died. I was—" She computed—"I was seven years old."

"Very young," Tweany murmured.

Grandfather Reynolds had loved the Czechs, and she had loved him; and, perhaps, he was the only human being she had ever had real affection for. Her father was a danger, not a person. Since one certain night when she had come home late, and he, in the living room, had caught her, had really caught her: not in a game. Since that night she had been afraid. And he, the grinning little man, knew it. And enjoyed it.

"Ed was working in a defense plant in San Jose," she said. "But my grandfather was home; he was old. He used to own a ranch in the Sacramento Valley. And he was tall." She felt herself drifting, falling away into her own thoughts. "I remember that . . . he used to lift me up and swing me around a long way off the ground. He was too old to drive; when he was a boy he rode on a horse." Her eyes shone. "And he wore a vest, and a big silver ring he bought from an Indian."

Getting to his feet, Tweany walked around the apartment pulling down the window shades. He leaned over Mary Anne to reach the window behind her; he smelled of beer and shirt starch and men's deodorant. "You're a nice-looking girl."

She roused herself a little. "I'm too thin."

"You're not a bad-looking girl," he repeated, looking down at her legs. Instinctively she drew them under her. "Do you know that?" he demanded, in an oddly hoarse voice.

"Maybe." She stirred fitfully . . . it was getting late. Tomorrow morning she had to be up early; she had to be alert and fresh when she went to see about the ad. Thinking of it, she took hold of her purse.

"You a friend of Nitz's?" Tweany asked.

"I suppose."

"You like him?" He settled himself facing her, his body slack. "You like Nitz? Answer me."

"He's all right," she said, feeling uncomfortable.

"He's little." The man's eyes were full of brightness. "I bet you prefer your men large."

"No," she said irritably, "I don't care." Her head had begun to ache, and Tweany's closeness seemed oppressive. And she hated his beer smell: it reminded her of Ed. "Why don't you clean this place up?" she demanded, shifting away from him. "It's an awful mess—junk everywhere."

He sat back and his face collapsed into itself.

"It's terrible." She got to her feet and collected her coat, her purse. The apartment was no longer interesting: she blamed him for spoiling it. "It stinks," she said. "And it's all littered and I'll bet the wiring is bad."

"Yes," Tweany said. "The wiring is bad."

"Why don't you have it fixed? It's dangerous."

Tweany said nothing.

"Who cleans up?" she demanded. "Why don't you have somebody come in?"

"I have a woman come by."

"When?"

"Once in a while." He examined his jeweled wristwatch. "It's time we were getting back, Miss Mary Anne."

"I suppose. I have to be up early tomorrow." She watched him go to get his coat; he had withdrawn back into his shell of formality, and it was her fault. "I'm glad your hot water heater's okay," she said, as a sort of apology.

"Thank you."

As they walked down the dark night street, Mary Anne said, "Tomorrow I'm going job hunting."

"Are you."

"I want to work in a record shop." She felt his disinterest, and she wanted to draw him back. "It's that new one that's opening." In the late air she trembled.

"What's the matter?"

"My sinuses. I'm supposed to go down and have them drained. Changes of temperature make them hurt."

"Will you be all right?" he asked. They had come to the edge of the business section; ahead, along the street of locked shops, she could see the red glow of the Wren.

"Yes," she said. "I'm going home and go to bed."

"Good night," Tweany said, and started away.

"Wish me luck," she called after him, suddenly feeling the need of luck. Loneliness closed in, and she had to force herself not to flee after him.

Tweany waved and continued on his way. For a moment she stood anxiously watching the diminution of his figure. Then, holding onto her purse, she turned toward her own neighborhood.

5

At eight-thirty the next morning Mary Anne entered the telephone booth in Eickholz's Creamery and dialed California Readymade Furniture. Tom Bolden answered.

"Let me talk to Edna," Mary Anne said.

"What? Who do you want?"

When she had got hold of Mrs. Bolden, Mary Anne explained: "I'm sorry, but I can't be at work today. It's my period and I always have a lot of difficulty."

"I see," Mrs. Bolden said, in a neutral voice that showed neither doubt nor belief, only an acceptance of the inevitable. "Well, there's not much we can do about it. Will you be back on your feet tomorrow?"

"I'll keep you posted," Mary Anne said, already hanging up. The hell with you, she thought. You and your factory and chrome chairs.

She left the creamery. High heels tapping against the pavement, she walked quickly up the sidewalk, conscious of her appearance, aware of the texture and style of her hair, her careful makeup, the scent of her perfume. She had spent two hours grooming herself, and she had eaten only a piece of toast with applesauce and a cup of coffee. She was on edge, but not apprehensive.

The new little record shop had been the Floral Arts Gift Shop. Carpenters were working busily in the newly decorated store, installing overhead recessed lighting and laying carpets. An electrician had parked his truck and was lugging phonographs inside. Cartons of records were piled everywhere; in the rear a pair of workmen were tacking squares of soundproofing to the ceiling of the half-completed booths. The work in progress was directed by a middle-aged man in a tweed suit.

She crossed the street and walked slowly back, trying to make out the figure that loomed over the carpenters. Waving a silver-handled stick, the man paced back and forth, giving instructions, laying down the law. He walked as if the ground came into existence at his feet. He was creating the store from the puddle of fabrics, boards, wiring, tiles. It was interesting to see this big man building. Was he Joseph R. Schilling? She gave up her prowling and approached the store. It was not yet nine.

Passing through the entrance was a sudden leaving of the emptiness of the street; she found herself in the midst of activity. Large and important objects had been collected here; she felt the tightness, the reassuring pressure that meant so much to her. While she was inspecting a newly built counter, the tweed-suited man glanced up and saw her.

"Are you Mr. Schilling?" she asked, a little awed.

"That's right."

All around them carpenters were hammering; it was noisier than California Readymade. She took a deep, pleased breath of the smell of sawdust, the stiff unfolding of new carpets. "I want to talk to you," she said. Her wonder grew. "Is this your store? What's all the glass for?" Workmen were carrying panes to the rear.

"For record booths," he answered. "Come in the office. Where we can talk better."

Reluctantly, she forgot the work in progress and trailed after him, down a hall past a flight of basement steps and into a side room. He closed the door and turned to face her.

* * *

MARY AND THE GIANT

It had been Joseph Schilling's first impulse to send the girl off. Obviously she was too young, not more than twenty. But he was intrigued. The girl was unusually attractive.

What he saw was a small, rather bony girl, with brown hair and pale, almost straw-colored eyes. Her neck fascinated him. It was long and smooth, a Modigliani neck. Her ears were tiny and did not flare in the slightest. She wore gold hooped earrings. Her skin was fair and unblemished and faintly tanned. There was no emphasis of sexuality; her body was not overly developed and there was an ascetic quality to her, a strictness of line that was refreshing and unusual.

"You're looking for a job?" he asked. "How old are you?"

"Twenty," she answered.

Schilling rubbed his ear and pondered. "What sort of experience have you had?"

"I worked eight months for a finance company as a receptionist, so I'm used to meeting the public. And then I worked over a year taking dictation. I'm a trained typist."

"That's of no value to me."

"Don't be silly. Is your business only going to be on a cash basis? You're not going to open charge accounts?"

"My bookkeeping will be done from outside," he said. "Is this your idea of the way to ask for a job?"

"I'm not asking for a job. I'm *looking* for a job."

Schilling reflected, but the distinction was lost on him. "What do you know about music?"

"I know everything there is to know."

"You mean popular music. What would you say if I asked you who Dietrich Buxtehude was? Do you recognize the name?"

"No," she said simply.

"Then you don't know anything about music. You're wasting my time. All you know is the Top Ten tunes."

"You're not going to be able to sell hit tunes," the girl said. "Not in this town."

Surprised, Schilling said: "Why not?"

"Hank is one of the smartest pop buyers in the business. People come down here from San Francisco, looking for tunes back-ordered all the way to L.A."

"And they find them?"

"Most of the time. Nobody can catch them all."

"How do you know so much about the record business?"

For an instant the girl smiled. "Do you think I know a lot about the record business?"

"You act as if you do. You pretend you do."

"I used to go with a boy who did Hank's stock work. And I like folk music and bop."

Stepping to the back of the office, Schilling got out a cigar, cut off the end, and lit up.

"What's the matter?" the girl asked.

"I'm not sure how good you'd be behind a counter. You'd try to tell people what they ought to like."

"Would I?" The girl reflected and then shrugged her shoulders. "Well, it's up to them. I could help them. Sometimes they want help."

"What's your name?"

"Mary Anne Reynolds."

He liked the sound of it. "I'm Joseph Schilling."

The girl nodded. "That's what I thought."

"The ad," he said, "gave only a phone number. But you found your way here. Had you noticed my store?"

"Yes," she said. There was tension surrounding her. He understood that this was of great importance.

"You were born here?" he asked. "It's a nice town; I like it. Of course, it's not large. It's not active."

"It's dead." Her face lifted, and he was confronted with her judgment. "Be realistic."

"Well," he said, "maybe it's dead to you; you're tired of it."

"I'm not tired of it. I just don't believe in it."

"There's a lot here to believe in; go sit in the park."

"And do what?"

"And listen!" he said with vigor. "Come out and hear . . . it's all around you. Sights to see, sounds, rich smells."

"What do you pay a month?" she asked.

"Two-fifty to start." Now he was annoyed. "Back to the practical?" It didn't fit his impression of her, and he thought now that it wasn't really practical: she was trying to find a reference point. Somehow he had upset her. "That's for a five-day week. It isn't bad."

"In California a woman can't work more than a five-day week. What about later? What does the salary go up to?"

"Two-seventy-five. If things work out."

"And if they don't? I have a pretty good job right now."

Schilling paced around the office, smoking and trying to recall when and if a situation of this sort had come up before. He was disturbed . . . the girl's intensity affected him. But he was too old to treat the world as ominous, and he enjoyed too many small things. He liked to eat good food; he loved music and beauty and—if it was really funny—a dirty joke. It pleased him to be alive, and this girl saw life as a threat. But his interest in her had grown.

She might well be the girl he wanted. She was alert; she would be an efficient worker. And she was pretty; if he could get her to relax she would freshen up the store.

"You'd like to work in a record store?" he asked.

"Yes," she said. "It would be interesting."

"By fall you'd know the ropes." He could see that she learned rapidly. "We might work out a trial basis. I'd have to see . . . after all, you're the first girl I've talked to." From the hall came the jangle of the phone, and he smiled. "That must be another job applicant."

The girl said nothing. But she seemed even more absorbed in her worry; she was like certain little concerned animals he had seen, those that huddled silently for hours.

"I tell you what," Schilling said, and even in his own ears his voice sounded rough and clumsy. "Let's go across the street and get something to eat. I haven't had breakfast. Is that restaurant all right?"

"The Blue Lamb?" Mary Anne moved to the door. "All right, I suppose. Expensive. I don't know if they're open this early."

"We'll see," Schilling declared, following her up the hall. A light-headedness seized him, a sense of adventure. "If not, then we can go somewhere else. I can't hire you without knowing more about you."

In the main part of the store the carpenters were hammering and pounding above the jangle of the phone. The electrician, surrounded by turntables and speaker systems, was trying vainly to hear the response of his amplifiers. Schilling caught up with the girl and took hold of her arm.

"Be careful," he warned her genially. "Watch out for that tangle of phono lead."

Her arm was firm within his fingers. He was conscious of her clothing, the dry rustling of the green knit suit. Walking beside her, he could catch the faint edge of her perfume. She was really surprisingly small. She plodded along, eyes on the floor; all the way to the street she failed to speak. He could tell she was deep in thought.

When they had reached the sidewalk, the girl halted. Awkwardly, Schilling released her arm. "Well?" he asked, as they faced each other in the bright morning glare. The sunlight smelled of moisture and freshness; he took a deep breath of it and found it better than cigar smoke. "What do you think? How will it look?"

"It's a nice little store."

"You think it'll be a financial success?" Schilling stepped agilely aside for workmen carrying in a cash register and carton of paper tapes.

"Probably."

Schilling hesitated. Was he making a mistake? Once he spoke it would be too late to back out. But he didn't want to back out. "The job is yours," he said.

After a moment Mary Anne said: "No, thanks."

"What?" He was shocked. "What's that? What do you mean?"

Without a word, the girl started off down the sidewalk. For an interval Schilling remained inert; then, tossing his cigar into the gutter, he hurried after her. "What is it?" he demanded, barring her way. "What's wrong?" Passersby gazed at them with interest; ignoring them, he caught hold of the girl's arm. "Don't you want the job?"

"No," she said defiantly. "Let go of my arm or I'll call a cop and have you arrested."

Schilling released her and the girl stepped back.

"What is it?" he begged.

"I don't want to work for you. When you touched me, I could tell." Her voice trailed off. "The store's lovely. I'm sorry—it started out fine. You shouldn't have touched me."

And then she was gone. Schilling found himself standing alone; she had slipped off into the stream of early-morning shoppers.

He made his way back into the store. The carpenters were banging mightily. The telephone shrilled. During his absence Max had appeared with a ham sandwich and a pasteboard carton of coffee (one lump of sugar).

"Here it is," Max said. "Your breakfast."

"Keep it!" Schilling retorted with fury.

Max blinked. "What's bothering you?"

Schilling fished in his coat pocket for a fresh cigar. His hands, he discovered, were shaking.

6

Whistling to himself, David Gordon parked the Richfield service truck and jumped to the pavement. Lugging a damaged fuel pump and a handful of wrenches, he entered the station building.

Sitting in the one chair was Mary Anne Reynolds. But something was wrong; she was too quiet.

"Are—" Gordon began. "What is it, honey?"

One single tear slid down the girl's cheek. She wiped it away and got to her feet. Gordon reached to take hold of her, but she drew back.

"Where were you?" she said in a low voice. "I've been here half an hour. The other man said you'd be right back."

"Some people in a Buick. Broke down on the old Big Bear Pass Road. What happened?"

"I went job hunting. What time is it?"

He located the wall clock; when anybody asked the time he could never seem to find it. "Ten."

"Then it's been an hour. I walked around for a while before I came here."

He was completely baffled. "What do you mean, you went job hunting? What about Readymade?"

"First," Mary Anne said, "can I borrow five dollars? I bought a pair of gloves over at Steiner's."

He got out the money; she accepted the bill and put it in her purse. He noticed that she had on nail polish, which was unusual. In fact, she was all dressed up; she had on an expensive-looking suit, and high heels, and nylon stockings.

"I should have known," she said. "The way he first looked at me. But I wasn't sure until he touched me. Then I was sure, and I got out of there as quickly as I could."

"Explain," he demanded. Her thoughts, like her activities, had become closed to him.

"He wanted to have relations with me," she said stonily. "That was what it was all for. The job, the record store, the ad. 'Young woman, must be attractive.' "

"Who?"

"He owns the store. Joseph Schilling."

Dave Gordon had seen her upset before, and sometimes he could calm her down. But he did not understand what was wrong; a man had made a pass at her—so what? He had made passes at girls himself. "Maybe he didn't have that in mind," he said. "I mean, maybe the shop is on the level, but when he saw you—" He gestured. "You're all dolled up; look at you. That suit, all that makeup."

"But an older man," she insisted. "It's not right!"

"Why not? He's a man, isn't he?"

"I thought I could trust him. You don't expect that from an older man." She got out her cigarettes, and he took her matches to light up for her. "Think of it—a respectable man like that, with money and education. Coming here to this town, picking this town for a thing like that."

"Take it easy," he said, wanting to help her but not really knowing how. "You're okay."

She paced around in a tight, aimless circle. "I feel sick. It's so—infuriating. I worked so damn hard fixing myself up. And the store . . ." Her voice faded. "It was so pretty. And the way he looked at first. He was so impressive."

"It happens all the time. All you have to do is walk along the street, by the drugstore. Guys hang out, watch."

"You remember when we were in high school? That bus incident?"

No, he didn't remember. "I—" he began.

"You weren't there. I was sitting next to a man, a salesman. He started talking to me; it was awful. Whispering to me, and everybody else just sitting there jiggling with the bus. Housewives."

"Hey," Gordon said. "I get off in half an hour. Let's drive over to Foster's Freeze and have a hamburger and a shake. That'll make you feel better."

"Oh, for Christ's sake!" she said, infuriated. "Grow up, will you? You're not a boy—you're a grown man. Can't you think of anything else? Milk shakes—you're a high school boy; that's all you are."

Gordon muttered: "Don't get sore."

"Why do you hang around with those fairies?"

"What fairies?"

"Tate and that bunch."

"They're not fairies. They just dress good."

She blew smoke at him. "Working in a gas station—that's no job for an adult. Jake; you're another Jake. Jake and Dave, the two pals. Be a Jake, if you want. Be a Jake until the army gets you."

"Lay off talking about the army. They're blowing on my ass."

"It wouldn't do you any harm." Restlessly, Mary Anne said: "Drive me out to Readymade. I have to be back at work; I can't sit around here."

"Are you sure you ought to go back? Maybe you ought to go home and rest."

The girl's eyes shrank with wrath. "I have to go back; it's my job. Take some responsibility, once in a while; can't you understand responsibility?"

* * *

On the trip Mary Anne had little to say. She sat bolt upright, gripping her purse and staring out the truck window at the countryside. Under her arms moist circles had formed, giving off the scent of rosewater and musk. She had wiped away most of her makeup; her face was white and expressionless.

"You look funny," Dave Gordon said.

"No kidding."

With a show of determination, he said, "How about telling me what's going on with you, these days? I never see you anymore; you always have some excuse. I guess what it is, is I'm getting the brush."

"I went by your house last night."

"And when I go by your house you're not there. Your family doesn't know where you are. Who does?"

"I do," Mary Anne said succinctly.

"Are you still hanging around that bar?" There was no rancor in his voice, only forlorn concern. "I even went down there, to that Wren Club. And sat around thinking maybe you'd show up. I did that a couple times."

Mary Anne softened minutely. "Did I show up?"

"No."

"I'm sorry." With a stir of longing, she said, "Maybe this will all clear away."

"You mean your job?"

"Yes. I suppose." She meant a great deal more than that. "Maybe I'll become a nun," she said suddenly.

"I wish I could understand you. I wish I saw more of you; I'd settle for that. I sort of miss you."

Mary Anne wished she missed Gordon. But she didn't.

"Can I say something?" he asked.

"Say away."

"I guess you don't want to marry me after all."

"Why?" Mary Anne asked, her voice rising. "Why do you say

a thing like that? My God, Gordon, where'd you get an idea like that? You must be crazy; you better go to a psychoanalyst. You're neurotic. You're in bad shape, baby."

Sulkily, Dave Gordon said: "Don't make fun of me."

She was ashamed. "I'm sorry, Gordon."

"And for Christ's sake, do you have to call me Gordon? My name's Dave. Everybody else calls me Gordon—you ought to be able to call me Dave."

"I'm sorry, David," she said contritely. "I wasn't really making fun of you. It's this whole awful business."

"If we got married," Gordon said, "would you keep on working?"

"I haven't thought about it."

"I'd prefer it if you stayed home."

"Why?"

"Well," Gordon said, twisting with embarrassment, "if we had kids, you ought to be home taking care of them."

"Kids," Mary Anne said. She felt strange. Her kids: it was a new idea.

"Would you like kids?" Gordon asked hopefully.

"I like *you*."

"I'm talking about real little kids."

"Yes," she decided, thinking about it. "Why not? It'd be nice." She contemplated at length. "I could stay home . . . a little boy and a little girl. Not just one kid; two at the least, and maybe more." She smiled briefly. "So they wouldn't be lonely. One kid is too lonely . . . he has no friends."

"You've always been lonely."

"Have I? I guess so."

"I remember when we were in high school," Dave Gordon said. "You were always by yourself . . . you never hung around with the group. You were so pretty; I used to see you sitting out there at lunchtime, with your bottle of milk and your sandwich, eating all by yourself. You know what I wanted to do? I wanted to go up and kiss you. But I didn't know you then."

With affection, Mary Anne said: "You're a pretty nice person." Then, urgently, she drew away. "I hated high school. I couldn't wait to get out of there. What did we learn there? What did they teach us we could use?"

"Nothing, I guess," Dave Gordon said.

"A lot of phony junk. Phony! Every word of it."

Ahead of them, to the right, was California Readymade. They watched it approach.

"Here we are," Dave Gordon said, pulling the truck to a stop at the edge of the road. "When'll I see you?"

"Sometime." She had already lost interest in him; stiff and tense again, she was preparing herself.

"Tonight?"

Climbing down, Mary Anne said over her shoulder: "Not tonight. Don't come around for a while. I have to do a lot of thinking."

Hurt, Gordon prepared to leave. "Sometimes I think you're riding for a fall."

"What do you mean?" She halted defiantly.

"Some people think—you're stuck up."

With a shake of her head Mary Anne dismissed him and trotted up the path to the factory office. Behind her, the sound of the truck motor faded as Gordon drove glumly back to town.

She felt no particular emotion as she opened the office door. She was a little tired, and her stomach was still upset; but that was all. As Mrs. Bolden got to her feet, Mary Anne began removing her gloves and coat. She could feel the mounting oppressiveness, but she continued, matter-of-factly, without comment.

"Well," Mrs. Bolden said, "you decided to come after all." At his desk, Tom Bolden peered around, listening and scowling.

"What do you want done first?" Mary Anne asked.

"I got to looking at the calendar," Mrs. Bolden continued, blocking the girl's way as she started toward her typewriter. "This isn't your period at all, is it? You just made that up to get time off. I marked the date down last time. My husband and I have been talking it over. We—"

"I quit," Mary Anne said suddenly. She tugged her gloves back on and started toward the door. "I have another job."

Mrs. Bolden's mouth fell open. "You sit down, young lady. Don't you walk out of here."

"Mail my check," Mary Anne said, tugging open the door.

"What's she saying?" Tom Bolden muttered, rising to his feet. "Is she leaving again?"

"Good-bye," Mary Anne said; without stopping she hurried out onto the porch and down the stairs to the path. Behind her, the old man and his wife had come to the doorway in bewilderment.

"I quit!" Mary Anne shouted back at them. "Go back inside! I have another job! Go away!"

The two of them remained there, neither of them knowing what to do, neither of them stirring until, to her own surprise, Mary Anne crouched down, swept up a chunk of loose concrete, and threw it at them. The concrete landed in the soft dirt by the porch; fumbling at the edge of the path, she found a handful of concrete fragments and showered them at the old couple.

"Go back in!" she shouted, beginning to laugh in amazement and fear at herself. Workmen had come out on the loading platform and were staring, openmouthed. "I quit! I'm not coming back!"

Then, clutching her purse, she ran down the sidewalk, stumbling in the unfamiliar heels, on and on until she was gasping and winded, blinded by red specks that swam in front of her.

Nobody had followed. She slowed down and stopped to lean against the corrugated iron side of a fertilizer plant. What had she done? Quit her job. All at once, in an instant. Well, it was too late to worry about it now. Good riddance.

Stepping into the street, Mary Anne waved down a pickup truck loaded with sacks of kindling. The driver, a Pole, gaped in astonishment as she opened the door and clambered in beside him.

"Take me into town," she ordered. Resting her elbow on the windowsill, she covered her eyes with her hand. After some hesitation, the truck started; she was on her way.

"You sick, miss?" the Pole asked.

Mary Anne didn't answer. Jogging with the motion of the truck, she prepared to endure the trip back to Pacific Park.

In the slum business section she made the Pole let her off. It was approaching noon, and the hot midsummer sun beat down on the parked cars and pedestrians. She passed the cigar shop and came to the padded red door of the Lazy Wren. The bar was closed and locked; going to the window, she began tapping with a quarter.

After an interval a shape made its appearance in the interior gloom: a paunchy, elderly Negro. Taft Eaton put his hand to the glass, surveyed her hostilely, then unlocked the door.

"Where's Tweany?" she asked.

"He's not here."

"Where is he, then?"

"Home. Anywhere." As Mary Anne started to push past him, he slammed the door and said through it: "You can't come in; you're a minor."

She listened to the door latch slide into place, stood indecisively, and then entered the cigar shop. Squeezing by the men clustered at the counter, she found the pay telephone. With difficulty, balancing the heavy phone book, she located his number and then dropped a dime into the slot.

There was no response. But he might be there asleep. She would have to go over. Right now she needed him; she had to see him. There was nothing else she could turn to.

The house, the great three-story house of gray fluting and balconies and spires, jutted from its yard of weeds, broken bottles, rusting tin cans. There was no sign of life; the shades on the third floor were down and inert.

Fear overtook her and she hurried up the path, across the cracked cement, past a bundle of newspapers and dying potted plants at the foot of the stairs. She climbed two steps at a time, holding fast to the banister. Gasping, she turned the corner of the long flight, felt the rotten slats sag under her, tripped on a broken step and pitched forward, scrabbling at the railing. Her shin struck the jagged old wood; pain made her scream and fall onto her open palms. Her cheek brushed a heap of dust-impregnated cobwebs that had caught over the green knit sleeve of her suit. A family of spiders clicked excitedly away; dragging herself to her feet, Mary Anne crept up the last steps, cursing and weeping, tears streaming down her cheeks.

"Tweany!" she screamed, "let me in!"

There was no response. From a long way off came the jangle of a traffic signal. And from the milk plant at the edge of the slums a clatter drifted up and spread over the town.

In a blind haze she reached the door. Below her the distant ground wheeled; for an interval she lay against the door, her eyes shut, trying not to let go and fall.

"Tweany," she gasped, her face against the closed door. "Goddamn it, let me in."

Through her suffering came reassuring noise: a person was stirring. Mary Anne settled in a heap on the top step, bent over, knees pulled up, rocking from side to side, the contents of her purse dribbling from between her fingers onto the steps, coins and pencils rolling out into the sunlight and dropping to the grass far below.

"Tweany," she whispered as the door opened and the dark, faintly luminous shape of the Negro appeared. "Please help me. Something's happened to me."

Frowning with annoyance, he bent down and gathered her up. With his bare foot—he had on only his pants—he kicked the door shut behind them. Carrying her, he padded down the hall, his blue-black face fragrant with shaving soap, his chin and furry chest dripping beads of lather. Around the girl's body his hands were brusque; she closed her eyes and clung to him.

"Help me," she repeated. "I quit my job; I don't have a job anymore. I met an awful old man and he did something to me. Now I don't have any place to stay."

7

At the corner of Pine and Santa Clara Streets was a swank hat shop. After the hat shop came Dwelley's Luggageware, and after that the Music Corner, the new phonograph record shop opened by Joseph Schilling in the early weeks of August 1953.

It was toward the Music Corner that the man and woman moved. The shop had been open two months: it was now the middle of October. In the display window was a photograph of Walter Gieseking and two long-playing records half-slid from their bright covers. Customers were visible inside the shop, some at the front counter, others in the listening booths. The Saint-Saëns Organ Symphony echoed through the open doorway.

"Not bad," the man admitted. "But he's got the loot; it should look okay."

In his thirties, he was dapper and fragile-looking, with shiny black hair, a bird-chested man who walked daintily. His eyes were quick and alive, and his hands, as he guided the woman into the store, fluttered against her coat.

The woman turned to see the sign over the doorway. It was a square of hardwood, with hand-carved fretwork, on which had been painted the words THE MUSIC CORNER, 517 PINE STREET. MA3-6041. OPEN 9–5. RECORDS AND CUSTOM-BUILT SOUND EQUIPMENT.

"It's cute," she said. "The sign, I mean."

She was younger than the man, a heavy, round-faced blonde who wore slacks and carried an immense leather bag which hung from her shoulder by a strap.

There was nobody behind the counter. Two young men were studying a record catalogue; they were involved in controversy. The woman did not see Joseph Schilling, but every aspect of the store's interior reminded her of him. The pattern of the wall-to-wall carpeting was characteristic of his taste, and many of the pictures on the walls—prints by contemporary artists—were familiar. The little vase on the counter—it held California wild iris—had been designed and fired by her. And the catalogues behind the counter were bound in a fabric of her choosing.

The woman seated herself and began reading a copy of *High-Fidelity,* which she found lying on a table. The man, less relaxed, inspected display racks and turned revolving wheels of records. He was poking at a Pickering cartridge when a familiar shuffling sound caught his attention. Up the flight of steps from the basement stockroom, his arms filled with records, came Joseph Schilling.

Tossing down the magazine, the woman rose to her feet. Plump and smiling, she advanced toward Schilling. The man joined her.

"Hi," the man muttered.

Joseph Schilling came to a stop. He was not wearing his glasses and, for a moment, he had trouble making them out. He imagined they were customers; their clothing informed him that they were fairly well off, fairly educated, extremely arty people. Then he recognized them.

"Yes," he said, in an unsteady, hostile voice. "The line forms . . . amazing, how fast."

"So this is it," the woman said, glancing around. Her smile, fixed and intense, remained; a frozen smile, made up of heavy lips and teeth. "It's lovely! I'm so glad you finally got it."

Stiffly, Schilling set down his records. He wondered where

Max was; they were afraid of Max. Probably down at the corner cocktail lounge, sitting in a booth constructing a tower of matches. "It's not a bad location," he said.

Her blue eyes danced. "This is what you always wanted, all these years. Remember," she said to her companion, "how he always talked about his store? The record store he was going to open up someday, when he got the money."

"I decided not to wait," Schilling said.

"Wait?"

"For the money." It didn't sound convincing; he was bad at games. "I'm broke. Most of this stuff is on consignment. My capital went into the remodeling."

"You'll struggle along," the woman said.

From his coat pocket Schilling got a cigar. As he lit up, he said: "Seems to me you've gained weight."

"I suppose so." The woman searched her mind. "How long has it been?"

"It was 1948," her companion said.

"We've all gotten older," the woman said.

Schilling went to wait on a middle-aged customer. Presently he returned. They were still there; they hadn't left. He hadn't really expected them to. "Well, Beth," he said, "what brings you here?"

"Curiosity. We haven't seen you in so long . . . when we read in the paper about your store, we said, 'Let's hop in the car and drive up there.' So we did."

"What paper?"

"The San Francisco *Chronicle.*"

"You don't live in San Francisco."

"Somebody sent us the clipping," she said vaguely. "They knew we'd be interested."

It had certainly been his mistake, five years ago, to mix with these people. He would never shake them, not now. They had found him and his store: he was a duck in a rain barrel. And he had tangible assets.

"Did you come out from Washington?" he asked. "Getting away from the winter?"

"God," Beth said, "we haven't lived in Washington in years. We lived in Detroit and then we moved to Los Angeles."

Following me, Schilling thought. Coming west with their noses to the ground.

"We stopped by to see you," Beth said, "when you were living in Salt Lake City. But you were having some sort of business meeting, and we couldn't stay."

"That was a nice spot you had there," Coombs, the man, said. "Did you own that place?"

"I had an interest."

"That wasn't a store, was it? Not that big brick building? It looked like a warehouse."

"Wholesalers," Schilling said. "We jobbed for a number of labels."

"And you built up capital for this shop?" Coombs was skeptical. "You were better off there; you won't do any business in a town this size."

"I guess you haven't seen the duck," Schilling said. "The duck in the park. He doesn't buy much, but he's fun to watch. What are you two doing these days? For a living, I mean."

"Different things," Beth said. "I taught for a while; that was in Detroit."

"Piano?" he asked.

"Oh, certainly. I stopped playing the cello years ago. I had stopped when—I met you."

"That's so," Schilling said. "There was one around your apartment, but you didn't play it."

"Two busted strings. And I lost the bow."

"It seems to me I had an old joke about lady cello players," Schilling said. "It had to do with their psychological motives."

"Yes," Beth agreed. "It was really a terrible joke, but I always thought it was funny."

Schilling felt himself mellow, remembering. "Freudian analysis . . . a popular indoor pastime, in those days. Not so popular now. What was it I said?"

"Women cello players. They have a subconscious need for something large between their legs." Beth laughed. "You were delightful. You really were."

It was hard to believe he had ever wanted this hefty girl, had carted her off for a weekend, found his way into that wonderfully avid cunt, and then returned her to her husband more or less intact. But she had not been hefty then; she had been small. Beth Coombs was still attractive—her skin was quite smooth and her eyes, as always, were clear. The affair had been brief and intense, and he had enjoyed it. If only there had been no aftereffects.

"What now?" he said, including the both of them. "Going to hang around town?"

Beth nodded, but Coombs pretended he hadn't heard.

"Oh, come on, Coombs," Schilling said. "Let's face it. You're that by which vinegar got from the bucket to Our Savior's mouth."

Coombs was still not hearing, but Beth laughed merrily. "It's good to hear you again, Joe. I've missed conversation."

Defeated, Schilling gave up. "Want an armload of records? Want the cash register?" He made a resigned, giving motion. "Want the diamond needles out of the cartridges? They're worth ten bucks apiece."

"Very funny," Coombs said. "Our business here is legitimate."

"You're still in the photography business?"

"Off and on."

"You didn't come here to photograph people."

After a pause, Beth said: "Well, we've been depending mostly on the music teaching."

"You're going to teach here?"

"We thought," Beth said, "that you could give us some help. You're fairly well settled. You have your store; you've probably built up contacts with the musical people in town. You're going to sell sheet music, aren't you?"

"No," Schilling said. "And I'm not going to give you a job. And I'm not going to fool around with this thing; I'm operating on a limited budget and I have all the expenses I can stand."

In a sputter of excitement, Coombs said: "You can give us a plug; that won't cost you anything. All the old ladies come around asking who's a piano teacher. What are you going to do at Christmas? You can't run your record store alone; you need somebody to help you."

"Surely you're going to hire somebody," Beth persisted. "I'm surprised you haven't already."

"I never was good at hiring."

"You don't feel you could use some help here?"

"I just said—I don't get that many customers. And I don't have that much money." Schilling kept his eye on the browsers among the display racks. "I'll paste a card over the cash register with your name and address. When someone wants a piano teacher, I'll send them around. That's all I can do."

Coombs said: "You don't feel you owe us something?"

"Good God, what?"

"No matter what you do," Coombs said rapidly, stumbling over his words, "you can never make up for the terrible harm you did us. You ought to get down on your knees and beg God to forgive you."

"You mean," Schilling said, "that because I didn't pay her then, I should pay her now?"

For a moment Coombs stood blinking, and then he melted altogether in a puddle of frenzy. "You should be destroyed," he said, his teeth chattering. "You're—"

"Let's go," Beth said, starting toward the door. "Come on, Danny."

"I heard a good one," Schilling said to Danny Coombs. "Right up your line. Somebody installed one of those one-way mirrors in a women's shower, one of those big mirrors, full-length. Maybe you can tell me how those work; one side is a mirror but the other is a window."

Pale but composed, Beth said: "Good luck with your store. Maybe we'll see you around."

"All right," he said. Reflexively he gathered an armload of records and began filing them.

"I don't see why we have to quarrel," Beth continued. "There's no reason why Danny and I can't come here; the Los Angeles job fizzled, and we were driving up the coast."

"But the same town," Schilling said. "And within a couple of months."

"Music is booming here. We're letting you do the groundwork."

"My grave or yours? Or all of ours?"

"Don't be nasty," Beth said.

"I'm not being nasty," Schilling answered. Well, this was his punishment for having lost—for a day or so—his better judgment. For having been weak enough to go to bed with another man's wife, and improvident enough to let the man find out. "Just being nostalgic," he said, and went on filing records.

8

• • • • • • • •

In the fall of 1953 Mary Anne Reynolds lived in a small apartment with a girl named Phyllis Squire. Phyllis was a waitress at the Golden State lunch counter, which was next door to the Lazy Wren, and Carleton Tweany himself had selected her. Thereby he had solved, in his own mind, Mary Anne's problems. He did not now have much to do with her. For Mary Anne there was little more than the passage of his presence; back and forth, not stopping, he went by and beyond her.

The telephone company job she had taken required her to work a split shift. At twelve-thirty at night she reached the apartment, and ate, and changed her clothes. As she changed, her roommate, in bed, read aloud from a copy of the sermons of Fulton Sheen.

"What's the trouble?" Phyllis asked, her mouth full of apple. In the corner, her white-enamel radio played a Perez Prado mambo. "You're not listening."

Ignoring her, Mary Anne slipped into her red culottes, stuffed in the tails of her shirt, and went to the door. "Don't go blind," she said over her shoulder, and closed the door behind her.

Noise and the movement of people flashed out into the dark street as she entered the Wren. Tables crowded with people, the line of men squeezed together at the bar . . . but Tweany was not singing. She was aware of it instantly. The upraised platform in the center was bare; he was nowhere in sight, and even Paul Nitz was absent.

"Hey," Taft Eaton said from behind the bar. "You get out of here; I'm not serving you."

Avoiding him, she began threading among the tables, searching for a place to sit.

"I mean it. You're a minor; you're not supposed to be in here. What do you want, you want me to lose my license?"

His voice faded as she reached the platform. Slouched at a table was Paul Nitz, conversing with a pair of patrons. He had apparently left his piano to talk to them; straddling a chair, leaning his bony chin against his arms, he was orating. ". . . but you have to make a distinction between folk songs and folk-*type* songs. Like jazz, and music in the jazz idiom."

The couple glanced up as she brought over a chair and seated herself. Nitz broke off what he was saying long enough to greet her. "How are you?"

"Fine," she said, "where's Tweany?"

"He just sang. He'll be back."

She felt a surge of tension. "Is he in the rear?"

"He probably is, but you can't go back there. Eaton'll throw you out on your ear."

At the side of the table appeared Taft Eaton, still fuming. "Goddamn it, Mary, I can't serve you. If the cops find you in here they'll close the Wren."

"Say I came in to use the john," she murmured. Pretending to ignore him, she began sliding out of her coat.

Eaton glowered at Nitz, who sat picking a bit of thread from his sleeve. "Don't you buy her anything. Contributing to the delinquency of minors—you and Carleton. You ought to be in jail." Taking her by the scruff of the neck, he said in her ear, "You ought to stay with your own race, where you belong."

Then he was gone, leaving Mary Anne to massage the back of her neck. "Drop dead," she muttered. It hurt, and she felt humiliated. But then, gradually, the pain left; and the need of Tweany resumed its usual dominance. "I'm going back and see if he's there."

"He'll be out," Nitz assured her. "Sit still . . . you and your hurry. Relax."

"I've got things to do. Where was he last night?"

"He was here."

"I don't mean here; I mean afterward. I went over to his pad at two-thirty and he wasn't home. He was out."

"Maybe so." Nitz dragged his chair around and returned to the listening couple. "Look at it this way, lady," he said, addressing the woman, a plump, somewhat pretty blonde. "Would you call Stephen Foster's stuff folk music?"

The blonde considered at excessive length. "No, I guess not. But it was based on folk themes."

"That's my point. Folk music is not what you have, but how you go about it. Nobody can plop himself down and write a folk song; and nobody can get up in white tie and tails in some plush cocktail lounge and sing a folk song."

"Does anybody sing folk music, then?"

"Not now. But they did, once. They sang, they added verses, they put together new material constantly."

She became aware of the nature of their discussion. It had to do with Tweany, and they were attacking him. "Don't you think he's a great folksinger?" she demanded, addressing the blonde. In her world, loyalty was a vital pillar. She could not understand this veiled undercutting of a friend; it seemed her responsibility to defend him. "What's wrong with him?"

"I've never heard him. We're still waiting."

"I'm not talking about Tweany," Nitz said, evidently aware of his moral lapse. "Not particularly, I mean. I'm talking about folk music in general."

"But this Tweany is a folksinger," the blonde said. "So where does he stand?"

Nitz uneasily sipped his drink. "It's hard to say. I'm just the intermission pianist . . . a mortal."

"You don't like his stuff," the blonde's companion said with a knowing wink.

"I'm a bop player." Nitz reddened and avoided the girl's accusing glare. "To me, folk music is like Dixie: a dead horse. It stopped growing back in the days of James Merritt Ives. Show me a folk song that's come down since then."

She was quite angry now; the need to defend Tweany, to keep the greatness of him intact, made her bristle and say: "What about 'Ol' Man River'?" Tweany sang "Ol' Man River" at least once a night, and it was one of her favorites.

At that, Nitz grinned. "See what I mean? 'Ol' Man River' was written by Jerome Kern."

He broke off, because at that moment there was applause, and Carleton Tweany appeared on the raised platform. Instantly, the girl forgot Nitz, forgot the blonde and everything else. The conversation fell into a vacuum.

"Excuse me," Nitz murmured. He crawled back to his piano, dwarfed, she observed, by the huge figure of Tweany.

"For my first number," Tweany rumbled in his furry singsong, "I will sing a work that expresses the bitter terror of the Negro people in their ages of bondage. You may have heard it before." He paused. " 'Strange Fruit.' "

A flutter of excitement stirred the room as Nitz picked out a few opening chords. And then, his arms folded, his head down, forehead wrinkled in contemplation, Tweany began. He did not raise his voice or shout; he did not bellow or snarl or shake his fist. Thoughtful, deeply moved, he spoke directly to the people around him; it was a highly personal communication and not a concert rendition.

When he had finished telling them the story of life in the South, there was silence. Nobody clapped; the people clustered around waited with fearful expectancy, as Tweany considered his next communication.

"My people," he murmured, "have suffered greatly in their chains and tribulations. Their lot has not been a happy one. But the Negro can sing about his privations. This is a song from the heart of the Negro people. In it he expresses his deeply felt sufferings, but, at the same time, his genuine humor. He is, innately, a happy person. What he wants is the simple things of life. Enough to eat, a place to sleep, and most important, a woman."

Carleton Tweany thereupon sang "Got Grasshoppers in My Pillow, Baby, Got Crickets All in My Meal."

Mary Anne listened tensely, following every word, her eyes on the man a few feet from her. In the last months she had not been close to Tweany; except for these public moments, she had seen little of him She wondered if he was singing to her; she tried to find in his words some special reference to herself and things they had done together. Bland and withdrawn, Tweany continued to sing, not noticing her, apparently unaware of her.

Beside her the blonde listened, too. Her companion was uninterested; sunk down in a brooding heap, he squeezed and pressed a piece of wax that had dripped from the candle.

"For my last number," Tweany declared when he had finished, "I shall sing a composition that has found special favor in the hearts of Americans, both Caucasian and Negro. It is a song that unites all of us in memories as we near the moment in which we celebrate the birth of One Who died to redeem us all, whatever our race, whatever our color."

Half-closing his eyes, Tweany sang "White Christmas."

At the piano, Paul Nitz plunked chords dutifully. Mary Anne, as she listened to the tune grind along, wished she could tell what was in the minds of the two men. Nitz, hunched over at the keys, seemed merely bored—as if he were pushing a broom, she reflected. She felt indignation at Nitz's betrayal of artistry. Was that all it meant to him? As if he were on an assembly line . . . she hated him for betraying Tweany. It was an insult to Tweany; he could show *some* feeling. And Tweany—what, if anything, was he thinking?

It seemed, almost, as if there was a cynical smile on Tweany's face, an emptiness that could have been the most muted kind of contempt. But contempt for whom? For the song? But he had picked it. For the people listening? As he sang—or rather muttered out the lyrics—Tweany's expression began to undergo a metamorphosis. The detachment began to fade; in its place appeared a fervor. His voice took on a throbbing sublimity, a grandeur that grew until he appeared to be vibrating with pain. There was no doubting his emotions: Tweany loved the song. He was terribly moved. And he was communicating that to the audience.

When he had finished there was once more the interval of silence, and then the applause exploded wildly. Tweany stood, shaken, his face impassioned. Then, gradually, grief sank and the half-cynical listlessness returned. Tweany shrugged, straightened his expensive hand-painted necktie, and stepped to the floor.

"Tweany!" Mary Anne called shrilly, jumping to her feet. "Where were you last night? I came over and you weren't home."

With a faint twitch of his eyebrows—two lines of expressive, cultivated black—Tweany acknowledged her existence. He stepped over to the table and stood for a moment with his hand on the chair Nitz had vacated.

The blonde said: "Why don't you join us?"

"Thank you," Tweany replied. He rotated the chair and seated himself. "I'm tired."

"Don't you feel good?" Mary Anne asked, concerned; he did look wilted.

"Not so good."

Nitz dropped down beside him and said: "I hate that goddamn 'White Christmas' worse than any other tune in the business. The joker that wrote that should be shot."

Sadness overcame Tweany. "Oh?" he murmured. "Do you feel that?"

Sipping his drink, Nitz said: "What do you know about the sufferings of the Negro people? You were born in Oakland, California."

The blonde, to Mary Anne's annoyance, leaned forward and

addressed Tweany. "That song about grasshoppers . . . that's an old Leadbelly tune, isn't it?"

Tweany nodded. "Yes, Leadbelly used to sing that, before he passed away."

"Did he record it?"

"He did," Tweany said absently. "But it's not available now. It's more or less a collector's item."

"Maybe Joe has it," the blonde said to her companion.

"Ask him," her companion said, without enthusiasm. "You're in there enough."

The discussion of folk music resumed, and Mary Anne managed to catch Tweany's attention.

"You didn't say where you were last night," she said accusingly.

A cunning smile settled over Tweany's face; the usual film glazed his eyes until they were a dulled, dispassionate gray. "I was busy. I've been rather occupied, the last few weeks."

"Months, you mean."

Half-listening to Nitz and the blonde rambling on about Blind Lemon Jefferson, Tweany asked: "How's the Pacific Tel and Tel?"

"Lousy."

"I'm sorry to hear that."

In a clear voice Mary Anne informed him, "I'm going to quit."

"Already?"

"No. Not until I have something else. I've learned my lesson."

"You wish you were back at the furniture place? Ask them—they'll take you back."

"Don't kid me. I wouldn't go back there on a bet."

"Suit yourself." Tweany shrugged. "It's your life."

"Why did you throw me out when I came to you that day?"

"I didn't throw you out. I don't recall doing that."

"You wouldn't let me move my things over. You made me

keep a separate address, and after a week you wouldn't let me stay all night. I had to get up and leave—that's what I call being thrown out."

He regarded her with wonder. "Are you out of your mind? You know the situation. You're under age. It's a felony."

"If it's a felony to do it at three o'clock in the morning, it's a felony to do it in the afternoon."

"I thought you understood."

"If it's a felony—"

"Keep your voice down," Tweany said, with a glance at Nitz and the couple. Now they were involved in a discussion of contemporary atonal experiments. "That was only—now and then. Not a thing they could catch."

"Now and then? *Temporary?*"

She was furious, really furious. Because she remembered what it was convenient for him to forget: that specific day he had taken her into his apartment, the two of them lost among the clutter that filled the rooms, two living creatures bedded together among the pack rat's hoard. And the hot summer sun baking the flies that crept up the windowpanes . . . lying, the two of them, slippery with sweat, covered by nothing, spread out on the bed with the glare blinding them into an indolent, careless stupor.

There, in that high loft, they had eaten their breakfast, had shared the old bathtub, had cooked and ironed, had roamed naked through the rooms, playing the little piano, had sat, in the evening, listening to the radio, staring into the red button of its dial light, the two of them combined on the couch, on the sagging, dust-sodden couch.

Although, according to Tweany, she was not much good that way. She had learned—been taught—to rest her weight on her shoulder blades and not on her coccyx; that way she could raise her hips higher. But other than purely muscular tensions, she had developed no responses; the experience brought her nothing, and nothing was what she gave back.

It was, to her, very like the time the doctor had stuck his metal probe into her nose to break off a polyp. The same pressure, the same too-large physical unit forcing its way inside her; then pain, and a little blood, and the crickets chirping in the grass of the yard below the window.

Tweany said she was no good: small and bony and frigid. Gordon, of course, had no opinion; he expected nothing but concavity, and that was what he got: no more and no less.

"Tweany," Mary Anne said, "you can't pretend we haven't been—"

"Don't get upset," Tweany said silkily. "You'll get ulcers."

Mary Anne leaned toward him until her small, tight face was almost touching his. "What have you been doing the last two months?"

"Absolutely nothing. Except my art."

"You're staying with somebody. You're never at home; I waited one night all night and you didn't show up. You didn't come home."

Tweany shrugged. "I was visiting."

Next to them, the discussion had become heated. "I never heard of that," Nitz was saying.

"You could have," the blonde told him. "Don't you have a radio? Every Wednesday night Joe has a program over that San Mateo good-music station. Listen to that. He writes up his material; he likes to do it all himself."

"I tried listening to that stuff," Nitz said, "but I can't get with it. It's—old."

Lapsing into silence, Mary Anne withdrew into her own thoughts; the conversation meant nothing to her.

"It's not old. It's still going on; the same material you're doing, only they don't call it by the same name. Milhaud, up in Oakland. And Roger Sessions is at Berkeley; go listen to him. Sid Hethel is at Palo Alto; he's about the best there is. Joe knows him . . . they're old friends."

"I thought it was nothing but Mozart," Nitz said.

The blonde continued: "On Sunday, when the shop is closed, Joe has a two-hour record concert. You should go."

"You mean people just walk in?"

"Fifteen or so people show up. He plays atonal, early baroque, whatever they want." With a flicker of her blue eyes she glanced up at Tweany. "I saw you there; you showed up once."

"That's so," Tweany admitted. "You brought out a tray of coffee for us, halfway through."

"Did you enjoy yourself?"

"Very much. That's an extraordinary shop he has."

"What's that?" Mary Anne said sharply. She woke up, then: the conversation had ceased to be abstract. Now it was dealing with reality, and she began to pay attention.

"The new record shop," Tweany said.

Mary Anne turned to confront the blonde. "Do you know that man?" she demanded, recalling in a rush the record shop, the looming shape of the man with his vest and gold watch and tweed suit.

"Joe?" The blonde smiled. "Oh, yes. We're old friends of Joe's."

"Where'd you meet him?" She experienced a kind of horror, as if she were being told about some personal crime.

"In Washington, D.C."

"You're from out of town, aren't you?"

"Yes," the blonde said.

"He's really on the level?" Her distress was real, again. But after four months it no longer had the same urgency. It had thinned as it receded into time; it was not immediate.

"Joe has been in the music business all his life," the blonde said. "His aunt sold harps in Denver during the Spanish-American War. Joe worked for Century Music in New York, in the twenties. Before you were born."

Brooding, Mary Anne said: "I don't like it in there."

"Why not?"

"It gives me the creeps." Not wishing to discuss it, Mary Anne said to Tweany: "When are you going to leave? Are you doing another set or not?"

Tweany pondered. "I believe I'll go lie down. No, I won't do another set. I've done enough for tonight."

The blonde was still studying Mary Anne with interest. "What do you mean? Why do you say that about Joe's store?"

Struggling, Mary Anne answered: "It's not the store." That was certainly true; she had loved the store.

"Did something happen?"

"No, nothing." She shook her head irritably. "Forget it, will you?" All at once the fear came back, and she said to Tweany: "Do you really go in there?"

"Certainly," Tweany said.

It seemed difficult to believe. "But that's the man I told you about."

Tweany had no comment.

"Did—you like him?" Mary Anne asked.

"A gentleman," Tweany stated. "We had quite an interesting talk about Bascom Lamar Lunsford. He played an ancient Lunsford record for me, cut around 1927. From his private collection."

Bewildered by this double set of images, Mary Anne said: "You never told me you went in there."

"Why? What's the importance?" Tweany seemed unconcerned. "I go wherever I care to."

Paul Nitz could no longer keep quiet. "You suppose he'd give me a few pointers?" he asked.

"Joe has worked with a number of young musicians," the blonde said. "He gave me a great deal of help—he got some pieces of mine published. Right now he's plugging a kid he heard singing up in San Francisco at one of the North Beach joints; he's been taping his routine and trying to get one of the lp companies to press it."

"Chad Lemming," her companion said.

"What sort of approach does he represent?" Tweany asked with professional interest.

"Chad does political monologues," the blonde said. "With a guitar. Sort of rhymed commentaries on the present state of affairs. Thought control, Senator McCarthy, topics like that. Would you care to hear him?"

"I suppose," Tweany said.

The blonde got promptly to her feet. "Come along, then."

"Where?"

"He's at our place—he's staying with us until he goes back up the peninsula. He'll only be down here a few days."

Mary Anne watched with dismay the response of Carleton Tweany. What was happening was obvious, but she could think of nothing to do. And then Nitz, mild, eyes half-shut, came to her rescue. "You've got another set, man," he said.

"I'm tired," Tweany said. "I'll let it go this time."

"You can't."

Hauteur overcame Tweany; he clearly was not giving up. "I can't perform creatively when I'm tired."

"Then come on," the blonde urged.

As if responding to an occult power, Taft Eaton approached the table, his bar rag oozing bubbles in a trail across the floor. "One more set, Carleton. You've not leaving."

"Certainly not," Tweany agreed.

Grinning, with a wink at Mary Anne, Nitz said, "Tough luck. Anyhow, this Lemming might start singing folk songs."

With his usual profound gravity, Tweany turned back to the blonde. She was still standing, still smiling at him, on the verge of leaving. "Perhaps," Tweany said, in a tone Mary Anne well recognized, "you could bring him over to my place. I'll be there directly I complete this final set."

"Then it's settled." A little quiver of her hips—a quite visible undulation of triumph—and then the blonde prodded her still-seated companion, saying: "Let's be going."

"My address," Tweany began artfully, but Nitz interrupted him.

"I'll take them over." Under the table he gave Mary Anne a comradely kick. "I'll be along; I want to have a look at this bird."

"Glad to have you," the blonde said.

"Just a moment," Taft Eaton began. "Paul, it seems strange to hear you talk about leaving."

"I don't have to accompany him," Nitz said. "I'm intermission pianist. He can sing some of those stomps and chain-gang hollers."

"Can I come?" Mary Anne asked, in a flurry of misery. She didn't want to be left out; she was helpless to prevent Tweany and the blonde from mingling, but at least she could be there, too.

"And my girl," Nitz said, rising. "I have to have her with me."

"Bring her." The blonde was already moving toward the street door.

"A party," her companion murmured, glancing at Nitz and Mary Anne. "Got any more friends?"

"Don't be rude." Halting beside Tweany, the blonde said: "My name's Beth, and this is my husband, Danny. Danny Coombs."

"How do you do," Tweany said.

"You can't leave," Taft Eaton repeated stubbornly, still there. "Somebody has to do something around here."

"I'm not leaving," Tweany said. "I explained it fully. I'll do the final set and then leave."

Putting his hand on Mary Anne's shoulder, Nitz said to her, "Don't feel bad."

She followed morosely after Beth and Danny Coombs, her hands in her pockets. "I don't want to go. But I have to."

"You'll live through it," Nitz said. He held the red-padded door open as Mary Anne stepped out onto the sidewalk. The Coombses had begun climbing into a parked Ford. "We'll give this guy a hotfoot."

He crawled into the backseat of the Ford and helped Mary Anne in. Hugging her comfortingly to him, he reached into his coat and got out his drink glass.

"Ready?" Beth inquried cheerfully over her shoulder.

"Here we go," Nitz said, settling back and yawning.

9

When they arrived at the Coombses' apartment, there was no sign of Chad Lemming.

"He's in the bathroom," Beth said. "Taking a bath." The sound of running water could be heard. "He'll be out in a few minutes."

The apartment was a single huge room with a grand piano at one end, two tiny bedrooms, and a kitchen no larger than a pea. The bathroom, in which Lemming was contained, was across the hall; it was a community bathroom, shared with the family downstairs. The walls of the apartment were spotted with prints, mostly by Theotocopuli and Gauguin. The floor, except at the extreme edges, was covered by a gray-green mat of woven fiber. The curtains were burlap.

"Are you an artist?" Mary Anne asked Beth.

"No. But I used to be."

"Why'd you stop?"

Glancing at Coombs, Beth strolled into the kitchen and started fixing drinks. "I got more interested in music," she answered. "What do you want to drink?"

"Bourbon and water," Nitz said, prowling around. "If you have some."

"How about you?" she asked Mary Anne.

"Anything's okay."

Four bourbons and water were brought out; each of them took

his awkwardly. Beth had tossed off her coat; now her figure emerged, mature and expanded. She wore a T-shirt and slacks. Seeing her, Mary Anne reflected on her own small bust. She wondered how old Beth was.

"How old are you?" she asked.

Beth's blue eyes widened with dismay. "Me? Twenty-nine."

Satisfied, Mary Anne dropped the subject. "Is this your piano?" She wandered over to the grand piano and plunked a few random notes. It was the first time she had ever touched a grand piano; the great blackness of it awed her. "How much do they cost?"

"Well," Beth said, a little amused, "you can pay up to eight thousand dollars for a Bösendorfer."

Mary Anne wondered what a Bösendorfer was, but she said nothing. Nodding, she approached one of the wall prints and scrutinized it. Suddenly from the hall came a swirl of motion; Chad Lemming, having completed his bath, was returning.

Lemming, a slender young fellow, dashed through the living room in a flapping cotton robe and vanished into the bedroom. "I'll be directly out," he fluttered. "I won't be long." He sounded, to Mary Anne, like a fairy. She resumed her examination of the print.

"Listen, Mary," Nitz said, close beside her. Beth and Danny Coombs were following Lemming into the bedroom, telling him at length what to sing. "Stop sticking nails in yourself. It's not worth it."

At first she couldn't imagine what he meant.

"Carleton Tweany," he said, "is a conceited posturer. You've been at his house; you've seen his jars of hair oil and his silk shirts. And his cravats. Those cravats."

Very thinly Mary Anne said: "You're jealous of him because he's big and you're a tiny-man."

"I'm no tiny-man, and I'm telling you the truth. He's stupid; he's snobbish; he's a fake."

Mary Anne floundered. "You don't understand him."

"Why? Because I haven't slept with him? I've done everything else; I've been up close to his soul."

"How?"

"By accompanying his 'Many Brave Hearts,' that's how."

Wavering, Mary Anne said: "He's a great singer. No, you don't think so." She shook her head. "Let's drop it."

"Mary Anne," Nitz said, "you're a hell of a sweet person. You realize that?"

"Thank you."

"Take your pal, that punk who chauffeurs you around. Dave something."

"Dave Gordon."

"Re-create him along useful lines. He's basically sound, just too young."

"He's dumb."

"You're way ahead of your pals . . . that's one of your troubles. You're too old for them. And you're so darn young it's pitiful."

She glared at him. "Keep your opinions to yourself."

"Nobody can tell you anything." He rumpled her hair, and she jerked away. "You're too smart for Tweany. And you're too good for all of us. I wonder who'll finally snare you . . . not me, I guess. Not very likely. You'll wind up with some donkey, some hulking pillar of bourgeois respectability you can admire and have faith in. Why can't you have faith in yourself?"

"Lay off, Paul. Please."

"Are you even listening?"

"I can hear you; don't shout."

"You're listening with your ears only. You don't even see me standing here, do you?" Befuddled, Nitz rubbed his forehead. "Forget it, Mary. I feel tired and sick and I don't make sense."

Beth rushed over to them, bright-eyed and excited, breasts wagging. "Chad is going to sing! Everybody shut up and listen!"

* * *

The young man had now emerged. His hair was crew-cut; he wore horn-rimmed glasses; a bow tie dangled under his protruding Adam's apple. Beaming at the people, he picked up his guitar and began his monologue and song.

"Well, folks," he said cheerily, "I guess you read in the papers a while back about the President going to balance the budget. Well, here's a little song about it I figured you might enjoy." And, with a few strums at his guitar, he was off.

Listening absently, Mary Anne roamed about the room, examining prints and furnishings. The song, in a bright metallic way, glittered out over everything, spilling into everyone's ears. A few phrases reached her, but the main drift of the lyrics was lost. She did not particularly care; she was uninterested in Congress and taxes. She had never seen anybody like Chad Lemming and the impression of him dulled against the closedness of her mind . . . she had her own problems.

The next ballad came almost at once. Now he was bleating about old-age pensions. That was followed by a spirited ditty about the FBI, then one about genetics, and finally an involved, rollicking jingle concerning the H-bomb.

"*. . . And if Mao Tse-tung makes trouble*
we will blow the world to rubble . . ."

Irritably, she wondered who cared about Mao Tse-tung. Who was he; wasn't he head of Communist China?

"*. . . I'll be lying in the ruin*
while disarmament is brewin' . . ."

Closing her ears against the racket, she wandered entirely out of the living room, into one of the gloomy bedrooms. Sitting on the edge of the bed—Beth's bed, from the looks of it—she prepared to endure the remainder of Lemming's routine. The title of the song, announced with much elaboration and fanfare, still dinned in her ears.

"What This Country Needs Is a Good Five-Cent H-bomb."

It failed to make sense. It had no meaning. Her mind reverted, instead, to prior thoughts. To the strong, dark presence of Carleton Tweany; and, drifting behind it, memories of the incident at the music shop, the large old man in his tweed suit. First striding about with his silver cane . . . then the pressure of his fingers as he took hold of her arm.

Gradually she became aware that the singing had died. Guiltily, she climbed to her feet and found her way back into the living room. Beth had disappeared into the kitchen for more drinks; Danny Coombs was off sulking in the corner, leaving Nitz and Lemming together.

"Who writes your stuff?" Nitz was asking.

"I do," Lemming said shyly. Now that he wasn't immersed in his act, he seemed to be a tame college freshman in a sports coat and slacks. Setting down his guitar, he removed his glasses and polished them on his sleeve. "I tried to do gag writing down in L.A., but I didn't click. They said I wasn't commercial. Apparently my material was too pointed."

"How old are you?"

"Twenty-seven."

"That old? You don't look that old."

Lemming laughed. "I graduated from Cal back in '48, in chemistry. For a while I worked up at the Project—" He explained: "The radiation lab. I could still work there, I guess. They never took away my clearance. But I prefer to keep moving around . . . I guess I never grew up."

"Is there any loot in this stuff?" Nitz asked.

"None that I'm aware of."

"Can you make a living?"

"Maybe so," Lemming said. "I hope so."

Nitz was puzzled. "A guy like you—you have an education, you could work at a big research project. But you want to bum around with this. You enjoy it? It's worth that much to you in terms of personal satisfaction?"

"These are troubled times," Lemming murmured, and Mary Anne lost the balance of it in words as well as thought. His talk, like his singing, made no sense. But Nitz was muttering away, asking the man questions, digging out answers. His interest was a mystery . . . she gave up and dismissed the subject.

"You never told us your name," Beth said, approaching her with a fresh drink.

Mary Anne declined the drink. She did not like the woman, and for good reason. But she felt an unhappy respect: Beth had gone directly after Tweany, and her obvious mastery left the girl participating out of her depth. "What's the matter with him?" she said, meaning Lemming. "Nothing at all, probably. But he's so—silly. Maybe it's me. I'm out of place here."

"Don't go," Beth said with condescension.

"I might as well. How long have you known Schilling?"

"Five or six years."

"What's he like?" She did want to find out, and Beth evidently knew.

"That depends," Beth said. "We had a lot of fun together. Years ago, when you were—" She measured the girl, until Mary Anne became offended. "Oh, about fourteen."

"He must have money, to open that store."

"Oh, yes. Joe has money. Not a lot, but enough for what he wants."

"What does he want?"

"Joe is a very thoughtful man. He's also a lonely man. In spite of everything—" She smiled her fixed smile— "I have the highest regard for his taste and intellect. He's highly educated; he's charming in an old-fashioned way. He's a gentleman . . . most of the time, at least. He knows a great deal about the music business."

"Then why isn't he running a big record company, like RCA?"

"Haven't you ever met a record collector?"

"No," Mary Anne admitted.

"Joe is where he always wanted to be: he's finally got a little store of his own where he has plenty of time to talk records, touch records, live records."

"He'll stay here, then?"

"Certainly. He's looked for this for years—a peaceful town, off the mainstream, where he can settle down. He's getting old; he wants to retire somewhere. He used to keep himself in the middle of things, running around to parties, concerts, social gatherings, traveling here and there. I suppose that's over . . . I don't know. He's always had a strong need for people; he's never liked being alone. He's not a naturally solitary person. He likes to talk and share his experiences. That keeps him reaching out . . . he can't be content."

"He sounds wonderful," Mary Anne said caustically.

"You don't sound convinced."

"I almost went to work for him."

"In many ways," Beth said, "it's hard for us to judge Joe Schilling. I once believed he was—well, ruthless."

"And he's not?"

"His needs are so strong. He hits you with such an impact."

"You didn't answer my question."

"I don't see why I should. Maybe some other time."

"Would it make a difference if I told you that something did happen in the store?"

"I know something happened. And I have a good idea what it was. Remember, you and I are the same age . . . we have similar problems. Similar experiences."

"You're twenty-nine," Mary Anne said reflectively. "I'm twenty. You're nine years older than I am."

Pained, Beth said: "But for all intents and purposes we're in the same group."

Subjecting the woman to her calm, pitiless scrutiny, Mary Anne said: "Would you help me pick out a bra sometime? I don't want to look so thin. I wish I had a good bustline, like yours."

"You poor kid," Beth said. She shook her head. "You just don't know what it's all about."

"I would, very much," Lemming was saying enthusiastically. "Here, you mean?"

"No," Nitz answered, "we'll have to go over there. It's been arranged by higher powers." He inspected his wristwatch. "He's probably home by now."

"I've heard a lot about him," Lemming said.

Rousing himself from his lethargy, Coombs protested, "The point escapes me. What are we going over there for?"

"Don't be a pill," Beth said.

"I don't want to see him. None of us want to see him. Just you."

"I'd sort of like to," Lemming said. "It might be a good thing professionally."

"It's almost two in the morning," Coombs said. "I'm ready for bed."

"Just for a while," Beth said, unrelenting. "Go get your camera—be a good boy. We told him we'd show up; he *asked* us to."

Coombs snickered. "He asked us?" He located his camera and tugged the strap on. "You mean, you asked him. The same old business—only this is the first one with a touch of the tarbrush. What's the matter, are you tired of—"

"Shut up," Beth said, walking away. "We're going; we said we'd go. Stop acting like a neurotic."

"I'm warning you," Coombs said. "If we go over there, no monkey business. You behave."

"Christ," Beth said.

"I mean it."

"Sure, you mean it," Beth said. "You always mean it. Come on," she said to Nitz and Mary Anne. "There's no point in sticking around here." She waved Lemming toward the door. "That's right, Chad. Just turn the knob."

Resignedly, Mary Anne had begun searching for her coat. "I'll show you how to get there," she murmured.

"Why, how sweet," Beth said with a lingering smile. "How very sweet of you, dear."

10

Tweany's house, when they arrived, showed only a faint blue haze in the region of the top floor.

"He's in the kitchen," Mary Anne said, pushing open the car door. The others followed, and, in a moment, they were tramping up the long flight of stairs.

There was no immediate response to Mary Anne's tap. Finally she opened the door and entered. Down the hallway glowed a pittance of light. The sounds of movement were audible; Mary Anne hurried in that direction and appeared breathlessly in Tweany's high-ceilinged kitchen.

Tweany, still wearing his pink shirt and hand-painted tie, was sitting at the table eating a sardine sandwich and drinking a bottle of Rheingold beer. In front of him, spread out among the litter of food, was a smeared copy of *Esquire,* which he was reading.

"We came," Mary Anne said, her heart aching to see him there, big and sturdy, his sleaves rolled up, his arms thick and heavy and powerful. "We brought what's-his-name along."

Nitz materialized in the doorway. "Get ready to be showed up," he announced, and then vanished back into the hall. The others, Beth and Lemming and Coombs, followed him into the disorderly living room, leaving Mary Anne and Tweany alone.

"He's no good," Mary Anne said loyally. "All he does is talk."

A placid superiority spread across the man's features. He shrugged and resumed his reading. "Help yourself. You know where the refrigerator is."

"I'm not hungry," Mary Anne said. "Tweany—"

Beaming, Chad Lemming entered the kitchen carrying his guitar. "Mr. Tweany, I've wanted to meet you for a long time. I've heard a lot about your style."

Untouched by the young man's flattery, Tweany looked slowly up. "You're Chad Lemming?"

Self-consciously, Lemming fingered his guitar. "I do a sort of political monologue."

Tweany studied him. Lemming, still grinning with embarrassment, started to speak and then changed his mind. A few plaintive squawks drifted from his guitar, as if it were getting away from him.

"Go ahead," Tweany said.

"Sir?"

Tweany inclined his head toward the guitar. "Go on. I'm listening."

Completely ill at ease, Chad Lemming began to tell the stories and sing the ballads he had produced at the Coombses' apartment. "Well," he croaked halfheartedly, "I suppose you read in the newspapers the other day about President Eisenhower going to cut taxes. That caused me to do some thinking." Stammering, his voice faint, he began to sing.

Tweany, after watching a moment, imperceptibly returned to his magazine. There was no particular instant when he did so; the change was so gradual that Mary Anne could not follow it. Suddenly there was Tweany eating his sardine sandwich and studying an article on big-league baseball.

The others, filling up the doorway, listened and peeped into the kitchen. Lemming, with a shudder of abandon, knowing that he had failed, did a final raucous number about a library that either burned all its books or never had any books—Mary Anne couldn't tell. She wished he would stop; she wished he would go.

He was making a fool of himself and it goaded her to a fever pitch. By the time he had finished she wanted to scream aloud.

The silence that followed Lemming's performance was total. In the sink the monotonous dripping of a leaky faucet increased the sense of futility that hung over the room. Finally, with a grunt, Coombs elbowed his way in, swinging his flash camera.

"What's that?" Tweany asked, taking an interest.

"I want to get some pictures."

"Of what?" Tweany's voice took on a formal edge. "Of myself and Mr. Lemming?"

"That's correct," Coombs said. "Chad, get over beside him. Tweany, or whatever your name is, get up so you're both in the picture."

"I'm sorry, but I can't oblige," Tweany said. "My agent won't permit me to pose for publicity shots without his consent."

"What the hell agent is that?" Nitz demanded.

There was an uncomfortable pause, while Tweany went on with his meal and Chad Lemming stood unhappily beside the table.

"Forget it," Beth said to her husband. "Do as Mr. Tweany says."

Coombs, staring down at Tweany, suddenly complied. He flipped the lens cover over his camera, turned his back, and walked off. "The hell with it," he said, and mumbled a few words that nobody caught.

Hoisting up his guitar, Lemming departed from the room. Presently they heard the mournful noises from a long way off; he was curled up in the living room, playing to himself.

"Tweany," Mary Anne said, exasperated. "You ought to be ashamed of yourself."

Tweany raised an eyebrow, shrugged, and finished the remains of his sandwich. Brushing crumbs from his trousers, he arose and went over to the sink to rinse his hands. "What would you people care to drink? Beer? Scotch?"

They accepted scotch and, with their drinks, joined Lemming

in the living room. The young man didn't look up; absorbed in his playing, he continued to crouch over his guitar.

"You play that pretty good," Nitz said sympathetically.

Lemming muttered a grateful, "Thanks."

"Maybe you ought to concentrate on that," Beth said, having ingested her cue from Tweany. "Maybe just the guitar would be better."

"I like that a lot better," Mary Anne said. "I can't see that talking."

In a quandary, Lemming protested: "But that's the whole point."

"Let it go," Beth said. Stalking around the untidy living room, she came upon the piano. No larger than a spinet, the piano was lost under heaps of magazines and clothing. "Do you play?" she asked Tweany.

"No. Sometimes Paul accompanies me. Practice."

"Not very often," Nitz said, wiping dust from the keyboard with his handkerchief. He struck a chord, expertly diminished it, and then lost interest. "You're going to have trouble getting this out of here," he remarked.

Instantly Mary Anne said: "Tweany isn't going anywhere."

"We got it up with ropes," Tweany said. "And we can get it down the same way. Through the kitchen window, if we have to."

"Where are you going?" Mary Anne demanded, panic-stricken.

"Nowhere," Tweany answered.

"Tell her," Nitz said.

"There's nothing to tell. It's just an . . . idea."

"Tweany's planning his big-time," Nitz said to the petrified girl. "He's moving along to L.A. Got an offer from Heimy Feld, the character who handles those jump concerts. Trial run at a bunch of test spots on Heimy's circuit."

"The word 'trial' never came up," Tweany corrected.

Seating herself at the piano, Beth started tapping out the G minor scale. A little island of sound came into being around her.

"Tweany," she said, with a toss of her hair, "I used to write songs. Did you know that?"

"No," Tweany said.

"She brought one along," Coombs said sourly. "She's going to trot it out and ask you to sing it."

At this, Tweany puffed up until he was even larger than usual. A bluish, steely nimbus shone out: a massive conceit. "Well," he said, "I'm always interested in new material."

Nitz belched.

As the sheet music was brought out of Beth's giant bag, Mary Anne said to Nitz: "You should have told me."

"I waited."

"What for?" She couldn't understand.

"Until he was here. So he could answer."

"But," she said helplessly, "he didn't answer." She felt swamped by what was happening; her reality was drifting and she was unable to stop it. "He didn't say anything."

"That's what I mean," Nitz said. His voice sank down as Beth began to play. Tweany, standing behind her, leaned forward to catch the words. He had already entered a stage of rigid concentration; to him, music was a serious matter. Whatever trifle Beth had concocted was going to receive his full attention. There was an innate grace that Mary Anne could not forget or ignore; belief in what he was doing added measure to the man's style.

"This song," Tweany intoned, "is called, 'Where We Sat Down,' and tells the story of a young woman walking through the countryside in autumn, remembering and visiting the places where she and her lover—now dead, killed in foreign lands—had been together. It is a simple song." And, taking a deep, meaningful breath, he sang the simple song.

"He doesn't usually do that," Nitz murmured as the song came to a finish. Beth began rippling out arpeggios and Tweany meditated over the enigma of existence. "It's hard to get him to do stuff on sight . . . he likes to give it the once-over."

Beth was saying to the man standing beside her: "You felt it, didn't you?" Her playing took on volume and emotion. "You felt what I meant, in that."

"Yes," Tweany agreed, eyes half-shut, swaying with the music.

"And you brought it over. You realized it."

"It was a beautiful song," Tweany said, in a trance.

"Yes," Beth murmured, "it takes on a beauty. An almost terrifying beauty."

" 'White Christmas,' " Nitz said, "that's the end of you. You're finished."

For the briefest interval Tweany wrestled with his composure. Then passion overcame him, and he turned from the piano. "Paul," he said, "a casual cruelty can do great harm."

"Only to a sensitive soul," Nitz reminded him.

"This is my house. You're a guest in my house, at my invitation."

"Only the top floor." Nitz was pale and tense; he was no longer joking.

The strained silence grew until Mary Anne at last went over to Tweany and said: "We all should go."

"No," Tweany answered, his geniality returning.

"Paul," Mary Anne said to Nitz, "let's get out of here."

"Whatever you want," Nitz said.

At the piano, Beth played a series of runs. "Don't you want to wait for us? We'll give you a ride back."

"I meant," Mary Anne said to her, realizing that it was hopeless, "if we *all* left. All five of us together."

"That would be nice," Beth agreed. "Gosh, I can't imagine anything nicer." She made no move to get up, and her playing continued. In the corner, his legs drawn under him, Chad Lemming sorrowfully picked at his guitar, ignored by the rest of the group. His sounds, drowned out by the overpowering piano, dissolved and were lost.

"You won't get her to go," Danny Coombs said to Mary Anne in a fit of excitement. "She's got herself planted; she's set."

"Shut up, Danny," Beth said good-naturedly, beginning a progression that formed into a Fauré ballade. "Listen to this," she said to Tweany. "Ever heard it? It's one of my favorites."

"I've never heard it," Tweany said. "Is it one of yours?"

Beth created a great shower of musical sparks: a Chopin prelude, followed at once by the opening of the Liszt B-flat sonata. Tweany, caught in the wind blazing around him, stood fast and survived, even managing to smile as the piece ended.

"I love good music," he declared, and Mary Anne, embarrassed, looked away. "I wish I had more time for it."

"Do you know Schubert's 'Erlkönig'?" Beth asked, playing furiously. "How wonderfully you could render it."

Lifting his camera, Coombs snapped a shot of the two of them at the piano. Tweany seemed not even to notice; he continued breathing in the music, eyes shut now, hands clasped together before him. Laughing, Coombs popped the exhausted bulb onto the floor and fitted in a fresh one from the leather pouch at his waist.

"Jesus," he said to Nitz, "he's completely left us."

"He does that," Nitz said, standing by Mary Anne, his hand on her shoulder. The friendly pressure made her feel a little better, but not much. "I'm afraid that's his way."

Suddenly Beth leaped from the piano. In ecstasy she seized Lemming by the hand and dragged him to his feet. "You too," she cried in his astonished ear. "All of us; join in!"

Gratified to find himself noticed, Lemming began playing wildly. Beth hurried back to the piano and struck up the opening chords of a Chopin "Polonaise." Lemming, over-powered, danced around the room; throwing his guitar onto the couch, he jumped high in the air, whacked the ceiling with the palms of his hands, descended, caught hold of Mary Anne, and spun her about. At the piano, rocking back and forth, Tweany roared out the lyrics:

". . . Til the *end* of time . . ."

Miserable and ashamed, Mary Anne struggled out of Lemming's embrace. She reached the safety of the corner and again stood beside Paul Nitz, collecting herself and smoothing down her coat.

"They're nuts," Nitz said. "They're hopped in another dimension."

Giggling, Coombs crept past them with his camera and stole a covert shot of Beth's emotion-contorted face. The dead bulb disappeared under Tweany's foot; Coombs crept on, past the Negro, over to the spot where Lemming was sprinting through his dance. Again a flash of light blinded them all; when Mary Anne could see again she found Coombs climbing up onto the piano to photograph the group from above.

"God," she said, shivering. "There's something wrong with him."

Nitz, withdrawn and bitter, said: "This is bad stuff, Mary. I should take you home. You don't deserve it."

"No," she said. "I'm not going."

"Why not? What do you want here?" His gaunt frame trembled; nauseated, he bent his head. "Him, still?"

"It's not his fault."

"You never give up, do you?" Nitz's voice cracked apart and he swallowed creakily. "I can't stand any more of this jumping; I'm leaving."

"Don't," Mary Anne said quickly. "Please, Paul, don't leave."

"Christ," Nitz implored, "I'm sick." He handed her his glass and, crouching over, hobbled out of the room and down the hall. Coombs, like some bony spider, gleefully took a picture of him as he passed.

"Look at me!" Lemming shouted, waving his arms and panting for breath. "What am I? Tell me what I am!"

Beth began to play "Poor Butterfly."

"No!" Lemming shrieked. "You're wrong!" He threw himself onto the floor and rolled under the piano; only his twitching legs were visible. "What am I *now?*"

Scuttling from the corner, Coombs squatted down and took a photograph of him. Eyes distorted, Coombs popped dead bulbs from his camera and fumbled new ones from his pouch. His skin had turned from white to a mottled red; his hair, disarranged and shiny, oozed down his temples.

Feeling ill herself, Mary Anne retreated into the kitchen, her hands over her ears, trying to shut out the noise. But it forced itself through the walls and floor; transmitted as vibration, it hammered around her. She could hear Nitz being sick in the bathroom, a tearing sound as if his body were being dragged apart.

Poor Nitz, she thought. Uncovering her ears, she stood listening to his agony and wondering what she could do. Nothing, apparently. And he was suffering for her, too. Behind her, in the living room, the delirium went on; Lemming appeared in the doorway, his face flooded with joy, held out his arms to her, and then vanished. The bull rumble of Carleton Tweany never abated, rising and falling, but contained within the frenzy of the little old piano.

To her, the sound of the piano was a friendly and familiar noise gone wrong. Sometimes, sitting alone in the apartment waiting for Tweany to appear—he seldom did—she had pecked out a few weak themes, jukebox melodies from her meager years. Now, the din of the piano was terrific; played by professionals, the racket grew in volume until the cups and plates in the cupboard above her vibrated.

At the moment they were playing "John Henry." Tweany was going into a routine: he stood beating his hands on the piano, eyes shut, head thrown back, body agitated with ecstasy. Coombs, sneaking around, took a picture of him and then one of Lemming, who was huddled over Beth, reaching past her to join with her on the keys of the piano. Four hands pounding . . . the enormous passion shook the house.

"Up!" Coombs's voice sounded in her ear. Startled, Mary Anne opened her eyes to find him leering at her from the doorway;

he was trying to take her picture. She grabbed a plate from the drainboard and hurled it at him; the plate burst against the wall above his head. He blinked and withdrew.

Shaking, she buried her face in her hands and took a labored breath. Now she wished she had gone; she shouldn't have stayed. In the living room, Lemming had swept Beth up from the piano; the two of them were leaping about the room, chanting meaninglessly, incoherent in their abandon. For Tweany it was still "John Henry"; the piano had ceased but he roared on. Around and around went the dancing couple; halting, Beth tore off her shoes, kicked them out of the way, and hurried on. Mary Anne closed her eyes and leaned wearily against the sink.

She was there, rubbing her eyes and trying to last, when she heard the crash in the bathroom.

Fully awake, she jumped randomly forward and stood in the center of the kitchen, listening, trying to hear above the din. There was no further sound; the bathroom, at the end of the hall, was silent. With a gasp of intuition she ran to the closed door, seized the knob, and rattled it. The bathroom door was locked.

"Paul!" she called.

There was no response. She kicked at the door with her toe; the sound echoed back to her, but still there was nothing from inside. Letting go of the knob, she turned and raced up the hallway to the living room.

"Tweany, for God's sake," she grated, catching hold of him as he stood leaning happily on the piano. No one paid any attention. Coombs was reloading his camera, his face blank with excitement; Lemming and Beth had whirled their way over to the corner and Lemming was now pushing her away and grabbing up his guitar.

Beating on Tweany's unresponsive shoulder, Mary Anne screamed: "Something's happened to Paul Nitz! He's killed himself!" Tweany stirred a little under the pressure of her fists; she caught hold of his shirt and tugged at him. "Tweany!" she wailed. "Help me!"

Gradually, with massive reluctance, Tweany awoke from his trance. "What?" he mumbled, blinking and focusing. "Where? The bathroom?"

Then she was scampering back down the hall; behind her Tweany strode along, collecting his wits. The door was still locked. She stepped aside as Tweany reached for the knob, turned it, and then hammered.

"Come on, Nitz," he bellowed, his cheek against the wood. There was no answer.

"He's dead," Mary Anne said.

"Christ," Tweany muttered, glancing around him. He made his way to the kitchen and returned with a key. The lock responded and the door fell open.

Stretched out on the bathroom floor lay Paul Nitz, but he was not dead. He had passed out and hit his head on the side of the toilet. There he lay, his eyes closed, arms outstretched, a puddle of vomit around him. He had been sitting on the rim of the bathtub, being sick into the toilet; the white porcelain was still streaked where he had clung to it.

Bending down, Tweany lifted the man and inspected the welt on his forehead. A drizzle of saliva and stomach juices leaked down Nitz's chin; he stirred and groaned.

"Go in the living room," Tweany instructed, "and phone a doctor."

"Yes," Mary Anne said, and hurried down the hall. At the entrance to the living room she halted; there was the telephone, resting on the small wooden table by the chair. But she could not go in.

In the rapture of the dance, Beth had given herself completely. She had pulled off her clothes, flung them in a heap on the floor, and gone on to greater heights without them. Naked, perspiring, she was lunging about the room, large and pale and gleaming, her breasts wiggling mightily, her bulging hips palpitating with delight. Lemming sat curled up on the carpet, his guitar in his lap, eyes glued happily on the instrument, strumming a weird cacophony that slithered and shimmered in time to the woman's orgy.

Coombs, still giggling, crept after the fluttering body of his wife, photographing her again and again, dead flashbulbs flying from his camera. None of the three noticed Mary Anne; each was involved in his own world. She remained in the doorway, unable to enter, unable to back out, until, finally, Tweany appeared beside her to find out what was wrong.

"Christ," Tweany said. He stood behind the girl, moved by what he saw, gazing until Coombs became aware of him and stopped his wary pursuit of his wife's hams.

An ugly discoloration fled up into Coombs's cheeks. He squinted, struggled to his feet, advanced a few uneven steps toward Tweany, and said in a thick, hoarse voice: "You nigger, what are you doing? You nigger—get out of here!"

Tweany said nothing.

The sound of Lemming's guitar dimmed into stillness. Shaking his head, Lemming turned, pulled his horn-rimmed glasses from his pocket, put them on, and peered around him. Beth, unwinding like a tardy mechanical device, came slowly to rest, mouth open, body shaking with fatigue and cold.

"Nigger!" Coombs squealed, trying to scuttle between Tweany and the sweating nakedness of his wife. "Get out! Get out or I'll kill you!" All of the man's hatreds rose to the surface; he tottered toward Tweany, peering blindly, circling in a crippled, jerky step that first took him closer and then farther away from the Negro.

"This is my house," Tweany murmured. His confidence began to seep back into him; pulling himself up he said almost sternly: "Don't talk to me like that in my house. I do what I want in my house."

From the stairs outside came a dull drumming; at the same time the whirr of sirens lapsed into a blur in the street below. Before any of them could move, there was a loud banging on the door of the apartment.

Mary Anne whirled to race down the hallway to the door. She twisted the lock back; the door was thrust in her face and she was thrown to one side. Three policemen pushed inside and thundered down the hall toward the living room, leaving her alone.

Without hesitation, she plunged out into the darkness of the porch and down the stairs. Gripping the invisible railing, she descended to the ground and, half-falling, half-rolling, shoved her way into the moist wall of shrubs that grew along the path.

Upstairs, in the darkness, sounded the rattle of voices. More police appeared, flashing lights and muttering commands. In a few minutes—astonishingly few—the first group plodded drearily down the flight of steps: Tweany and Beth Coombs. After them came Danny Coombs and the shivering individual that was Chad Lemming. The four of them were herded into a patrol car; the car came to life and shot away. Porch lights winked on here and there as neighbors, aroused from sleep, appeared.

"That's them?" one of the policemen was asking. From his patrol car came the enlarged mutter of his radio; he stalked over to it, slid in behind the wheel, and addressed the police operator at the station.

They were leaving. One by one the police assembled, spoke a few words to each other, and climbed back into their cars. In a doorway on the bottom floor of the building stood a dignified Negro man; he watched with righteous solemnity as the police departed. One of them halted long enough to speak to him; the Negro nodded in satisfaction and closed his door.

After a long wait Mary Anne stirred. She was shivering with cold; damp night mist clung to her hair and bits of gravel cut into the palms of her hands as she crawled forward and out of the shrubbery. Her coat was torn and fragments of leaves were embedded in her hair. Shuddering, she stood up, hesitated, and then began ascending the stairs to the third floor.

The living room was a shambles. The lights, still on, blazed impotently. From the open door a chill gust of wind billowed in; Mary Anne closed the door, locked it, and passed on inside. Beth's clothing lay where she had shed it; she had been hustled down the stairs in Tweany's overcoat. There, in the corner, was Coombs's camera, a dead flashbulb still in the holder. The floor was strewn with broken bulbs; drops of blood glinted where Beth's naked feet had dripped, cut by the particles of glass.

Automatically, Mary Anne picked up Lemming's guitar and placed it upright in the corner. Then she went to the bathroom and looked timidly in.

Paul Nitz was sitting up, leaning his head against the side of the tub. Partly conscious, he was feebly exploring the injured bump where his head had struck the toilet. Noticing her, he blinked, grinned a little, and tried to stand.

"Don't," Mary Anne said, hurrying in and bending down beside him. "I'll help you."

"They missed me," Nitz murmured. "Thanks, Mary. I'm okay—I got sick and passed out."

Holding onto him, she got him from the bathroom into the chaotic living room. There she dropped down on the couch, pulled him down beside her, and dragged his damaged head into her lap. For a while he passed into semiconsciousness; she sat clinging to his limp shoulders, rocking back and forth, gazing vacantly ahead of her. Finally he stirred and pulled himself up.

"Thanks," he repeated weakly. "You're good."

She said nothing.

"They missed me," Nitz declared with pride. "I got the door shut and I didn't make any sound. They didn't know I was there."

Hugging him futilely, Mary Anne pressed her face against his forehead.

"Nobody else but us," Nitz murmured defiantly. "They took them all. All gone. Only the two of us left, now."

Outside, in the darkness, a bird made a few dismal noises. In an hour or so it would be dawn.

11

Daniel Coombs, as soon as his wife had left the apartment, put on his hat and coat and departed. It was his first full day of freedom. They had, all four of them, been booked on one count of disturbing the peace and one count of disorderly conduct. Each had spent the night in jail, in a separate cell.

Now, on his way downtown, Daniel Coombs brooded over the imbalances of the universe. His wife had the morals of a pig. She had slept with men as they came along, had exhibited and then opened herself for Joseph Schilling and then an Italian boy who ran a vegetable concession and then a music pupil and another music pupil and after that a confused procession that had wound up with a Negro named Carleton Tweany. It could go no further.

He recalled the depravity of that night, and his pace increased. By the time he had reached the business section of Pacific Park, he was almost running.

On a side street in the slum area, among cafés and pool halls and cigar stores, was a gun shop. Coombs entered and stood at the glass-topped display case, waiting for the proprietor. Presently a bald person in vest and pin-striped trousers made his appearance.

"Yes, sir," he said, in a New England twang. "What can I do for you?"

Coombs spent an hour selecting the gun he wanted. It was a tarnished Remington .32 repeating pistol, which cost him more than he had anticipated. An additional fifteen minutes was spent haggling over the price. Finally, the sale completed, he left the gun shop.

On foot, he tramped out of the slum section, past the residential area, and into the open country beyond. A meager tangle of trees and brush grew a few miles from the highway; Coombs crossed the fields in that direction. Soon he was wandering in the cold gloom, looking for something to shoot, something to practice on. He hadn't fired a gun since his days in the National Guard.

Some birds fluttered overhead and he shot into the group at random. Nothing came of it, except a startled panic and a rain of detached feathers. Moodily, he poked around, kicking the damp underbrush and wondering if a bird had fallen anywhere. Apparently not. Now the woods were still. He could hear, from the distant highway, the swish of tires and occasionally the burble of a truck horn.

Two boys came thrashing their way along, followed by a scampering springer spaniel. Coombs retired behind a heap of rusting trash and vines until the boys had passed. The dog, nosing, stopped within a few yards of him. Coombs raised his pistol and shot the dog. A cloud of gray smoke drifted up from his gun; ears ringing from the noise, Coombs backed away into the shadows.

Startled by the sound, the two boys began to circle cautiously back. One of them, in a low, abashed voice, called again and again: "Corky! Corky!" The wounded dog, not yet dead, whined dismally and tried to crawl toward the voice. Coombs was reloading his gun when the boys burst out into the clearing and gathered around the remains of their pet.

Watching the boys try unsuccessfully to collect the animal, Coombs reflected on the vanity of life. Finally they located a rotting board and laid the dog on it. Each holding an end, the boys lugged the board and its bleeding occupant from the clearing toward the highway. Having nothing else to do, Coombs followed.

At the edge of the woods the boys, exhausted, halted and laid down the board. While they were resting, Coombs, on impulse, stepped out and said: "What's the matter? What happened?"

Face streaked with tears, one of the boys cried: "Somebody shot our dog!"

The other said nothing; he was staring at the gun in Coombs's hand.

"That's terrible," Coombs said. Again on impulse, for reasons unknown to him, he brought out a ten-dollar bill and pushed it into the first boy's hand. "Go flag down a car," he instructed him, although neither boy seemed able to hear. "It's still alive; you can get it to the vet."

Both boys, smeared with blood, gazed dumbly after him as he departed. A quarter mile away—across an open marsh—he stopped and lifted his gun; taking aim toward the figures at the edge of the woods, he fired. The shot dissolved into the morning air, and Coombs went on.

By ten o'clock he was back in Pacific Park. His Ford was still parked on Elm Street, in front of the great slatternly house in which Carleton Tweany lived. Coombs, the gun in his pocket, stood undecidedly by the car; then, his mind made up, he walked over to the stairs and proceeded to climb.

There was no response to his knock. He shielded his eyes against the window of the door and peered in. A littered hall and room were visible; clothes were strewn everywhere. But nothing stirred; there was no evidence of Tweany. Coombs tried the knob, but the door was locked. Resigned, he descended the stairs, got into his car, and drove away.

When he reached a Standard station he shifted into second and drove up onto the concrete. He had been intending to do this all week; the appearance of the gas station had tripped a suprarational reflex. Climbing out, he said to the service station attendant: "How long would it take to get my car greased? It's been two thousand miles at least."

The man pondered. "About half an hour."

"Fine," Coombs said, reaching back to put the car in gear. He wandered next door to a lunch counter, but after he had ordered he discovered he wasn't hungry. Leaving his soup untouched, he paid the tab and walked out.

Gratifyingly, his Ford was already up on the rack. Strolling over, he critically supervised the men as they squirted grease up into the transmission. He created a lively discussion about weights of motor oil, heatedly demanding, in spite of their advice, a crankcase full of detergent oil, ten-thirty weight. Fussily he paced around until he had what he wanted. The attendants finished the greasing, lowered the car, and wrote out a bill.

At eleven-thirty he drove up Elm Street and parked a block from Tweany's house. He was close enough to see who came in and who went out. Clicking on the car radio, he tuned in the good-music station at San Mateo and listened to the Brahms Third Symphony. Now and then somebody passed along the sidewalk, but for the most part there was no sign of life.

Doubt assailed him. Perhaps Tweany had appeared during his absence.

His gun bumping around in his pocket, he climbed out, crossed the street, and walked toward the house. But again, when he tapped on the door, there was no response. Satisfied, he returned to the car and clicked the radio back on. Now they were playing the Berlioz *Roman Carnival* Overture. He wondered if there was an opera called *Roman Carnival* or if it was one of *those* overtures. Schilling would know. Schilling knew everything there was—about music, at least. Outside of that, he wasn't too bright; he certainly was a pushover for a piece of tail. For the space of one Berlioz overture Coombs considered driving around to the record shop, but then he changed his mind. Max Figuera would be hanging close by. It was, as always, too risky.

Slightly after noon, a figure came hurrying up the sidewalk, a brown-haired girl in a cloth coat, with hooped earrings and heels. It was Tweany's friend Mary Anne Reynolds.

Without hesitating, the girl left the sidewalk and dashed up the flight of wooden stairs to Tweany's apartment. She didn't bother to knock; producing a key, she unlocked the door and pushed it open. Disappearing inside, she slammed the door after her. For a time the street was silent. Then, one after another, the windows of Tweany's apartment flew open. The sounds of activity filtered out. At last came the roar of a vacuum cleaner: the girl was cleaning the apartment.

Lounging in the warmth of his Ford, Coombs continued to wait. Time passed, so much and so uniform that he lost all sense of it and drifted into a doze. Somewhere along the line his car battery gave out and the radio faded away. Coombs was unaffected. He remained inert until two o'clock in the afternoon, when, without warning of any kind, Carleton Tweany hove into sight at the far end of the block, his arm around a woman. The woman was Beth Coombs. The two of them, chattering, ascended the stairs and, like a pair of mud wasps, squeezed into the apartment. The door closed after them.

Pulling himself together, Coombs stepped from the car. One leg was asleep; he had to stamp it on the pavement to restore circulation. Then, one hand in his coat pocket, he started at a jog toward the three-story house.

12

That morning, not having to be at the telephone company until three o'clock, Mary Anne showed up at the business office of the Pacific Park *Leader*.

Evading the information counter, she went directly into the inner offices. "Hello, Mr. Gordon. Can I come inside and sit down?"

Arnold Gordon was pleased to see what he imagined and hoped was his son's fiancée. "Certainly, Mary," he said, getting up and showing her to a chair. "How are you today?"

"Great. How's the newspaper business?"

"Expanding all the time. Well, what can I do for you?"

"You can give me a job. I'm sick and tired of the telephone company."

Her request was no surprise to him. Gravely, Arnold Gordon said: "Mary, you know how much I'd like to."

"Sure," Mary Anne said, recognizing that it was indeed a lost cause.

"But," Arnold Gordon said, and it was true, "this is a small-town newspaper operating on a small budget. We have sixteen employees, not counting carriers. Most of those are typesetters and union men working in the shop. You don't mean that kind of job, do you?"

"Okay, I'm convinced." She got to her feet. "I'll see you again, Mr. Gordon."

"Going?" Eyes twinkling, he observed: "When you're finished with something, you're really finished."

"I have a lot to get done."

"How've you and David been getting along?"

She shrugged. "The same as usual. We went dancing last Thursday."

"Any date set, yet?"

"No, and there isn't going to be unless he wises up."

"What do you mean?"

"That gas station. He could be taking some kind of correspondence course. If I was a man I would; I wouldn't sit around doing nothing, just drifting, waiting. He could take business management. He could learn TV repairing, like you see in the ads."

"Or grow giant mushrooms in your basement? You're not really a practical person, Mary. You appear very efficient and realistic, but underneath that you're—" He searched for the term. "You're an idealist. If you had been born earlier, you'd have been a New Dealer."

Mary Anne started out the door. "Can I drop over for dinner some Sunday? I get sick of my roommate."

"Any time you want," Arnold Gordon said. "Mary—"

"What?"

"I think in spite of our differences you and I are going to get along well."

Mary Anne disappeared, and he was alone. Chuckling self-consciously, Arnold Gordon seated himself and lit his pipe. She was quite a girl. Were they all that way, now? A generation of oddly mature young people, more adult in some ways than he approved of. Blunt, without piety, unable to find anyone or anything they could respect . . . looking for something real enough to believe in: looking for something worth their respect. And, he realized, they could not be fooled. They could see through sham.

Uncomfortably, he realized how his way of life looked to her. False and empty platitudes, ceremonies without content. A world of hollow manners. She made him feel slow and foolish. She made him feel that he had somehow fallen short, had not, in some mysterious fashion, lived up to a standard. She made him feel ashamed.

"What's yours, lady?" the tow-headed boy behind the Bobo's window inquired, when she approached.

She ordered a hamburger and milkshake. "Thanks," she said, accepting her order. He watched her move carefully away from the window, holding onto her purse and hamburger and container of milkshake.

"You go to Pacific High?" he asked.

"I did once."

"That's what I mean. I think I used to see you."

Stopping a few feet from the window where the big, brightly painted sign cast a square of shade, she began eating.

"It's hot," the boy said.

"No kidding." She moved a little farther off.

"When did you graduate?"

"Years ago."

"What's your name?"

With great reluctance, she said: "Mary Anne Reynolds."

"I think we were in a class together." He turned up a radio by his elbow. "Dig this." Progressive jazz drifted out and mixed with the sounds of traffic. "Recognize it?"

"Naturally. Earl Bostic's 'Sleep.' "

"You're good."

Mary Anne sighed.

"What's the matter?" the boy asked.

"I've got ulcers."

"You drink cabbage juice?"

"Why should I drink cabbage juice?"

"That's what cures ulcers. My uncle has had ulcers all his life; he drinks it by the gallon. You have to go up to the health food store in San Francisco to get it."

"Sleep" ended and a new tune took its place, a Dixieland number. Mary Anne finished her milkshake and dropped the container into the wire basket.

"What are you doing?" the boy asked, resting his arms on the counter of the window. "Going to work?"

"Not until three."

"Where?"

"Phone company." She wished he would stop pestering her; she hated to be pestered.

"That's a long way; that's across town. How are you going to get there?"

"Walk!"

The boy hesitated, and a strange expression fell over his face. Clearing his throat, he said squeakily; "You want a *ride* over?"

Mary Anne sneered. "Take off."

"I'll be done with my shift in a couple of minutes. I've got a cool '39 Chevy; it's my brother's, but I get to use it. What do you say?"

"Go fly a kite." He reminded her of Dave Gordon; they were all alike. Wiping her hands with a paper napkin, she examined her appearance in the plate-glass window of the drive-in.

"You going?" the boy asked.

"You're a wizard."

"Sure you don't want a ride? I'll take you somewhere; anywhere you want. You want to drive up to San Francisco? We could go to a show and then maybe to dinner."

"No, thanks."

An elderly white-haired gentleman approached the window, leading a little girl by the hand. "Two ice cream sandwiches," the elderly gentleman said.

"Strawberry!" the child shrilled.

"There's no strawberry," said the counter boy. "Just vanilla."

"Vanilla is quite satisfactory." The elderly gentleman brought out his purse. "How much will that be?"

The child, noticing Mary Anne, started a few hopeful steps after her. "Hello," she piped.

"Hello," Mary Anne said. She didn't mind talking to children; they, like Negroes, seemed to mean no harm. She could feel close to them. "What's your name?"

"Joan."

"Tell the young lady your whole name," the elderly gentleman instructed.

"Joan Louise Mosher."

"That's a nice name," Mary Anne said. She bent down, being careful of her nylons, and held out her hand. "What's that you have?"

The child studied the drooping camellia she clutched. "A flow'r."

"It's a camellia," the elderly gentleman said.

"It's sweet," Mary Anne said, straightening up."How old is she?" she asked the elderly gentleman.

"Three. My great-granddaughter."

"Gee," Mary Anne said, touched. It made her think of her own grandfather. The image of his marvelous tallness . . . and herself, tagging along, running to keep up with his giant strides. "What's it like, having a great-granddaughter?"

"Well," the elderly gentleman began, but then the ice cream came, and he found himself involved in removing wrappers and giving out money.

"Good-bye," Mary Anne said to the child, and patted her on the head. Then, with a wave of her hand, she started in the direction of the slum area and Elm Street.

As always, she located the house by the ragged palm tree growing in the front yard. Holding tight to the banister, she mounted the stairs. The door, of course, was locked. She got out her key and made her entrance.

Nothing stirred. In the living room stood a card table heaped with beer bottles and ashtrays. A chair, one leg broken, was overturned; she righted it. On the piano, among the clothes and newspapers, was a plate of sandwich crumbs; something small dived out of sight as she approached.

In the kitchen the remains of a meal were drying on the table. A man's hand-painted necktie lay over the back of a chair, and a pajama top was on the floor beside the table; with it was a cigarette lighter—Tweany's—and two wire coat hangers. The sink was filled with dishes, and sacks of garbage spilled out from below.

Removing her coat, Mary Anne wandered into the bedroom. The shades were still down and the room was amber dark, slightly damp with the presence of sheets. There, in the gloom, she began listlessly removing her clothing. She folded her skirt and blouse across the bed and, opening the closet, rummaged among the mothball-clouded fabrics.

Soon she had what she wanted: women's jeans and a heavy checked shirt that reached to her knees as she buttoned it around her. In a pair of moccasins, she padded over to the windows and let up the shades. For the other rooms she did the same, lifting, in addition, the windows she could budge.

First, before anything else, she washed the dishes. After that came scrubbing down the wooden drainboard with steel wool and soap. Rivulets of grime dripped from her bare arms as she worked; pausing, she pushed her hair from her eyes, rested, and then searched the cupboards for rags. In the closet she found a heap of clean shirts; she ripped them up, filled a bucket with soapy water, and began scrubbing the kitchen floor.

When that was done, she got a broom and swept down the cobwebs from the walls and ceiling. Bits of soot rained on the newly scrubbed floor; panting, she halted and examined the situation. Of course she should have done the ceiling first, but it was too late now.

She gathered up the garbage and made her way downstairs to the backyard. The can was full; she heaped her armload on top and started back. Cans and bottles lay everywhere; in the weeds under her foot a light bulb burst, sending fragments of glass flying. Wearily, she climbed the stairs, glad to be away from the shrub-sized weeds; there was no telling what lived in the wet boards and litter.

Now she began dragging out the decrepit vacuum cleaner. Clouds of dust rolled from it as she snapped it on; she spread out newspapers and located the catch that opened it. A vast ball of dust bloomed in her face, and she scrambled back miserably. It was just too damn much. It wasn't worth it.

Through a blur of exhaustion she surveyed what she had accomplished. Virtually nothing. How could she put in order the corruption of years? It was too late, and it had been too late as long as she had been alive.

Giving up, she forced the vacuum cleaner together and carried it back to its place in the closet.

The hell with Tweany's pigsty. The hell, she thought, with Tweany. Let him clean up his own mess. She went into the bedroom and began searching the dresser for clean sheets and blankets. The dirty sheets she threw out into the hall, stumbling as she did so, and then began turning the mattress.

When she had finished making the bed, she smoothed a coverlet over it and threw herself down. She kicked off her moccasins, stretched out, and closed her eyes. It was peaceful and quiet. The hell with you, Carleton Tweany, she thought again. Paul is right: you are a jerk. A great big grinning jerk. But, she thought, that isn't all. Not at all it isn't all. Daddy, she thought, you could have done a lot better by me, but what the hell, who ever has?

She had come to a dead end. Belief in Tweany was no longer possible. She couldn't go on pretending he was what she wanted him to be: a great, kindly man whom she could count on. He had let her fall back into her old fear and isolation.

Thinking that, she fell asleep.

At two o'clock in the afternoon the stairs shook with the sound of people; a moment later the door burst open and Carleton Tweany, his arm around Beth, appeared.

"Jesus," Beth said, wrinkling her nose. "What's all the

dust?" She halted at the pile of dirty sheets lying in the hall. "What's going on?"

"Somebody's been here," Tweany grumbled, letting go of her and peering into the living room. "Probably Mary Anne; she shows up all the time."

"Does she have a key?"

"Yeah, she shows up and cleans. She likes to." Tweany made his way into the bedroom and halted. "Well, I'll be damned."

"What is it?" Beth came and looked over his shoulder.

Mary Anne lay asleep on the bed. On her face was a troubled, unhappy frown. Beth and Tweany stood in the doorway, dumb with astonishment.

Then, very quietly, Tweany began to titter. He tittered in a high-pitched falsetto, his teeth showing in a broad, flashing grin. The laughter spread to Beth; she chuckled in low, short barks.

"Poor Miss Mary Anne," Tweany said, trying not to laugh, trying to hold it back. But it couldn't be held back. The laughter spread across his face—and then he and Beth were shrieking in spasms of merriment. On the bed Mary Anne stirred; her eyelids fluttered.

"Poor Miss Mary Anne," Tweany repeated, and the laughter bubbled out in gusts.

While the two of them stood rocking back and forth, the door flew open and Daniel Coombs bounded into the apartment.

Tweany, identifying him, pushed between him and Beth, as Coombs, his head down, raised the Remington .32 and aimlessly fired. The noise awakened Mary Anne; sitting up, she saw Coombs hurry past the doorway of the bedroom toward Tweany and Beth.

"I'm going to kill you, nigger!" Coombs raved, trying to shoot once more. He tripped over a heap of magazines and stumbled; Tweany, pushing Beth out of the hall, caught him around the neck. Arms flailing, Coombs struggled to get his head loose. Without emotion, Tweany dragged him down the hall to the kitchen.

"Tweany!" Mary Anne shrieked. *"Don't!"*

Then she and Beth were clawing at him. Tweany continued to

drag his burden, paying no attention. Coombs's face could not be seen; it was buried in Tweany's coat. Feet scraping the floor, Coombs was yanked against the kitchen table—it spilled salt shaker and sugar bowl to the floor—and over to the sink.

"For God's sake," Mary Anne pleaded, kicking at the Negro's shins; Beth's long red nails gouged into his face. "Don't do it, Tweany, they'll put you in jail the rest of your life; they'll string you up and lynch you and burn your body in gasoline and spit on you; spit on your body. Tweany, *listen* to me!"

Holding Coombs with one arm, Tweany snatched open the drawer under the sink and fumbled among the silverware until he found an ice pick. Coombs managed to jerk free. He skittered away, reached the door, and then the hall. His thrashing sounds diminished as he vanished out the door, onto the flight of wooden steps.

Coombs squealed, a shrill, high-pitched bleat, followed by the sound of old wood splintering. After that, a distant *plop,* as if some wad of organic waste, voided, had dropped a long way.

"He fell," Beth whispered. "My husband."

Mary Anne ran down the hall to the door. The railing was intact, but at the bottom of the steps lay Daniel Coombs. He had plunged the length; he had, along the stairs, missed his footing.

Beth appeared. "Is he dead?"

"How would I know?" Mary Anne said frigidly.

Shoving her aside, Beth scampered down to the ground level beside her husband. Mary Anne watched for a moment, and then turned back to the apartment. Tweany was still in the kitchen; he emerged, straightening his shirt and smoothing his tie. He looked disconcerted but not apprehensive. "Those cops," he said, "they're going to be mad."

"Want me to call them?"

"Yes, maybe you better."

She picked up the phone and dialed. When she had finished she hung up and faced the man. "You were going to kill him." It was, for her, the final straw.

Tweany said nothing.

"It's lucky for you he got loose." A lethargy lay over her. "Now you don't have to worry."

"I guess not," Tweany agreed.

Mary Anne seated herself. "You better put something on your face." The side of his head was bleeding where she and Beth had clawed him. "What did you do with the ice pick?"

"Put it back in the drawer, naturally."

"Go down and make sure she won't say anything about it. Hurry—before they get here." She could already hear sirens.

Obediently, Tweany went off down the hall. Mary Anne remained, rubbing the instep of her right foot; she had twisted it floundering after Tweany. After a time she got to her feet and went into the bedroom. She had changed back into her skirt and blouse and was stepping into her heels when the police arrived.

The first policeman—one she remembered from the other night—studied her searchingly as she descended the stairs.

"I don't remember you," he said.

Mary Anne didn't answer. She stopped to glance at Coombs's body . . . thinking, in a corner of her mind, that it would not be possible to get to her job today.

13

On a morning in early December, Joseph Schilling stood inspecting his window display. The sun was shining brightly, and he frowned, thinking of the records warping in their envelopes. Then he remembered that he had, before setting up the display, taken the records out and used the envelopes alone. Heartened, he unlocked the door and entered the shop.

Records were heaped on the front counter. Temporarily ignoring them, Schilling got the push broom from the back closet and began sweeping away the debris that had piled up before his door during the night. When he had finished he reentered and plugged in the high-fidelity phonograph system mounted above the door. From the records on the counter he selected Handel's *Water Music* and started it playing.

He was outside again, rolling down the awning, when Mary Anne Reynolds appeared at his elbow. "I thought you opened at eight," she said. "I've been sitting over there for half an hour." She indicated the Blue Lamb.

"I open at nine," Schilling said, carefully going on with his awning unwinding. "Or thereabouts. No fixed schedule, actually. Sometimes when it's raining I don't open until noon."

"Who did you hire?"

Schilling said: "Nobody."

"Nobody? You're doing all the work?"

"Sometimes a former friend of mine stops by and helps. A music teacher."

"Beth Coombs, you mean."

"Yes," Schilling said.

"You heard about her husband, didn't you?"

"Yes."

"Do you remember me?"

"Certainly I remember you." He was deeply moved, and he had difficulty speaking. "I've thought about you every once in a while, wondering what became of you. You're the girl who wanted a job."

"Can I go inside and sit down?" Mary Anne asked. "These heels hurt my feet."

Schilling followed her into the store. "Excuse the mess . . . I haven't had time to clear things up." The music dinned, and he bent to decrease the volume. "You're acquainted with Mrs. Coombs?" He spoke conversationally, wanting to put this anxious, tense girl at her ease. "Where did you meet her?"

"At a bar." Mary Anne seated herself on the window ledge and kicked off her shoes. "I notice you removed some of the listening booths."

"I was pressed for space."

The girl's blunt attention focused on him. "Will three booths be enough? What happens when you get a crowd?"

Candidly, he admitted: "I'm waiting to find out."

"Are you making a profit?" She massaged her foot. "Maybe you shouldn't hire anybody."

"I'm currently preparing for Christmas. If I'm lucky this store may yet see some activity."

"What happened to what's-his-name, that singer? Did he go over?"

"Chad? Not exactly. We sent the tapes down to L.A., but nothing has come of it yet."

The girl pondered. "Paul Nitz liked him. I thought he was silly." She shrugged. "It doesn't matter."

Neither of them said anything for a while, as Schilling began sorting records on the counter.

There she was, sitting on the window ledge as if she had gone to work for him after all, as if she had not turned and run out of the store. He had made a blunder, that day. He had liked her and he had frightened her off. This time he was going to be careful; this time—he hoped—he had the situation under control.

"You like it?" he asked. She certainly looked as if she belonged there on the ledge; like a cat, she had entered and taken possession. Now she was busy making herself comfortable.

"The store?" she said. "I told you. Yes, I like it very much. It looks lovely." There was a crisp, businesslike quality in her voice. It embarrassed him.

"You feel hostility toward me," he said.

The girl didn't answer. She was trying on her shoe.

"You say you met Beth in a bar," Schilling said, steering the conversation back to safer topics. "That was here in Pacific Park, wasn't it? You didn't know her before?"

"No, not before."

"Did you know her, that day?"

"She wasn't around, that day," the girl reminded him. "They didn't show up until later."

"How does she strike you?"

"She's attractive." A shade of envy touched the girl's voice. "Such a lovely figure."

"She's fat."

"I don't call that fat," Mary Anne said, closing the subject. "That little man, that Danny Coombs, he was a creep. There was something wrong with him."

"I agree," Schilling said. He slid an lp from its sleeve and, holding it by its edges, examined it for scratches. "Coombs tried to kill me once."

She was interested. "Really?"

Putting down his record, Schilling pushed back his coat sleeve; he unscrewed his gold cuff link, parted his clean white cotton shirt-sleeve, and showed her his wrist. A bumpy line made its way among the hairs. "He broke my wrist at that point, by hitting me with a tire iron. Then my man Max showed up."

Impressed, she studied the scar. "He tried to kill Tweany, but—" She broke off. "It didn't work out."

"Beth told me a number of the details." He reset his cuff link and smoothed down his coat. "Coombs had a pathological streak . . . the sight of a Negro evidently brought it out. The Negro is a musician, I understand."

"Sort of. Why did Coombs try to kill you? Were you hanging around his wife?"

Schilling was embarrassed. "Nothing like that at all. Coombs was always on the verge of the brink. He lived in a world of vitriolic distortion."

"Why did she marry him?"

"Beth is a little mixed up, too. Their manias jigsaw." He explained: "She told me Danny was expelled from his grade school for peeping the girls' gym. Later on that camera was his roaming eye."

"And she likes to—exhibit herself," Mary Anne said, with aversion.

"Beth was an artists' model. That's how Coombs met her . . . he was running a girl-picture agency. He wanted a model who would pose nude. You can imagine how happy that made her. It was a satisfactory arrangement for both of them."

He was, of course, relieved that Coombs was dead. Beth, alone, was little or no menace; the mistake of five years ago had finally ceased to plague him. It meant a turning point in his life.

"I'm not sorry to have him gone," he said.

"That's the wrong attitude," Mary Anne informed him.

"Why?" He was surprised.

"It's just wrong, that's all. He was a human being, wasn't he? Nobody should be killed; capital punishment and all that, it's wrong." With a shake of her head she dismissed the topic. "I'm going to have to change into some other shoes; I wore these so I'd look older."

Amused, he said: "I know how old you are. You're twenty."

"You're a wizard." She hobbled to the door. "I'm going home and change. Is the job decided? Everything's set, isn't it?"

His humor departed. "The job is open, yes."

"Well, I'm applying. Do I get it or not?"

"You get it," he said, with a tug of emotion. "At two-fifty a month, a five-day week, everything we talked about when you were in before." Good God, it had been four months. He had waited for her that long. "When do you want to start?"

"I'll be back this afternoon, as soon as I've changed." For a moment she lingered. "What should I wear? How formal do you want me to dress? Heels, I suppose."

"No, not necessarily." But he experienced a kind of delight at the idea. "You can wear flats, if you want. But definitely stockings."

"Stockings."

"Don't go overboard . . . but don't come in wearing jeans. Whatever you'd wear to go shopping downtown."

"That's what I thought," she said, consulting with herself. "How often do you pay, every two weeks?"

"Every two weeks."

Without embarrassment, she asked: "Can I have ten dollars right now?"

He was partly captivated, partly outraged. "Why? What for?"

"Because I'm broke, that's what for."

Shaking his head, he got out his wallet and handed her a ten-dollar bill. "Maybe I'll never see you again."

"Don't be silly," Mary Anne said, and disappeared out the doorway, leaving him alone, as he had been before.

At one-thirty in the afternoon the girl returned, wearing a cotton skirt and a short-sleeved blouse. Her hair was brushed back and her face was shiny with eagerness; she looked ready to go to work. But with her was an indolent-looking young man.

"Where can I put my things?" she asked, meaning her purse. "In the back?"

Schilling showed her the steps leading to the basement stockroom. "That's the safest place, down there." Reaching into the stairwell, he snapped on the light. "The bathroom's down there, and a closet. Not very large, but enough for coats."

While Mary Anne was absent, the young man sauntered up to him. "Mr. Schilling, they told me you'd give me the word on music."

From his coat pocket the man got out a crumpled envelope; he began flattening it on the counter. It was a list of composers, Schilling saw; all contemporary and all individualistic experimentalists.

"You're a musician?" Schilling asked.

"Yeah, I play bop piano over at the Wren." He scrutinized Schilling. "Let's see how good you are."

"Oh," Schilling said, "I'm good, all right. Ask me something."

"Ever heard of a fellow named Arnie Scheinburg?"

"Schönberg," Schilling corrected. He couldn't tell if he was being made fun of. "Arnold Schönberg. He wrote the *Gurrelieder.*"

"How long have you been in this racket?"

He computed. "Well, in one form or another since the late twenties. This is my first retail shop, though."

"You like music?"

"Yes," Schilling said, worried in an obscure way. "Very much."

"Don't you do anything else? Don't you get outdoors?" The young man strolled around, taking in the store. "This is an elegant little shop. Shows good taste. But tell me, Schilling, don't you sometimes feel cut off from the broad masses?"

Mary Anne appeared from the back."Well? Let's get with it."

Having loaded the young man up with records, Schilling steered him into a booth. At the counter Mary Anne was busily opening the cash register.

"Friend of yours?" Schilling asked, amused that, in her world, introductions did not exist.

"Paul plays over at the Wren," she answered, starting to count the one-dollar bills. As soon as she had left the store she had gone home to her apartment, changed, and then hurried to the Wren to pay Paul back his ten dollars . . . money that had kept her going since she cashed her final check from the telephone company.

"That place?" Nitz had said. "That record shop? That's the fellow they said I should talk to."

"Come along," Mary Anne had urged him, timid at the idea of returning to the store alone. "Please, Paul. As a favor to me."

He had raised an eyebrow. "What's the matter?"

"Nothing."

"You scared?"

"Sure I'm scared. It's a new job; it's the first day."

"What do you know about this character?"

Evasively, she had said; "I met him once. He's an older man."

Tossing down his paperbacked Western, Paul Nitz had climbed to his feet. "Okay, I'll go along and chaperone you." He clapped her warmly on the back. "I'll even challenge him to a duel—just give me the nod."

"What are you doing?" Schilling asked, watching her fingers fly as she counted the bills.

"Seeing what we need from the bank."

When she had completed her list, Schilling showed her the miniature safe by the night-light. "I go to the bank once a week. Otherwise I draw from this."

"You should have told me." Finishing with the money, she went to get the broom. "I'm going to clean up this place," she informed him. "It really needs it . . . how long has it been since you swept out?"

Disconcerted, Schilling went on sorting records. Later he stepped into the back office and plugged in his Silex coffeemaker. In the first listening booth Mary's friend had barricaded himself behind his records; he stared blankly out.

Here was a girl, Schilling reflected, who, on her first day at work, had borrowed money from her employer, had set her own moment of appearance, and, when she finally appeared, had brought along a friend prepared to spend all day listening to the store's records. And now, instead of waiting dutifully for instructions, she was announcing her own tasks.

"Why don't you move the counter back?" Mary Anne said as he appeared with the coffee.

"Why?" He began filling two cups.

"So you can get directly to the window." She gave the counter a fretful swat. "It blocks the way."

"Miss Reynolds," Schilling said, realizing that he was entering a pattern that must have included all her employers, "put down your broom and come over here. I want to talk to you."

She smiled at him, a quick flash of her very small lips. "Wait until I'm finished," she said, and disappeared out the front door with the dustpan. When she returned she found a dust cloth and began going over the surface of the counter.

Nettled, Schilling sipped his afternoon coffee. "I think you should learn how my inventory is handled and what I expect in customer relationships. I'm trying out something new of my own; I want a personal, more individual arrangement. We should know every customer by name, and we should learn to use those names as soon as they set foot inside the store."

Mary Anne nodded as she dusted.

"When the customer asks for something, you've got to be able to respond with information, not a slack-jawed stare. Suppose I come in here and say to you: 'I heard a Bach piano concerto played on the violin. What is it?' Could you do anything with that?"

"Of course not," Mary Anne answered.

"Well," he conceded, "I don't really expect you to. That's my job. But you've got to learn enough to handle the regular classical buyer. You'll have to know how to meet requests for the standard symphonic works. Suppose somebody comes in and asks you for a good Dvořák symphony. You better be sure how many he wrote, which are the best recordings, and what we have in stock. And you've got to know Smetana and Brahms and Suk and Mahler and all the other composers a buyer of Dvořák might enjoy."

"That's what Nitz is doing," Mary Anne said.

"Nitz? What's that?"

"Paul Nitz, in the booth. He never heard any of that serious music before."

"My point," Schilling said sharply, "is that whenever a buyer is introduced to a new field by a salesperson, the buyer becomes dependent on that salesperson. That means you have a responsibility not to sell the buyer short by simply pushing merchandise on him for the sake of getting rid of it. That's where this business becomes an art with standards. We're not selling gum or soda pop—we're selling, to some people at least, elements that make up a way of life."

"What's the name of that?" Mary Anne asked. "That music he's playing."

"What are you talking about?" The girl was paying no attention to him. "Miss Reynolds," he said, "have you heard anything I've said?"

"Of course I have," she answered, industriously dusting. "You said I have to kow what it is we're selling. But I can't learn that overnight . . . you're going to have to help me."

"Do you *want* to find out what's on these records? Do you care?"

"Yes, I care."

"Listen to what your friend is playing." The rattle of a Chávez percussion experiment was audible. "Can you honestly tell me you like that? Damn it," he protested, "stop that dusting. You don't like that kind of music; it doesn't mean anything to you."

"It's terrible," Mary Anne agreed.

In despair, Schilling said: "Then what can I do with you? I can't *make* you like it."

She scrutinized him shrewdly. "Do you like it?"

"No," he admitted. "I don't care for experiments in pure sound."

"What do you like, then?"

"I'm a vocal collector. I'm interested in lieder."

"But you can sell this stuff." She resumed her dusting. "Do you really believe music is important?"

"Well," Schilling said, "it's my whole life."

"Your whole life?" Again she fixed her intense eyes on him. "You mean there's nothing more important to you than music?"

"That's what I mean," he said, with a stir of belligerence. There was no comment from the girl; she heard and accepted his statement, filed it away somewhere in her mind. "Why not?" he demanded, following her around as she dusted.

"That's the way it is with Paul. Sometimes I wish I had something like that."

"Why not?"

She shrugged. "No reason, I guess. Except that around here, this town—well, who ever heard of that stuff you gave Paul? He never heard of it, and he's a musician."

"That's why I came here. That's why I settled here."

"Anyone who would live here is a moron."

"Am I a moron for coming here?"

"I mean somebody growing up here, not seeing anything, not knowing anything. Like Jake Lovett. Like Dave Gordon . . . all the rest of them. Drinking malts, hanging around the drugstores and gas stations. But you're different. You've seen enough to know what you want and what you enjoy. You came from outside."

She had stopped dusting; now she stood deep in thought. Joseph Schilling went over and firmly took the dust cloth from her. Taking her hand, he led her over to the counter and stationed her behind it. She went obediently.

"Now, Miss Reynolds," he said, "you listen to what I'm going to tell you. We're going over the mechanics of selling a record."

She nodded.

"All right." He laid an LP down on the counter before her. "I'd like to buy that; I'm an elderly customer. What's your first step?"

Mary Anne picked up the record and gazed at the brightly colored jacket with its drawing of violins. "What is it?" Lips moving, she worked out the composer's name. "Prokofiev."

"We're selling the record; this has nothing to do with the music. What do you do when a customer brings his purchase to the counter?"

Mary Anne groped under the counter and found a record bag.

"No," Schilling said, "first you examine the record to make certain it isn't scratched." He showed her how to draw the record from its envelope and hold it by the edges. "See?"

She did so.

"What next?" he asked, again laying the record down.

"Then," she said, "I put it in the bag."

"No, then you write up a sales slip. So we can get the customer's name and address." He presented her with a mechanical pencil and showed her how to use the machine that rolled out duplicate sales slips. "Then," he said, "you put the record and his copy of the slip in the bag. Our copy goes on that spindle." He did that for her, too.

Mary Anne slid the LP into the bag and folded the handle. Suddenly she looked up at Schilling and gave him the warmest smile he had ever seen in his life. "Thank you," she said, and pushed the record bag across the counter.

"What?" he murmured.

Still smiling, she gave a little half-curtsy."Thank you for buying the record."

Gruffly, Schilling said: "You're welcome."

She continued to smile at him, a sweet and utterly guileless glow that charmed him and, at the same time, made him uncertain of himself. "The next step," he went on, "is the cash register. You suppose you can work it?"

She didn't answer immediately. "Sure," she said, at last.

"What else?" He couldn't seem to collect his mind. "Do you know where to find record prices?"

"No."

He got the Schwann LP catalogue open and showed her the price list at the back. "They're all here. Until you've learned them, always look them up."

"Would you like to buy another record?" she asked.

"No," he said, "one is fine, thanks."

From a nearby pile, she selected the top record. "Buy this." She read the title. *"Schubert Piano Music for Four Hands.* Buy that . . . it's pretty."

"Is it?"

"Yes," she said, "very pretty."

"Maybe I will, then."

"Want me to put it on the phonograph for you?"

"Yes," he said, with a kind of eagerness.

She stuck her tongue out at him. "Put it on the phonograph yourself; you're grown up."

Schilling laughed unsteadily. "Apparently you'll do all right."

With a flounce of dismissal, Mary Anne went to get her dust rag.

At four-thirty Paul Nitz emerged from the smoke-drenched record booth, loaded down with records, which he deposited on the counter. "Thanks," he said to Schilling.

"Did you enjoy them?"

"Yeah," he said. "Some of them."

Schilling began grouping the records by brand. "Why don't you come around Sunday? I'll be playing some new Virgil Thomson."

Nitz was fumbling in his pocket. "I'll buy that top one there."

"Paul," Mary Anne said sharply, "you don't have a phonograph."

Nitz hung his head. "That has nothing to do with it."

Dropping the stock covers she had been making out, Mary Anne hurried over and took the record away from Nitz. "You can't do it; I know what you're going to do, you're going to just sit home and look at it. What'll looking at it do for you?"

Nitz muttered: "You sure are bossy, Mary Anne."

"I'll put it under the counter," she told him. "You go buy a phonograph; when you have a phonograph, come back and get your record."

Schilling stood watching as she pushed the man out of the store and onto the sidewalk. The episode, to him, had a fabulous and unreal quality; it could not really happen in a store. In its own way, it seemed funny.

"He has to go to work," Mary Anne explained, hurrying back inside. "He plays bop piano over at the Wren."

"You cost me a sale," Schilling said, feeling still a little bewildered.

"Look . . . if he bought that record he would have just gone home and sat looking at it. I know him; take my word. He never would have bought any more records; now he'll go get a phonograph and then he'll buy records all the time."

"Either you're very far sighted," he said, "or you're an exceptionally fast talker. Which is it?"

They faced each other.

"Don't you trust me?" she inquired.

He smiled grudgingly. "Some. But you're too intricate for me."

That seemed to intrigue her. "Intricate? In what way?"

"You're partly very young, very inexperienced and naive." He studied her intently. "And at the same time you're completely practiced. Even somewhat unscrupulous."

"Oh," she said, nodding.

"Why did you change your mind? Why did you decide to come back and work for me?"

"Because," she said, "I got tired of working at the phone company."

"Is that all?" He didn't believe it.

"No. I—" She floundered. "A lot of things happened to me. Somebody I depended on let me down. Now I don't feel the same way about him, or about anything."

"You were afraid of me, weren't you?"

"Yes," she admitted, "very much."

"But not now?"

She pondered. "No. I see you differently, and I see myself differently."

Schilling hoped it was true. "What did you do with the ten dollars?" he asked.

"Gave it to Paul Nitz."

"Then you're broke?"

She smiled. "Yes, broke."

"So I suppose you're going to borrow another ten dollars tomorrow."

"Can I?"

"We'll see."

Her eyebrows went up. "We will, will we?"

The store was empty. Outside, the late afternoon sun sent up a glare from the sidewalk. Schilling walked over to the window and stood with his hands in his pockets. Finally, to quiet his various emotions, he lit a cigar.

"Put that stinky thing out," Mary Anne ordered. "How do you suppose that smells to customers?"

He turned around. "If I invited you to dinner, what would you say?"

"It depends where." She seemed, instantly, to fold up in wariness; he was aware of her change in mood.

"What's a good place?" he asked.

She reflected. "La Poblana, up along the highway."

"All right, we'll go there."

"I'll have to change to go there. I'll have to get my heels and suit again."

He demolished her anxieties with the hand of quiet reasonability. "When we close the store, I'll drive you over to your apartment and you can change."

With relief he heard her say: "Fine." Pleased and gratified, he put out his cigar and, going into the back office, began preparing the Columbia order sheet.

It was a routine job he did not usually enjoy, but he enjoyed it this time; he enjoyed it very much.

14

That night he took her to dinner. And four nights later, on Saturday, he took her with him to a wholesaler's party in San Francisco.

As the two of them drove up the peninsula, Mary Anne asked: "Does this car belong to you?"

"I bought this Dodge back in '48. A package deal; it came along with Max." He added: "I gave up heavy driving." His eyes had become bad and he had, one night, hit a parked milk truck. He didn't tell the girl that.

"It's a nice car. It's so big and quiet . . ." She watched the dark fields passing on either side of the highway. "What will this party be like?"

"You're not scared, are you?"

"No," she said, sitting very upright beside him, her hands around her purse. She had put on what looked to him like a pair of black silk pajamas; the trousers were tied around her bare ankles and the shirt flared out into a great pointed collar. On her feet were little flat slippers, and her hair was tied back in a foreshortened ponytail.

As she had skipped out of her apartment house and into the car he had observed: "Your hair is too short for a ponytail."

Breathlessly, she had settled beside him and slammed the car door. "Is this too arty? Am I dressed wrong?"

"You look wonderful," he had said in all honesty as he started up the car.

But she was, in spite of what she said, a little frightened. In the gloom of the car her eyes were large and serious, and she had almost nothing to say. Once, she got her cigarettes from her purse and bent toward the dashboard lighter.

"This may be fun," he said, to cheer her up.

"That's what you told me."

"Leland Partridge is a fanatic, what we call an 'audiophile.' There'll be speakers as large as houses, diamond cartridges, hi-fi recordings of freight trains and glockenspiels."

"Will there be very many people there?" she asked again, for the third time.

"People from retail, plus some of the San Francisco musical crowd. There'll be drinks and plenty of talk. You may hear some good arguments when the sound boys and the legitimate musicians tangle."

"I love San Francisco," Mary Anne said with ardor. "All those tiny bars and restaurants. Once I went to a place out in North Beach, with Tweany. Something called The Paper Doll. We heard a Dixieland pianist . . . he was cool."

"Cool," Schilling echoed, grimacing.

"He was quite good." She tapped her cigarette with her finger; sparks swept out the window into the darkness. From the car radio filtered the sounds of a Haydn symphony.

"I like that," she said, inclining her head.

"Do you recognize it?"

She meditated. "Beethoven."

"It's the Haydn *Drumroll* Symphony."

"Do you think I'll ever learn to tell what a piece is? Will I be as old as you?"

"You're learning," he said, as lightly as possible. "It's a question of experience; nothing more."

"You really love that music. I've watched you . . . you're not pretending. It's the same way Paul is about his music. You sort of—drink it up. You try to get all of it."

"I like your friend Nitz," he said, although, in some ways, he was disturbed by the man.

"Yes, he's a lovely person. I don't believe he could ever do anybody harm."

"You admire that."

"Yes," she said, "don't you?"

"I admire it in the abstract."

"Oh, you and your abstract." She settled in a heap against the door, her legs drawn up under her, one arm resting on the windowsill. "What are those lights up there?" She sounded apprehensive. "Are we almost there?"

"Almost. Pull your courage together."

"It's together. Don't make fun of me."

"I'm not making fun of you," he said gently. "Why should I make fun of you?"

"Will they all laugh at what I say?"

"Of course not." He couldn't help adding: "They'll be making so much racket with their sound effects records they won't hear what you say."

"I don't feel good."

"You'll feel better when we get there," he assured her with fatherly sympathy, speeding up the car.

The party was already in progress when they arrived. Schilling noted the transformation in the girl as she climbed the steps to Partridge's house. Her fear vanished below the surface; face impassive, she lounged against the iron railing of the porch, purse in one hand, the other hand draped over her trousered knee. As soon as the door opened she slipped to her feet and passed by the man at the entrance. She had already gone into the hall and was approaching the living room full of noise and laughter when Schilling stubbed out his cigar and stepped inside.

"Hello, Leland," he said to his host, shaking hands. "What became of my girl?"

"There she goes," Partridge said, closing the door. He was a tall, middle-aged man with glasses. "Wife? Mistress?"

"Counter girl." Schilling removed his overcoat. "How's the family?"

"About the same." Arm on Schilling's shoulder, he led him into the living room. "Earl has a cold, again; it's the same flu we all got last year. How's the store?"

"Can't complain."

They both stopped to watch Mary Anne. She had picked out Edith Partridge and was accepting a drink from her hostess's tray. Apparently at ease, Mary Anne turned to meet a band of young record clerks grouped around a table. On the table was a display of sound components: turntables, cartridges, tone arms. Elements of the Diotronic binaural system.

"She's got savoir faire," Partridge said. "For a girl that young it's unusual. My oldest is about her age."

"Mary," Schilling said, "stroll over and meet your host."

She did so, and the introductions were made.

"Who's that terribly fat man?" she asked Partridge. "Over in the corner there, sprawled on the couch."

"That?" Partridge smiled at Schilling. "That's a terribly fat composer named Sid Hethel. Go over and listen to him wheeze . . . he's worth hearing."

"That's the first I've heard you admit that about Sid," Schilling said. He always found Partridge a shade offensive.

"His conversation is exquisite," Partridge said drily. "It's a pity he didn't decide to go into literature."

"Do you want to meet him?" Schilling asked Mary Anne. "He's an experience, even if you don't care for his music."

Accompanied by Partridge, they made their way over. "What's his music like?" Mary Anne asked nervously.

"Very sentimental," Partridge declared, his beaked face rising above her as he steered the two of them between the groups of people. "Somewhat like a breakfast of maraschino cherries." Over the mutter of voices roared the titanic Mahler Symphony No. 1, amplified by the network of horns and speakers mounted throughout the large, well-furnished living room.

"What Leland means," Schilling said, "is that Hethel hasn't run out of melody, as his compatriots have."

"Ah," Partridge said. "How it takes me back to hear you talk, Joe. The good old days, when a little man used to run out at the beginning of each record and shout the name of the selection."

Sid Hethel was involved in conversation. Legs stuck out, cane resting against his fleshy groin, he was jabbing a ponderous finger at his circle of listeners. Hethel was a continent of tissue; from deep fat his eyes, black and sharp, peered out. It was the Hethel that Schilling remembered; he had, to accommodate his belly, unsnapped the two top buttons of his fly.

". . . oh, no," Hethel was sputtering, wiping his mouth with a wad of white handkerchief, which he held in his hand, close to his chin. "You've got me wrong; I never said anything like that. Frankenstein's a good reviewer, a good music reviewer; the best in the area. But he's a chauvinist; if you're local talent, you're the cream of the crop; if you're Lilly Lombino from Wheeling, West Virginia, however, you can play the violin like Sarasate and Alf won't give you a tumble."

"I hear music and art reviewing don't keep him occupied," a member of Hethel's circle supplied. "He's going to kick out Koltanowski and do the chess column."

"Chess," Hethel said. "This is possible; with Alf Frankenstein it could be everything but cooking." He caught sight of Partridge, and a wicked gleam sparkled in his eyes. "Now, this binaural business. If only Mahler were alive today . . ."

"With binaural," Partridge broke in gravely, "Mahler would have been able to listen to his music as it really sounded."

"You have a point," Hethel conceded, turning his attention to his host. "Of course, we must remember that to Mahler his music sounded good. Is there a knob or dial on your system that makes Mahler sound good? Because if there is—"

"Sid," Schilling said, feeling the potency of their years of friendship, "you realize you're drinking Leland's liquor and you're insulting him at the same time."

"If I wasn't drinking his liquor," Hethel said rapidly, "I wouldn't be insulting anybody. What brings you up here, Josh? Still trying to put Maurice Ravel under contract?" His vast pulpy hands, both of them, snaked out; Schilling accepted them and the two men gripped each other warmly. "It's good to see you," Hethel said, equally moved. "Still carry a box of contraceptives around in your briefcase?"

"What you call a briefcase," Schilling said, "is a large, leather, custom-appointed douche bag."

"Once," Hethel confided to his group, "I saw Josh Schilling sitting in a bar . . ." His voice trailed off. "Good God, Schilling! I want to see the woman who goes with *that* douche bag!"

A little embarrassed, Schilling glanced at Mary Anne. How was she weathering the spectacle of Sid Hethel, the great contemporary composer?

Standing with her arms folded, she listened and did not seem amused nor offended. It was impossible to tell what she thought; her face was expressionless. In her black silk trousers she was remarkably slender . . . there was balance in her straight back and elongated neck, and above her folded arms her breasts were very small, very sharp, quite visibly uptilted.

"Sid," Schilling said, bringing the girl forward, "I've opened a little new record shop down in Pacific Park. Remember, I always wanted to? One day when I pried up the lid of a shipping carton this elf popped out."

"My dear," Hethel said to her, the banter all at once gone from his voice, "step over here and tell me why you're working in that old man's record shop." He put his hand out and closed his fingers around hers. "What's your name?"

She told him, quietly, with the innate dignity Schilling had come to expect of her.

"Don't be elusive," Hethel said, smiling around at the circle of people. "Doesn't she look elusive to you?"

"What's that mean?" Mary Anne asked him.

Hethel scowled. "Mean?" He sounded baffled. "Well," he said, in a cross, overly loud voice, "it means—" He turned to Schilling. "Tell her what it means."

"He means you're a very pretty little girl," Edith Partridge said, appearing with a tray of drinks. "Who's run dry?"

"Here," Hethel muttered, groping at the tray for a glass. "Thanks, Edith." He focused his attention on her, letting go of Mary Anne's hand. "How're the kids?"

"How does he strike you?" Schilling asked the girl as he maneuvered her back through the ring of people, away from Hethel. "He didn't upset you, did he?"

"No," she said, shaking her head.

"He's had too much to drink, as usual. You find him repulsive?"

"No," she said. "He's like Nitz, isn't he? I mean, he's not like most people . . . whatever it is about them. The hard part. The part I'm afraid of. I wasn't afraid of him."

"Sid Hethel is the gentlest man in the world." He was gratified by her reaction. "Can I get you anything?"

"No, thanks." Suddenly, with a rush of pessimism, she said; "They all can tell how old I am, can't they?"

"How old are you?"

"I'm *young.*"

"That's good. Think of yourself and then think of us—Partridge and Hethel and Schilling, three old dodderers, reminiscing about the days of the cylinder record."

"I wish I could talk about that," Mary Anne said fervently. "What have I got to say? All I can do is tell people my name . . . isn't that wonderful?"

"It's good enough for me," he said, and meant it.

"Do *you* know who Milhaud is?"

"Yes," he admitted.

She wandered away from him and, after some hesitation, he followed. Now she had halted at the edge of a group of audio engineers and was listening to their conversation. Her face was drawn up in the troubled frown he was beginning to know.

"Mary Anne," he said, "they're comparing the roll-off of the new Bogen and Fisher amplifiers. What do you care about that?"

"I don't even understand what it is!"

"It's sound. And sometimes I wonder if they understand." He led her over to a window seat in the deserted corner of the room and sat her down. She held onto her glass—Edith Partridge had taken her purse—and stared at the floor.

"Cheer up," he said.

"What's that awful racket?"

He listened. All he could hear was the noise of human voices; and, of course, the torrent of Mahler's symphonic texture. "That must be it. There's a speaker horn mounted near here." He felt around with his hands until he located a grille set in the wall behind a print. "See? It's emerging from that."

"Does it have a name?"

"Yes, it's the Mahler First Symphony."

Mary Anne brooded. "You even know the name. Would you teach me that?"

"Of course." He felt sad and touched.

"Because," Mary Anne went on earnestly, "I want to talk to that man and I can't. That fat man." She shook her head."I guess I'm tired . . . all those people coming in and out of the store today. What time is it?"

It was only nine-thirty. "Want to leave?" he asked.

"No, that wouldn't be right."

"It's up to you," he said, meaning it.

"Where would we go? Back?"

"If you want."

"I don't want."

"Well," he said softly, "then we won't. We could go to a bar; we could go get something to eat; we could simply walk around San Francisco. We could do any number of things."

"Could we ride on a cable car?" she asked in a wan, discouraged whisper.

At the far end of the room an argument had broken out. Angry voices burst through the curtain of symphonic sound; it was Partridge and Hethel.

"Let's try to be rational about this," Partridge was complaining in his scolding voice. "I agree that we have to keep means and ends clear. But sound is not a means and music the end; music is a value term applied to recognized patterns of sound. What you call *sound* is simply music you don't like. And furthermore—"

"And furthermore," Hethel's response boomed out, "if I kick over a stack of bottles twice in succession I'm entitled to claim I've composed something called 'A Study in Glass'—is that it? Isn't that what you're saying?"

"There's no need to make a personal attack out of this." Turning his back on Hethel, Partridge flounced off, smiling in a set, mechanical fashion, going from group to group, saying hello and greeting people. The talk and music gradually resumed; Hethel, surrounded by his ring of neophytes, ceased to be audible.

"God," Partridge breathed, approaching Schilling and Mary Anne. "He's drunk, of course; I should have known better."

Schilling said: "Known better than to invite him?"

The characteristic sound of a piano rose up; somebody was starting to play. Partridge's exasperation boiled up anew. "Damn him. That's Hethel—he finally found the piano. I told Edith to get it completely out of the house."

"That's pretty hard to do," Schilling said, feeling scant sympathy for the man, "unless you have plenty of notice."

"I'll have to stop him; he's ruining the entire thing."

"What entire thing?"

"The demonstration, of course. We're here to inaugurate a new dimension in sound; I don't intend to permit his infantile—"

"Sid Hethel," Schilling said, "plays the piano, in public, on the average of once a year. I can name a few students in composition who would give their right eyes to be here."

"That's my point. He's picked this time on purpose; of course he doesn't play in public. How did he get over to the piano? The man's so obese he can scarcely stagger."

"Come on," Schilling said, bending over Mary Anne. "This is unique . . . you won't have this opportunity again."

"I wish Paul was here," she said, as they pushed over. An eagerness had set in among the guests; men and women, forgetting their talk, strained close to see. Standing on tiptoe, those in back succeeded in catching a glimpse of the great mound of flesh slouched at the keyboard.

"Here," Schilling said. "I'll boost you up." He caught hold of the girl around her waist; she was slim, very slim and firm. His hands passed almost around her as he lifted her up against him, raising her until she could see over the ring of heads.

"Oh," she said. "Oh, Joseph . . . look at him."

When the playing had finished—Hethel soon ran out of breath—the crowd dispersed and flowed off. Her face flushed, Mary Anne trailed after Schilling.

"Paul should have seen this," she said wistfully. "I wish we could have brought him. Wasn't he wonderful? And he looked as if he was asleep . . . his eyes were shut, weren't they? And those big fingers—how did he manage it? How could he play the keys?"

Over in the corner Sid Hethel sat gasping, his face mottled and dark. He hardly glanced up as Schilling and Mary Anne appeared in front of him.

"Thanks," Schilling said to the man.

"Why?" Hethel wheezed. But he seemed to understand. "Well, at least I interfered with the future of binaural sound."

"It was worth coming," Mary Anne said to him quickly. "I never heard anybody play like that."

"What sort of store is this?" Hethel demanded, coughing into his handkerchief. "You used to be in publishing, Josh; you were with Schirmer."

"I left them a long time ago," Schilling said. "For a while I was in wholesale records. I prefer this . . . in my own store I can talk to people as much as I want."

"Yes, you always loved to waste time. I suppose you still have your damn record collection . . . all those Deutsche Grammophons and Polydors. And that girl we liked to listen to back in the old days. What was her name?"

"Elisabeth Schumann," Schilling said, remembering.

"Yes, the one who sang like a child. I never forgot her."

"I wish," Schilling said, "I could get you down to see my place."

"A store? We've got stores up here."

"I've been trying to stir some sort of interest in music down there. Every Sunday I have open house—records and coffee."

"You desire me to die?" Hethel demanded. "I'd travel down there and expire. You remember what happened that time in Washington when I fell getting off the train. You remember how long I was laid up."

"I've got a car; I'll drive you both ways. You can sleep the whole trip."

Hethel reflected. "You'll hit bumps," he decided. "You'll pick out bumps and run over them; I know you."

"On my word of honor."

"Really? Let's have that good old Boy Scout oath. In these times of shifting moral values there's got to be something stable we can count on." Hethel's eyes gleamed with nostalgia. "Remember the time you and I got lost in that Chinese whorehouse on Grant Avenue? And you got drunk and tried to—"

"Seriously," Schilling said, not wishing such topics discussed before Mary Anne.

"Seriously, I'll have to mull it over. I want to get out of the Bay Area; this parochial climate is murder. I could come and dazzle people. Maybe between us we could lick the sound boys." He patted Schilling on the arm. "I'll call you, Josh. It depends on how I feel."

"Good-bye," Mary Anne said as she and Schilling started away.

Hethel opened his tired eyes. "Good-bye, little Miss Elf. Josh Schilling's elusive elf . . . I remember you."

The party was breaking up. A few scattered people were gathered around Partridge's hi-fi, examining the Diotronic Binaural Sound System, but the majority had drifted off.

"You want to go?" Schilling said to the girl.

"Maybe so."

"You feel better, don't you?"

"Yes," she said, and shivered.

"Cold?"

"Just tired. Maybe you could get me my purse . . . I think she put it in the bedroom."

He went to get her purse and his own overcoat. In a moment they had said good evening to the Partridges and were starting down the front steps onto the sidewalk.

"Brrrr," Mary Anne said, jumping into the car. "I'm freezing."

He started the motor and clicked on the heater. "You want to go back? Tomorrow's Sunday; you don't have to get up early."

Restlessly, Mary Anne said: "I don't want to go back. Maybe we could go somewhere." But she looked tired and drawn; a scrawny, almost gaunt quality had crept up into the hollows of her face.

"I'll take you home," Schilling decided. "It's time you were in bed."

Without protest, she sank down against the seat, brought up her knees, and pressed her chin into the fabric. Arms folded, she stared at the steering column.

Once, as they drove along the peninsula highway between towns, Mary Anne lifted her head and murmured: "If he does come down, Paul could hear him."

"Absolutely," he agreed.

"Did he write some of the music Paul listened to in the booth that day?"

"I gave Paul one of Hethel's pieces, yes. A sonata for small chamber orchestra. His 'Rustic' Sonata."

"You told me sonatas were for piano."

"Most of them . . . but not with Sid Hethel."

"Jesus," Mary Anne sighed. "It's so darn confusing . . . I'll never get it."

"Don't worry about it."

The girl lapsed into silence.

"Still cold?" he asked presently.

"No, but I should have worn a coat. Only I wanted you to see my outfit. Do you like it?"

"It's fine," he said, as he had said before. "It's just right."

She became despondent again. "Wednesday is the inquest, or whatever they call it."

"What inquest?"

"For Danny Coombs. I have to go down and explain what happened, so they'll know if they want to arrest anybody."

"Will they want to?"

"No, because it was an accident. Coombs ran out and fell. There was a laundry delivery man who saw him. It seems so remote . . . but it was only a couple of weeks ago. Now it sounds like something I made up. Except that if we don't say the right thing, Tweany will go to the flea-bee." Her voice trailed off.

"You don't want him to be tried."

"Of course not. Well, they won't. He's strutting around; he got rid of Coombs. Now he has a free field with Beth. Good for him." With a sigh, she rolled herself up in a ball and lay back against the seat; in a few moments she had drifted off into a troubled doze.

When he brought the car to a halt in front of her apartment building she was still asleep. She didn't stir as he shut off the motor and pushed open the door; he had already begun to gather her up before she blinked and opened her eyes.

"What are you doing?" she asked warily. "Going to carry me inside?"

"Do you mind?"

"I guess not." She yawned. "But be careful . . . don't kill yourself."

She weighed, he discovered, about as much as four cartons of records, probably not much more than a hundred pounds. Without difficulty, he pushed open the front door of the building and carried her upstairs. Here and there light showed under doors, but her own apartment was dark. And the door, when he tried the knob, was locked.

"I have the key," she murmured. "In my purse. Set me down and I'll get it."

He set her down; stumbling a little, she leaned against the door, eyes half-shut. Presently she smiled, opened her purse, and groped inside it.

"Thank you for the nice time," she said.

"That's perfectly all right."

"We went out together, didn't we?"

"I suppose so. Did you have fun?"

"I wish—" Again she yawned, showing her small white teeth and pink cat's tongue. "I wish I could have understood more. Will we ever see that fat man again . . . Sid Hethel? Will he come down here?"

"Maybe. I hope so." Putting his hands on her shoulders, his fingers touching her neck, he bent over her and kissed her close to the mouth. She gave a little soundless cry of surprise and wonder; one hand came up in a gesture of defense, as if she intended to scratch him. Whatever it was, she changed her mind. For an interval she leaned drowsily against him, clinging to him in her half-sleep; then, all at once, she was awake. She had reached some kind of decision; her body stiffened and she pulled back.

"No," she said, slipping away from him, out from under his hands, becoming shadowy and insubstantial in the gloom of the hall.

"No what?" he echoed, not understanding.

"We can't go in there; she's in there." Taking hold of his hand, Mary Anne led him back along the hall, away from the locked door of her apartment.

15

Still clutching his hand, she hurried down the stairs of the apartment building and outside to the darkness of the street. Schilling started toward his parked car, but she led him away from it and down the sidewalk.

"Not the car," she gasped, veering away from the misty black-metal hull. "It isn't far; we'll walk."

"Where are we going?"

Her answer was lost; he couldn't make it out. In the night silence her breathing was labored. Not letting go of him, she led him across the street and around the corner. Ahead of them glowed the lights of the downtown business section, stores and bars and gas stations.

She was taking him to the record shop. Rushing through the darkness, she was carrying him closer and closer to his own store. What she had said, he realized, was *stockroom*. They were going there, to the converted basement under the street level. Already she was struggling with her purse, getting out her store key.

"Let me take you home," he protested. "To my place."

"Please, Joseph—I don't want to go there."

"But why the store?"

She slowed a little, her face very pale in the glare of the streetlight. "I'm afraid," she said, as if that explained everything. And it did, for him. She was becoming panic-stricken, as she had been that first day. But this time he was ready for it: it was no surprise.

"Look," he told her reasonably, pulling her to a halt. "Go on back to your apartment. I'll leave you . . . there's nothing to worry about." He untangled her fingers until his own hand was free. "See? It's as simple as that."

"Don't leave," she said instantly. "Can't we go to the store? I'll be all right there; I want to be downstairs, where it's safe." And then she was hurrying on again, the silk of her clothes shining and rustling ahead of him.

He followed. When he caught up with her she had crossed the street to the far side; the record shop was visible now, its window lights glaring.

"Here," she said. "You unlock the door." She jabbed her key at him; accepting it, he turned the lock, and swung the door aside.

The store was cold. Except for the window display everything lay in darkness. An acrid haze of cigarette smoke hung in the listening booths, a stale smell mixed with the presence of onions and human perspiration: reminders of customers. To his left was the counter, laden with records. As he reached for a light switch, the corner of a display table caught him against the knee; snorting, he stopped to reach painfully down.

In the back of the store the hall light came on. Mary Anne disappeared into the office and then emerged almost at once, a wool jacket around her shoulders. "Where are you?" she asked.

"Here." He located the overhead light and pulled it on. Grunting, he limped to the door, pulled down the shade, and released the lock. The heavy bolt jumped into place.

"Yes," she agreed. "Lock it. I forgot. Can I turn on the heater in the office?"

"Certainly." Sitting down on the window ledge, he rested and rubbed his knee. Mary Anne had already vanished into the office; the soft blue shimmer of the fluorescent lamp above his desk became visible. He could hear her stirring around, lifting out the electric heater, lowering the window shade.

"Find it?" he asked, when she reappeared.

"It's on; it's getting warm." She came up and dropped beside him, crouched against the counter, half-kneeling, half-leaning against the upright surface behind her. "Joseph," she said, "why did you kiss me?"

"Why?" he echoed. "Because I love you."

"Do you? I wondered if that was why." She settled down and sat gazing at him with a worried, preoccupied frown. "Are you sure that's it?" Then she had scrambled up to her feet. "Let's go in the office where it's warm."

The little electric heater beamed and radiated, creating a nimbus of heat around itself. "Look at it," Mary Anne said. "Getting itself warm . . . nothing else."

"Are you afraid of me?" he asked her.

"No." Harassed, she paced around the office. "I don't think so, at least. Why should I be afraid of you?"

Outside the store a car rushed along the empty street, its headlights spilling across the display tables and racks, the shelves of records behind the counter. Then the car was gone; the store returned to darkness.

"I'm going downstairs," she announced, already starting out into the hall.

"What for?"

There was no response; she had turned on the basement light and was hurrying down the stairwell.

"Come on back up here," he ordered.

"Please don't shout at me," she said in a clipped voice. But she had paused on the stairs. "I can't stand being shouted at."

"Look at me," he said.

"No."

"Stop this damn neurotic business and look at me."

"You can't order me around," she said. But gradually her head turned. Eyes dark, lips pressed tight, she faced him.

"Mary Anne," he said, "what's the matter?"

The darkness in her eyes blurred. "I'm afraid something will happen to me." One small hand came up; frail and trembling, she was holding onto the banister. "Oh, hell," she said, her lips twitching. "It goes back a long way. I'm sorry, Joseph."

"Why?" he repeated. "Why do you want to go downstairs?"

"To get the coffeepot. Didn't I say?"

"No, you didn't say."

"It's still down there . . . I was washing it out today. It's drying on the packing table by the gummed tape. On some pieces of cardboard."

"Do you want coffee?"

"Yes," she said eagerly. "Then maybe I wouldn't be so cold."

"All right," he said. "Go on and get it."

Gratefully, she let go of the banister and hurried down into the stockroom. Schilling followed after her. When he reached the basement he found her sitting on the edge of the rickety packing table, fitting the Silex coffeepot together. A few drops of water shone on her wrist; she had filled the coffeepot up and it was sloshing over.

For a moment he thought of getting the tin of Folger's coffee down for her; she was starting to search the shelves behind her, reaching up and pushing aside the boxes of twine and Scotch tape. He went over, half-intending that and half-intending something else, something that remained diffused in his mind until he had almost reached her and she was lifting the Silex up for him to take. He took it and then, without hesitation, set it down again, this time on the edge of the table, and put his arms around the girl's shoulders.

"How thin," he said aloud.

"I told you." She shifted until more of her weight rested on the table. "What is it they call it when you want to run? Panic? That sounds like the word. But I always wanted a place I could run to, a place I could hide . . . but when I got there, nobody would let me in, or it wasn't where I wanted to be after all. It never worked out; there was always something wrong. And I gave up trying."

"Have you been coming down here at night?"

"A couple of times."

"Doing what? Just sitting?"

"Sitting and thinking. I never worked where they gave me a key before. I played a few records . . . I tried to remember what you told me about them, what I was supposed to listen for. There was one I liked very much; I put it on the machine and then I went in the office and listened from there because it was warmer. Are you mad at me?"

"No," he said.

"I'll never be able to figure all that out, all the things you know. But that wasn't why I came down, anyhow. I just wanted to listen and be in here by myself, with the door locked. One night—last night, I think—the cop came around and shone his flashlight on me. I had to go and unlock the door and prove who I was."

"Did he believe you?"

"Yes, he had seen me working during the day. He asked me if I was okay."

"What did you tell him?"

"I told him I was about as okay as I had ever been. But not really okay enough."

"What can I do?" he asked.

"You don't have to do anything."

"I want to do something."

"Well, you could find the coffee."

"Can't I do more than that?"

She pondered, her head against his, one hand resting against her cheek, the other in her lap. He could feel her breath rushing and see the slight motion of her lips. Like a child, she was breathing through her mouth. She was so close to him that, even in the dim light, he could make out the tiny, perfectly formed strands that grew from the nape of her neck and were lost in the general darkness of her hair. Along the edge of her jaw, beneath her left ear, was an almost invisible scar, a thin line of white that disappeared into the faint fuzz of her cheek.

"What was that?" he asked, touching the scar.

"Oh." She smiled up at him, lifting her chin. "When I was eleven I bumped into a glass cupboard door and the glass broke." Her eyes roamed mischievously. "It didn't hurt, but it bled a lot, all down my neck in big red drops. I had a cat who used to sneak into the dish cupboard and go to sleep in the big mixing bowl, the one my mother mixed her cakes in. I was trying to get him out, but he wouldn't come. I was pulling on his paw, and all of a sudden he scratched me. I backed away and broke the glass door."

She was still meditating over her childhood injury when he turned her face upward and kissed her, this time directly on her dry lips. Nowhere on her was there any excess flesh; her bones were close to the surface, just beneath the skin: first came the silk of her clothing and then the immediate hardness of her ribs and shoulder blades and collarbone. Her hair, as it swept close to him, smelled faintly of cigarette smoke. Close to her ears lingered the remnant of some perfume, long since evaporated. She was tired, and there was a presence of tiredness about her, a drooping passivity and silence.

At first he held her lightly because he thought she might want to get away, and it was important that she be able to get away. But, after a time, he realized that she was falling quietly asleep, or, at least, into a kind of unwinding stupor. Her eyes were still open—she was gazing at the cardboard cartons of adding machine tape above his head—but there was no particular focus of consciousness in them. She was aware of him, aware of herself too, but only in a nebulous way. Her mind was turned inward, still revolving around thoughts, and around memories of thoughts, meditating over experiences that had long ago existed.

"I feel safe," she said at last.

"Yes," he agreed. "You are."

"Because of you?"

"I hope so. Because of the store, too. It feeds us."

"But mostly because of you. I didn't always feel this way. Not at all, before. Remember?"

"I frightened you."

"You scared hell out of me. And you were so—stern. You lectured me; you were like—" She searched her memory, brightness dancing in her eyes. "When I was very little . . . the picture of God in Sunday school. Only you don't have a long beard."

"I'm not God," he said. He was an ordinary man; he was not God or even like God, in spite of the picture she had seen in Sunday school. An unhappy anger grew inside him. Her odd, warm, totally childish ideal . . . and there was really so little he could do to help her. "Disappointed?" he asked.

"I guess not."

"You wouldn't like God. He sends people to hell. God's an old-fashioned reactionary."

She pulled back and wrinkled her nose at him. Again he kissed her. This time she stirred; moving her face away, she smiled and blew a mouthful of warm breath up at him. Then her smile, without warning, vanished. Ducking her head she trembled and sat with her back stiff, hands clenched together, and, moaning, rose up until her bare throat was against his eyes.

Joseph Schilling knew that she was frightened now, that the old image had come back. But he did not stir. Motion would have been a mistake. He kept that fixed in his mind.

"Joseph," she said. "I—" The spoken sound faded into a stammer of confusion; shaking her head, she tugged fretfully upward, as if her body were caught.

"What is it?" he asked, rising with her as she slid from the table and caught at him. Her nails dug into his sleeves; she struggled with herself, swallowing rapidly, eyes shut.

Schilling saw his own hands tearing at the clasps that held her shirt together. How strange, he thought. So that was it. What an eerie sight it was, his large, reddish hands plucking so industriously. The girl, opening her eyes, looked down and saw. Together they watched the hands twitch aside her shirt and spread out across the hollow of her shoulders, until they had pushed her clothes down to her elbows.

"Oh, dear," the girl whispered. Schilling, unable to comprehend, drew back and sat rubbing his hands together.

Mary Anne took a deep breath and began to gather her shirt back around her. A wondering expression appeared on her face; turning to him, she asked: "Did you do that? You did do it, didn't you?"

"Yes," he said. And then he reached out, drew the fabric of her shirt completely away from her, and unfastened the remaining clasps. She made no protest; with curiosity she watched his hands as they traveled across her stomach to the snap that held her slacks in place. Once she made a motion of unclipping her bra; she stood groping behind her back without accomplishing anything until Schilling turned her partly around, pushed her fingers away, and undid the hooks.

"Thanks," she murmured. Her bra fell forward and she caught the cups. In a few brief motions she had pulled her slacks all the way off and, with a shiver, worked down her underpants. Collecting her clothes, she folded them in a bundle and pushed them away. For an instant her slightly luminous column danced in front of him; then she hurried forward, very smooth, very alive, creeping up onto the table.

"Yes," she told him. "Don't wait; hurry, Joseph, for heaven's sake."

He did not have to wait. By flattening her back she was able to receive him; she guided him in with her own fingers, pushed until she could go no farther, and, supporting herself upon her fists, stiffened her body. She was warm inside, warmer than he had ever found anywhere, with anyone. Her eyes were shut and she was involved in the rhythms of her body. Across her pelvis rippled a sheet of fine, energetic muscles; the activity spread until it reached her breasts and dilated each nipple. He had entered her in so short a time that neither of them had spoken a word.

It was accomplished, then. Something rushed to the surface of her body and was gone; she constricted, became hard, then soft again. Sighing, the girl lowered herself and relaxed. She withdrew her fists and contentedly laid her palms flat across her belly.

Schilling waited, and then he carefully withdrew himself. Mary Anne said nothing. Finally, after he had got his clothes back around himself and was stepping to the floor, she stirred, opened her eyes, and sat up.

In a low, timid voice she said: "That never happened to me before. I never felt anything inside me come. It was always something that happened to me; nothing I did."

"It's good," he assured her.

Presently she located her clothes and began to dress. He couldn't help looking at his watch. Only ten minutes had gone by since they descended to the storeroom. It did not seem possible, but it was actually no longer than that. If they had, instead, gone up and put on the coffee, it would just now be ready.

When the girl had finished dressing, he said to her: "How do you feel, Mary Anne?"

She stretched her arms, shook herself like an animal, and then trotted toward the stairs. "I feel fine, but I'm hungry. Can we go have something to eat?"

He laughed. "Right away?"

Halfway up the stairs she halted to gaze down at him. "Why not? What's wrong with that?"

"Nothing." Mounting the stairs, he stopped behind her. She did not seem to mind; there was no objection as he reached up and put his arm around her waist. Leaning back, she rested against him, making a breathy whirr of satisfaction. He covered her right breast with his fingers and she did not seem to mind that, either; in fact, she closed her hand over his and pressed him against her until he could feel the line of ribs under her flesh. "Where do you want to go?" he asked, releasing her.

"Anywhere. Someplace we can get hotcakes and ham and coffee. That's what I want; plenty of it, too." Excitedly, she scampered up the stairs to the top. "Okay?" she demanded, outlined above him.

"Okay," he said happily, and reached to switch off the basement light.

16

The Pacific Star Diner was a little wooden café on the rim of the slum business section. Mary Anne opened the screen door and entered. A taxi driver and two workmen in black leather jackets sat at the counter drinking coffee and reading the sporting green of the San Francisco *Chronicle.* In one of the booths was a solemn Negro couple.

"Can I order anything I want?" Eyes sparkling, she slid into an empty booth at the rear.

"Of course," Schilling said, reaching for the menu.

"I want what I said, still. Will they give it to me?"

"If they don't, we'll go somewhere else."

The counter man, a middle-aged Greek wearing a soiled white apron, approached and took their order.

"How long will it be?" Mary Anne asked Schilling as the Greek went back to get ham from the refrigerator. "It won't be long, will it?"

"Only a couple of minutes."

"I'm starving." She began to read the titles on the jukebox selector. "Look—these are all jump tunes. All 'Jazz at the Phil' stuff . . . could I play one? Could I play this Roy Brown tune? 'Good Rockin' Tonight,' it's called. Would you mind?"

He found some change and pushed it across to her.

"Thanks," she said shyly, dropping a coin into the selector

and rotating the dial. Presently the café boomed with the noise of an alto saxophone.

"I guess it's pretty terrible," Mary Anne said as the racket finally subsided. She made no move to pick up any more money from the little heap, and Schilling asked:

"Aren't you going to play any others?"

"They're no good."

"Don't say that. Those men are artists in their field. I don't want you to give up what you enjoy in favor of what I like."

"But what you like is better."

"Not necessarily."

"If it isn't better, then why do you like it?" Mary Anne reached eagerly for a paper napkin. "Here comes the food. I'm going to ask Harry to sit down and eat with us." She explained, "That's Harry carrying the food."

"How do you know his name is Harry?"

"I just know; all Greeks are named Harry." When the man had reached the table and his long arms were beginning to push out the platters of food, Mary Anne announced: "Harry, please sit down; we want you to join us."

The Greek grinned. "Sorry, Miss."

"Come on. Whatever you want; we'll pay for it."

"I'm on a diet," the Greek told her, wiping off the table with his damp rag. "I can't eat anything but orange juice."

"I don't believe he's really a Greek," Mary Anne said to Schilling as the counter man went off. "I'll bet his name isn't even Harry."

"Probably not," Schilling agreed, starting to eat. The food was good and he ate a great deal. Presently, across from him, the girl finished the last of her coffee, pushed away her plate, and said:

"I'm through."

She had already finished, and completely so. Lighting a cigarette, she sat smiling at him across the yellow-moist table.

"Still hungry?" he asked. "Want more?"

"No. That's enough." Her attention wandered. "I wonder what it's like to run a little café . . . you could get all you wanted to eat, any time of the day. You could live in the back . . . do you suppose he lives in the back? Do you suppose he has a big family?"

"All Greeks have big families."

The girl's fingers drummed restlessly on the surface of the table. "Could we take a walk? But maybe you don't like to walk."

"I used to walk all the time, before I got the car. And I didn't find that it hurt me." He finished his food, wiped his mouth with his napkin, and got up. "So let's go take our walk."

He paid Harry, who lounged at the cash register, and then they strolled outside onto the dark street. Fewer people were visible and most of the stores had shut off their lights for the night. Hands in her pockets, purse under her arm, Mary Anne marched along. Schilling followed behind her, letting her choose her own direction. But she had no particular course in mind; at the end of the block she halted.

"We could go anywhere," she declared.

"That's so."

"How far do you suppose we could walk? Would we still be walking when the sun came up?"

"Well," Schilling said, "probably not." It was eleven-fifteen. "We'd have to walk for seven hours."

"Where would we be then?"

He calculated. "We might make it to Los Gatos, if we kept on the main highway."

"Have you ever been in Los Gatos?"

"Once. That was back in 1949, when I was still working for Allison and Hirsch. I had a vacation, and we were on our way to Santa Cruz."

Mary Anne asked: "Who is 'we'? "

"Max and myself."

Walking slowly across the street she said: "How close were you and Beth?"

"At one time we were very close."

"As close as you and I?"

"Not as close as you and I." He wanted to be honest with her, so he said: "We spent a night together at a cabin up along the Potomac, in a little old lock-keeper's cabin on the old canal. The next morning I brought her back to town."

"That was when Danny Coombs tried to kill you, wasn't it?"

"Yes," he admitted.

"You weren't telling me the truth before." But there was no rancor in her voice. "You said you hadn't been with her."

"Beth—wasn't his wife then." This time he couldn't tell her the truth, because he couldn't expect her to understand. The situation had to be experienced.

"Did you love her?"

"No, absolutely not. It was a mistake on my part—I always regretted it."

"But you love me."

"Yes," he said. And he meant it very much.

Satisfied, the girl strolled on. But after a time she seemed to fall back into worry. "Joseph," she said, "why did you go with her if you didn't love her? Is that right?"

"No, I suppose not. But with her it was a regular event . . . I wasn't the first, nor the last." So he had to explain anyhow. "She was—well, available. Physical acts of that sort happen. Tensions build up . . . they have to be expiated in some fashion. No personal element is involved."

"Did you ever love anybody before me?"

"There was a woman named Irma Fleming who I loved a great deal." He was silent for a moment, thinking back to his wife, whom he hadn't seen in years. He and Irma had legally separated in—good God—1936. The year Alf Landon ran for president. "But," he said, "that was a long time ago." It certainly was.

"How long ago?" Mary Anne asked.

"I'd rather not say." There were a lot of things, related things, he would rather he didn't have to say.

"If I asked, would you tell me your age?"

"I'm fifty-eight years old, Mary."

"Oh." She nodded. "That's about what I thought."

They had reached the car wash at the edge of the main highway. Seeing it, Schilling recalled the first hour he had spent in Pacific Park: the Negro named Bill who had owned the car wash, and his assistant who had been somewhere getting a Coke. And the dark-haired high school girl.

"Did you go to this high school?" he asked.

"Sure. It's the only one around."

"When was that?" He could, easily, picture her as a high school girl; he could imagine her in sweater and skirt, carrying a few textbooks, roaming, as the dark-haired girl had roamed, from the high school to Foster's Freeze at three o'clock in the warm midsummer afternoon.

Fresh little breasts, he thought almost sadly. Like cakes of yeast. The lightly downy body, growing and budding . . . and, from it, the smell of spring.

"That was a couple of years ago," Mary Anne said. "I hated school. All the dumb kids."

"You were a kid, too."

"But I wasn't dumb," she said, and he could well believe it.

Beyond the closed-up car wash was a small roadside ceramics shop. A few lights were still on; a woman in a long smock was carrying pottery into the building.

"Buy me something," Mary Anne said suddenly. "Buy me a cup or a flowerpot—something I can have."

Schilling approached the woman. "Is it too late?" he asked.

"No," the woman said, continuing. "You can have anything you see. But excuse me if I don't stop."

Together, he and Mary Anne walked among the bowls and vases and plates and jars and wall planters. "Do you see anything you want?" he asked. Most of it was the usual garish oddities sold to motorists.

"You pick it out," Mary Anne urged.

He looked and found a simple clay dish glazed a light speckled blue. Paying the woman, he carried it to Mary Anne; she stood waiting at the edge of the field.

"Thank you," she said shyly, accepting the dish. "It's nice."

"It isn't ornate, at least."

Carrying her dish, Mary Anne wandered on. Now they had left the stores behind; they were approaching a dark square of trees at the edge of town. "What's that?" Schilling asked.

"A park. People come and eat picnics here." The entrance was barred by a hanging chain, but she stepped over it and continued on toward the first table. "Nobody's supposed to be in here at night, but they never bother to check. We used to come here all the time . . . us kids from school. We used to drive up here at night and park and leave the car and go on inside on foot."

Beyond the table was a stone barbecue pit, a trash can, and, after that, a drinking fountain. A tangle of trees and shrubs grew around the picnic area, a chaotic blur of night.

Sitting down on the bench beside the table, Mary Anne leaned back and waited for him to catch up. The dirt slope was an upgrade, and he found himself short of breath by the time he had reached her. "It's pleasant here," he said, lowering himself to the bench beside her. "But the other one has the duck."

"Oh, yes," she said. "That big drake. He's been there for years. But I can remember when he was a baby."

"You like him?"

"Sure, but he tried to bite me once. Anyhow, that park's for the pensioners." She looked around her. "In summer we used to sit here, when it was nice and hot, drinking beer and listening to a Zenith portable we carried around. I forget who it belonged to. It fell out of the car one day and got smashed."

Holding her blue dish on her lap, she carefully examined it. "At night," she said, "you aren't able to tell what color it is."

"It's blue," Schilling said.

"Is it painted?"

"No," he explained, "it's a fire-baked glaze. It's put on with a brush and the whole affair is stuck in a kiln."

"You know almost everything there is."

"Well, I've seen pottery fired, if that's what you mean."

"Have you been all over the world?"

He laughed at the thought. "No, only to Europe. England, France, a year or so in Germany. Not even all of Europe."

"Can you speak German?"

"Fairly well."

"French?"

"Not so well."

"I took two years of Spanish in high school," Mary Anne said. "Now I can't remember any of it."

"You'd get it back if you ever needed it."

"I'd like to travel," she said. "I'd like to visit South America and Europe and the Orient. What do you suppose it's like in Japan? My roommate has a brother who was in Japan after the war. He sent her a lot of ashtrays and trick boxes and lovely silk curtains and a silver letter opener."

"Japan would be nice," Schilling said.

"Let's go there, then."

"All right," he agreed, "we'll go there first."

For a period Mary Anne was silent. "Do you realize," she said finally, "that if I dropped this dish it would smash to smithereens?"

"It probably would."

"What then?"

"Then," Schilling said, "I'd get you another."

Abruptly, Mary Anne hopped down from the bench. "Let's walk. Will we get hit and killed if we walk along the highway?"

"It's possible."

She said: "I want to, anyhow."

It was eleven-forty-five. They walked two hours, neither of them saying much, concentrating instead on the cars that rushed past them every now and then, stepping off the highway, standing on the weedy ground, and then starting back again when each car was gone.

Shortly before two o'clock they neared an island of lights growing by the highway. Presently the lights resolved into a Shell station, a closed-up fruit stand, and a tavern. A pair of autos were parked in the lot outside the tavern. A GOLDEN GLOW neon sign gleamed in the window; the sound of voices and laughter drifted out into the night.

Walking across the lot, Mary Anne threw herself down on the steps of the tavern. "I can't go any farther," she said.

"No," Schilling agreed, halting beside her. "Neither can I."

He went inside and telephoned the Yellow Cab people. Fifteen minutes later a cab drove into the lot and slowed to a stop beside them. The driver threw open the door and said: "Hop in, folks."

As they rode back toward Pacific Park, Mary Anne lay watching the dark highway move past. "I'm tired," she said once, very softly.

"You must be," Schilling said.

"These weren't the proper shoes." She had lifted her feet up and tucked them under her. "How do you feel?"

"I'm fine," he said, which was true. "I don't even think I'll be stiff tomorrow," he added, which was probably not true.

"Maybe we could go hiking again sometime," Mary Anne said. "When we have the proper shoes and all the rest. There's a nice place over toward the mountains . . . it's up high, and you can see for miles."

"That sounds wonderful." It really did, tired as he was. "If you want, we could drive part of the way, park the car, and walk on from there."

"Here you are, folks," the driver said cheerfully, drawing to a stop in front of Mary Anne's apartment building. "You want me to wait?" he asked, opening the door.

"Yes, wait," Schilling instructed him. He and the girl climbed the stairs; he held the door open for her and she glided on inside, under the arch of his arm.

In the lobby she halted. She still had tight hold of her blue dish. "Joseph," she said, "good night."

"Good night," he said. Leaning forward, he kissed her on the cheek. Smiling, she raised her face expectantly. "Take care of yourself," he said to her. That was all he could think of.

"I will," she promised and, turning, hurried up the stairs.

Schilling found his way back out onto the porch of the building. There was the cab, its parking lights on, waiting for him. He had descended the concrete steps and was starting to climb into it when he remembered his own car. The Dodge, moist and dark, was parked only a few yards up the street; it had completely slipped his mind.

"I'll walk," he said to the taxi driver. "How much do I owe you?"

The driver slammed the meter arm down and tore off the paper receipt. "Nine dollars and eighty-five cents," he said with benign pleasure.

Schilling paid him and then walked stiffly to his own car. The upholstery, as he got in, was cold and repellent. And the motor sputtered unevenly when he started it. He allowed it to warm for several minutes before he released the parking brake and drove out into the silent, empty street.

17

The next morning, Sunday morning, she telephoned him at ten o'clock.

"Are you up?" she asked.

"Yes," Schilling said; having shaved, he was now dressing. "I was up at nine."

"What are you doing?"

Truthfully, he answered: "I was about to go downtown and have breakfast."

"Why don't you drop over here? I'll fix breakfast for you." Her voice ebbed. "Maybe you could pick up the Sunday paper."

"I'll do that." He was afraid to ask if her roommate would be there. Instead, he said: "Anything else I can get for you? How do you feel today?"

"I'm fine." She sounded lazy and contented. "It looks like a nice day."

He hadn't, as yet, looked. "I'll see you in a short while," he said. Hanging up, he began finding his overcoat.

The door to her apartment, when he arrived, was standing open. A warm, sweet smell of frying bacon and eggs drifted out into the hall, along with the sound of the New York Philharmonic. Mary Anne met him in the living room; she had on brown slacks and a white shirt, and her sleeves were rolled up to her elbows. Face shiny with perspiration, she greeted him and hurried back into the kitchen.

"Did you drive over?"

"I drove," he answered, laying the Sunday *Chronicle* down on the couch and removing his overcoat. He went over and closed the door to the hall. There was no sign of the roommate.

"The blimp—my roommate—is out," Mary Anne explained, noticing his prowling. "She's at church, and then she's having lunch with some girl friends, and then she's going to a show. She won't be back until late this afternoon."

"You don't like her very much," he said, lighting a cigarette. He had decided to stop smoking cigars.

"She's a drip. Why don't you come into the kitchen? You could set the table."

When they had finished eating breakfast the two of them sat listening to the closing minutes of the Philharmonic. The apartment still smelled of warm coffee and bacon. Outside in the driveway, a neighbor in a sports shirt and dungarees was washing his car.

"It's nice," Mary Anne said, profoundly peaceful.

Schilling felt the amount of their understanding. Not much—almost nothing—had been said, but it was there. It was there, and both of them were aware of it.

"What's that?" Mary Anne asked. "That music."

"A Chopin piano concerto."

"Isn't it good?"

"It's somewhat cheap."

"Oh." She nodded. "Will you tell me which ones are cheap?"

"Gladly; that's half the fun. Anybody can enjoy music; it's disliking it that takes training."

"I have some records," she said, "but they're all pops and jump tunes. Cal Tjader and Oscar Peterson. My roommate listens to mambo records."

"Why don't you get rid of her?" He had nothing in mind, only an awareness of the quiet of the apartment. "Find a place of your own."

"I can't afford it."

On the radio, the music had reached an end. Now the audience was clapping and the announcer was describing next week's program.

"Who is Bruno Walter?" Mary Anne asked.

"One of the great conductors of our day. He left Austria in '38 . . . about three weeks before he recorded the Mahler Ninth."

"Ninth what?"

"Symphony."

"Oh." She nodded. "I heard his name; somebody asked what we had by him."

"We have plenty. One of these days I'm going to play you the recording of Mahler's *Song of the Earth* that he made with Kathleen Ferrier."

Mary Anne leaped up from the table. "Play it for me now."

"Now? This instant?"

"Why not? Don't we have it at the store?" She skipped over to the radio and turned it off. "Let's do something."

"You want to go out somewhere?"

"No more walking—I want to lie around listening to music." Eyes sparkling, she ran and got her red jacket. "Could we? Not here—the blimp will be back. Where are all your records, your collection? Home?"

"Home," he said, rising from the table.

She had never seen his apartment. Impressed, she gazed around at the carpets and furnishings. "Gee," she said in a small voice as she entered ahead of him. "How nice it all is . . . are those real pictures?"

"They're prints," he said. "They're not originals, if that's what you mean."

"I guess that's what I mean." She began peeling off her jacket; he helped her with it and hung it up in the closet. Wandering about, she came to Schilling's giant oak desk and stopped there. "Is this where you sit when you write your radio program?"

"Right in that spot. There's my typewriter and reference books."

She inspected the typewriter. "It's a foreign typewriter, isn't it?"

"It's German. I picked it up when I was with Schirmer's. I represented them in Germany."

Awed, she ran her fingers over the type bars. "Does it make that funny mark?"

"The umlaut?" He typed an umlaut for her. "See?"

He put on his big Magnavox phonograph, set the record changer for seventy-eight speed, and then, while it was warming up, entered the pantry and looked over his wine. Without consulting her he selected a bottle of Mackenzie's Fino Perla sherry, found two small wineglasses, and returned to the living room. Presently they were sprawled out listening to Heinrich Schlusnus singing "Der Nussbaum."

"I've heard that," Mary Anne said when the record ended. "It's cute." She was seated on the rug, her back against the side of the couch, wineglass beside her. Absorbed in the music, Schilling barely heard her; he put on another record and returned to his chair. She listened attentively until it was over and he was turning the record.

"What was that?" she asked.

"Aksel Schiøtz." Then he added the title of the work.

"You're more interested in who sings it. Who is he? Is he still alive?"

"Schiøtz is alive," Schilling said, "but he's not singing much anymore. Most of his highs are gone . . . all he has left now is his lower range. But he's still one of the really unique voices of this century. In some ways, the finest of all."

"How old is he?"

"In his late fifties."

"I wish," Mary Anne said energetically, "that I could get rid of my darn roommate. Do you have any ideas? Maybe I could find a smaller place somewhere that wouldn't cost too much."

Schilling lifted the needle from the record; it had not yet reached the grooves. "Well," he said, "the only solution is to search. Read the ads in the paper, go around town finding out what exists."

"Will you help me? You have a car . . . and you know about these things."

"When do you want to look?"

"Right away. As soon as possible."

"You mean now? Today?"

"Could we?"

A little amused, he said: "Finish your wine first."

She drank it down without tasting it. Resting the glass on the arm of the couch, she scrambled to her feet and stood waiting. "It's seeing your place," she told him as they left the apartment. "I can't go on living with that fool—her and her Oregon apples and her mambo records."

At the corner drugstore Schilling picked up Saturday's edition of the *Leader;* there was no Sunday edition. He drove through town as Mary Anne, settled down beside him, scrutinized every ad and description.

Within half an hour they were tramping up the stairs of a great modern concrete apartment building on the edge of town, part of a newly developed improvement area, with its own stores and characteristic streetlamps. A tinted fountain marked the entrance of the area; small trees, California flowering plums, had been planted along the parking strips.

"No," Mary Anne said when the rental agent showed them the barren, hygienic suite of rooms.

"Refrigerator, electric range, automatic washer and drier downstairs," the agent said, offended. "View of the mountains, everything clean and new. Lady, this building is only three years old."

"No," she repeated, already leaving. "It has no—what is it?" She shook her head. "It's too empty."

"You want a place you can fix up yourself," Schilling told

her as they drove on. "That's what you're looking for, not just something you can move into, like a hotel room."

It was three-thirty in the afternoon when they found what she wanted. A large home in the better residential section had been divided into two flats; the walls were redwood-paneled and in the living room was an immense picture window. A smell of wood hung over the rooms, a presence of coolness and silence. Mary Anne roamed here and there, poking into the closets, standing on tiptoe to peek into the cupboards, touching and sniffing, her lips apart, body tense.

"Well?" Schilling said, observing her.

"It's—lovely."

"Will it do?"

"Yes," she whispered, only half-seeing him. "Imagine how this would look with a Hollywood bed over there, and Chinese mats on the floor. And you could find me some prints, like those you have. I could build a bookcase out of boards and bricks . . . I saw that once. I've always wanted that."

The owner, a gray-haired woman in her sixties, stood in the doorway, gratified.

Schilling walked over to Mary Anne and put his hand on her shoulder. "If you're going to rent it, you're going to have to give her a fifty-dollar deposit."

"Oh," Mary Anne said, dismayed. "Yes, that's so."

"Do you have fifty dollars?"

"I have exactly one dollar and thirty-six cents." Defeat settled over her; shoulders drooping, she said mournfully: "I forgot about that."

"I'll pay for it," Schilling said, already producing his wallet. He had expected to. He wanted to.

"But you can't." She followed after him. "Maybe you could take it out of my salary; is that what you mean?"

"We'll work it out later." Leaving Mary Anne, he crossed over to the woman with the idea of paying her.

"How old is your daughter?" the woman asked.

"Eh," Schilling said, staggered. There it was again, the reality under the surface. Mary Anne—thank God—hadn't heard; she had wandered into the other room.

"She's very pretty," the woman said, writing out the deposit receipt. "Does she go to school?"

"No," Schilling muttered. "She works."

"She's got your hair. But not quite so red as yours; much more brown. Shall I make this out in your name or hers?"

"Her name. She'll be paying for it." He accepted the receipt and herded Mary Anne out of the building and downstairs to the street. She was already plotting and planning.

"We can haul over my things in the car," she said. "I don't have anything very large." Rushing ahead of him, turning and skipping back, she exclaimed: "It doesn't seem possible—look what we've done!"

"Before you unpack your things," Schilling said practically, but experiencing the same spur of excitement, "the ceilings should be painted, wherever there isn't the wood paneling. I noticed the paper's beginning to decay."

"That's so," Mary Anne agreed, sliding into the car. "But where can we get paint on Sunday?" She was prepared to start work at once; he had no doubt of that.

"There's paint in the back of the store," he said as they drove toward the business section. "Left over from the redecorating. I kept it for touch-up. There's probably enough, if you don't object to the limited assortment. Or if you'd prefer to wait until Monday—"

"No," Mary Anne said. "Could we start today? I want to move; I want to get in there *right away.*"

While Mary Anne wrapped dishes in newspaper, Joseph Schilling carried the loaded cardboard cartons down the stairs and put them into the back of the Dodge. He had changed from his suit to wool work pants and a heavy gray sweatshirt. It was a shirt he had owned for years, given to him as a birthday present by a girl living in Baltimore. Her name was long forgotten.

In the back of his mind was the realization that, customarily, he should be in the store providing his Sunday afternoon record concert. But, he said to himself, the heck with it. He found it hard to concentrate on records or business; it was impossible to imagine himself going through the motions of lecturing on Renaissance modality.

They had dinner together at Schilling's apartment. Mary Anne, rummaging in the refrigerator, found a veal roast and prepared it for the oven. It was now six o'clock; outside, the evening street was fading. Standing by the window, Schilling listened to the sounds of the girl fixing dinner. Busily she opened drawers and brought out his various pots and pans and bowls.

Well, a lot had happened. He had gone a long way since the previous Sunday. He wondered what he would be doing in another week. He now had a certain life to lead, and a certain person to be. That person had to be careful of what he did and said; he had to be careful to keep on being that person. Could he keep it up? Anything could happen. He recalled his lecture to Mary Anne on the responsibility of opening up whole new fields for someone . . . smiling at the irony, he turned from the window.

"Need any help?" he asked.

She appeared, a very slim, very high-breasted little figure, outlined in the kitchen doorway. "You could mash the potatoes," she said.

Watching her scurry about the kitchen, he was impressed. "You must have helped your mother a lot."

"My mother's a fool," she said.

"And your father?"

"He—" The girl hesitated. "Little shrimp. All he does is drink beer and watch TV. I hate TV because of him; every time I see it, I see him and his black leather jacket. And his glasses, his steel glasses. Watching me. And grinning."

"Why?"

She seemed unable to speak. Her face was dark and strained, convoluted with tiny lines of worry that pulled her features together. "Teasing me," she said.

"About what?"

Struggling, she said: "Once—I guess I was fifteen or sixteen. I was still in high school. One night I came home late, around two o'clock. There was a dance, a club dance, up in the hills. When I opened the door I didn't see him. He was in the living room, asleep. Not in their room. Maybe he had been drinking and passed out; he had his clothes on, even his shoes. Lying on the couch, spread out. Newspapers and beer cans."

"You don't have to tell me," he said.

She nodded. "I went by him. And he woke up. He saw me; I had on my long gown. I think he was confused, and he didn't realize it was me. Anyhow." She shuddered. "He—grabbed hold of me. It happened so fast I didn't understand. I didn't realize it was him at first. Two other people." She smiled mournfully. "So, anyhow, he put me down on the couch. In just a second. I couldn't even yell or anything. He used to be very good-looking. I've seen pictures of him when he was young, when they were first married. He was a lot of times with different women. They talked about it openly. They yell about it, back and forth. Maybe it was reflexive; you know?"

"Yes," he said.

"He certainly moved fast. And he's still strong; he works in a pipe factory, with big sections of pipe. Especially his arms. There wasn't anything I could do. He got my dress up over my face and he held my hands. You want me to tell you?"

"If you want," he said.

"That's about all. He didn't—really do it. My mother must have heard or something. She came in and turned on the living room light. He hadn't had time. Then he saw it was me. I guess he didn't know. Every once in a while I think about that. But—it's a joke, as far as he's concerned. He thinks it's funny. He teases me.

He sneaks up and grabs me, and gets a big charge out of it. Like a game or something."

"Your mother doesn't mind?"

"She does, but she never stops him. I guess she can't."

"Christ," Schilling said, deeply disturbed.

Mary Anne hauled out the small stepladder and got down plates and cups. "They're all here in town: my family, my friends. Dave Gordon—"

"Who is Dave Gordon?"

"My fiancé. He works over at the Richfield station, driving a truck. His idea of getting somewhere is borrowing the truck for the weekend."

"That's so," Schilling admitted. "You did mention him." He felt uncomfortable.

"Go sit down," Mary Anne said, catching up a pot holder and kneeling to peer into the oven. "Dinner's ready."

18

At eight o'clock, after they had eaten, Schilling drove the girl to the closed-up record shop. Together they loaded cans of paint into the trunk compartment of the Dodge, both of them feeling fearful and intimidated by what was happening.

"You're so quiet," he said to her.

"I'm scared."

"Where does your friend Paul Nitz hang out?" It seemed like a good idea. "Let's go pick him up."

Nitz, with his usual amiability, was glad to drop what he was doing and tag along with them. "I got to be at the Wren before twelve, though," he warned them. "Eaton says I have to show up once in a while."

"We're not going to work much later than that," Schilling said. "Tomorrow's Monday."

The three of them trudged up the stairs with Mary Anne's possessions and piled them in the redwood-paneled kitchen. Presently they were stirring cans of paint and softening brushes. An unlit cigarette between his lips, Paul Nitz poured rubber-based paint into a roller pan and began sloshing it with a broken coat hanger.

Cold night air billowed around them as they painted; all the windows and doors were wide open to let out the fumes. Standing on chairs, each of them labored at the ceiling, one person in each room, saying very little to one another as they worked. Occasionally, beyond the windows, a car passed along the street, its headlights flashing. The inhabitants of the downstairs flat were out; there was no sound and no light showing.

"I'm out of paint," Schilling said once, halting.

"Come and get more," Mary Anne answered from the living room. "There's a lot left in the bucket."

Wiping paint from his arms and wrists with a rag, Schilling stepped from his chair and walked toward the sound of her voice. There she was, standing on tiptoe, reaching above her head with both hands. Her short brown hair was tied in a bandana; drops of pale yellow paint streaked her cheeks and forehead and neck; moist trails of paint had slithered down her arms and down her clothes and across her bare feet. She wore jeans, rolled up at the bottom, and a T-shirt; that was all. She seemed tired but cheerful.

"Help yourself," she gasped, indicating the bucket of paint in the center of the floor. Newspapers, sloppy and yellow, were spread everywhere. The redwood paneling oozed globs of rubber-based paint, but a rag dipped in water would remove them.

"How's it coming?" he asked her.

"I'm almost done in here. Do you see any places I missed?"

She had, of course, missed no places; her work was thorough and scrupulous.

"I'm anxious to get my stuff unpacked," she said to him, painting vigorously away. "Will we have time tonight? I don't want to sleep over there . . . anyhow, all my bedding and personal stuff, all my clothes, are here."

"We'll get you unpacked," Schilling promised. He headed back toward his own room and resumed his work. In the bedroom Paul Nitz labored in isolation; Schilling halted long enough to pay him a visit.

"This stuff really covers," Nitz said, dropping from the chair onto the floor. He got a crumpled pack of cigarettes from his pocket and, offering Schilling the pack, lit up himself. Schilling, accepting the cigarette, felt a disturbing flow of memory. Five years ago he had stood in Beth Coombs's apartment watching her paint a kitchen chair. He, in his vest and wool tie, his briefcase under his arm, had come to visit her officially: he was a representative for the music publishers Allison and Hirsch, and she had submitted a group of songs.

There she had been, crouched on the kitchen floor in halter and shorts, her bare flesh streaked with paint. He had wanted her furiously: a healthy blonde who had chatted with him, poured him a drink, rubbed up against him as the two of them examined drafts of her songs. The pressure of her living, woman's body; breasts to be kneaded and gripped . . .

"She's a hard worker," Nitz said, indicating the girl.

"Yes," Schilling agreed, startled back to the present. He was confused; old images blurred with new ones. Beth, Mary Anne, the girl with long red hair he had lived with in Baltimore. He wished he could recall her name. Barbara something. She had been like a field of wheat . . . a dancing orangeness around him and beneath him. He sighed. He hadn't forgotten *that.*

"What do you think of her?"

"Well," Schilling said. For a moment he wasn't certain who Nitz meant. "Yes, I think a lot of her."

"So do I," Nitz said, with a shade of emphasis that eluded Schilling. "She's a nut, but she's okay."

Schilling said: "How do you mean, nut?" It didn't sound gallant, and he wasn't sure he approved.

"Mary takes things too seriously. You ever in your life heard her laugh?"

He tried to remember. "I've seen her smile." He had her very clearly, now. Which was a good thing.

"None of the kids laugh anymore," Nitz said. "It must be the times. All they do is worry."

"Yes," he agreed, "she always worries."

"Are you talking about me?" Mary Anne's voice came in. "Because if you are, cut it out."

"She'll tell you what to do," Nitz said. "She's got a mind of her own. But—" he began painting again— "in some ways she's two years old. It's easy to forget that. She's a little kid wandering around lost, looking for somebody to find her. Some kindly cop with brass buttons and a badge to lead her home."

"Stop it!" Mary Anne ordered, leaping down and padding into the bedroom, the paint roller leaking a trail of yellow after her. Rubbing her cheek with her wrist, she reminded them: "This is my house, you know; I could throw both of you out."

"Little Miss Wise," Nitz said to her.

"You shut up."

Handing Schilling his cigarette, Nitz jumped forward and grabbed the girl around the waist. Sweeping her up, he carried her to the open window and lifted her over the sill. "Out you go," he said.

Screaming and clutching at him, Mary Anne kicked wildly, her arms around his neck, her bare feet thumping against the wall. "You let me down! You hear me, Paul Nitz?"

"Can't hear you." Grinning, he lowered her to the floor. Shaky and winded, Mary Anne sank down in a heap; pulling her knees up, she rested her chin on them and clasped her arms around her ankles.

"All right," she grumbled, panting for breath, "I think you're just funny as *hell.*"

Stooping over her, Nitz untied her bandana. "That's what you need," he told the indignant girl, "a good taking-down. You're getting too uppity."

Mary Anne sneered at him and then climbed to her feet. "Look," she proclaimed. "I'm going to have a bruise on my arm where you grabbed me."

"You'll live," Nitz said. He picked up his roller and climbed back on his chair.

Momentarily, Mary Anne glowered up. Then, all at once, she smiled. "I know something about you."

"What?"

"You're no good at painting." Her smile increased. "You can't see well enough to tell where it's uneven."

"That's true," Nitz admitted fatalistically. "I'm nearsighted as hell."

Pivoting on her bare heel, Mary Anne padded back to the living room and resumed her toil.

At ten-thirty Schilling went downstairs to the parked car and got the fifth of Glayva scotch from the glove compartment. At the sight of it, Nitz's face turned an avid, delighted gray. "Jesus," he said, "what do you have there, man? Is that on the level?"

Schilling rummaged among the cartons of dishes and pots until he found tumblers. Half-filling each with tap water, he placed the three of them on the tile sink and then opened the bottle.

"Hey, hey, man," Nitz protested. "Don't put any of that dirty old water in mine."

"That's your chaser," Schilling said, passing him the bottle. "It's good stuff . . . see how it strikes you."

Nitz's throat expanded as he drank from the bottle. "Whoooee," he gasped, snorting and shaking his head. Wiping his mouth with the back of his hand, he returned the bottle to Schilling. "Man, oh, man. You know what I call that? That's angel pee, pure and simple."

Curious, Mary Anne appeared in the kitchen doorway. "Where's mine?"

"You can have a tablespoonful," Schilling said.

The girl's eyes blazed. "Tablespoonful, nothing! Come on—" She grabbed at the bottle. "You gave me some of that other stuff, that wine."

"This is different." But he found a plastic measuring cup among the dishes and poured an inch or so for her. "Don't choke," he warned her. "Sip it, don't drink it. Pretend it's cough medicine."

Mary Anne glared at him and then cautiously lifted the rim of the cup. Wrinkling her nose, she said: "It smells like gasoline."

"You've had scotch before," Nitz said. "Tweany drinks scotch—you've had it over there."

Each deep in his own thoughts, the two men watched her gulp down a mouthful of scotch. Mary Anne made a face, shuddered, and then reached for her glass of water.

"You see?" Schilling chided. "You didn't want it after all; you didn't like it."

"It ought to be mixed with something," she answered speculatively. "Fruit juice, maybe."

Nitz shook his head. "You better stay away from me awhile."

"Oh, you'll recover." Mary Anne disappeared into the living room; clambering back up on her chair, she resumed work.

The men each had a go at the scotch once more. "It's superb stuff," Schilling said.

"I already told you my opinion," Nitz said. "But it's not for kids."

"No," Schilling agreed, feeling uneasy. "I didn't really give her any."

"Okay," Nitz said, and walked off, leaving Schilling standing alone. "Well, back to the salt mine."

"Maybe we better call it quits," Schilling said, looking after him. With a kind of sorrow he felt the man's deep jealousy of him—and knew also that it was just and right. He had come in and taken the girl away from her world, her town, away from Nitz. He couldn't blame him.

"Not quite quits," Nitz said. "I want to finish the bedroom."

"All right," Schilling said, resigned.

The three of them worked until eleven-thirty. Schilling, as he crept along the floor, touching up the baseboard, found himself almost unable to straighten his legs. And the bruise on his knee, where the store counter had struck him, was swollen and sore.

"I'm getting old," he said to Nitz, halting and throwing down his paintbrush.

"Are you stopping?" Mary Anne called anxiously. "Both of you?"

Apologetically, Nitz entered the living room. He was tugging on his frayed sports coat; he was departing. "Sorry, sweetheart. I've got to get to the Wren; Eaton'll fire me."

Schilling sighed with secret relief. "I'll drive you over. It's time we knocked off anyhow; we've done all we can for one night."

"My God, I've still got to play." Nitz displayed his paint-stained fingers. "Some of these should be replaced."

Walking into the kitchen with Nitz, Schilling said, "Do me a favor?"

"Sure," Nitz said.

"Take the scotch with you." It was a gesture of propitiation . . . and he wanted now to get rid of the thing.

"Hell, I didn't do *that* much painting."

"I meant for us to drink it up, but I lost track of the time." He placed the bottle in a brown paper bag and presented it to Nitz. "Is it a deal?"

Mary Anne came pattering into the kitchen. "Can I ride along?" she begged. "I want to go along with you."

"Better wipe the paint off your face," Schilling said.

She blushed and began searching for a damp rag. "You don't mind, do you? It's so lonely here . . . no furniture, and everything messy and confused. Nothing finished."

"Glad to have you," Schilling murmured, still a little upset by Nitz's behavior.

She cleaned the paint from her face, and he helped her into her jacket. Then she followed the two men out the door of the apartment; together they descended the stairs to the dark street. The drive took only a few moments.

"Looks like a fair crowd," Schilling said as the fat red doors of the Wren were pushed aside to admit a couple. It was the first time he had seen this place, the girl's old hangout. Suddenly he said to her: "Want to go in for a while?"

"Not like we are."

"Who cares?" Nitz said, stepping from the car onto the pavement.

"No," she decided, with a glance at Schilling. "Some other time; I want to get back. There's too much to do."

"It'll keep," Nitz said, halting by the car. "Take it easy, Mary."

"I'm taking it easy."

"You can't do everything in one day, baby doll."

"That's easy enough for you to say," Mary Anne said. She moved closer to Schilling, and he was grateful. "You don't have to sleep there."

Nitz said: "Neither do you."

"I—want to sleep there."

"Be careful where you sleep," Nitz said, and Schilling leaned forward because he could see what was coming. But he heard it now; Nitz was saying it already. "It's no good. I'm sorry, Mary. I wish to hell it was. He's just too old."

"Good night, Paul." She didn't look at him.

"I've got to say."

"It *is* good," she said tightly.

"What's good about it? Well, a lot of things, maybe. But not enough. Go ahead and hate me."

"I don't hate you." Her voice was faint, aloof. She seemed to be watching something a long way off. Nitz reached out to tweak her nose, but she pulled away.

"We can talk about it some other time," Schilling said. "We're all tired. This isn't the best time."

"Not the best time," Nitz agreed. "Nothing's best. Nothing's as good as you think, Mary. Or want."

Schilling started up the motor. "Leave her alone."

"Sorry," Nitz said. "I really am sorry. You suppose I enjoy this?"

"But you have your duty," Schilling said. He let out the

clutch and the car moved forward. Reaching past Mary Anne, he slammed the door. She made no motion, no protest. Behind them, on the sidewalk, Nitz stood clutching the brown paper bag. Then he turned and vanished inside the bar.

After a time, Schilling said: "Some of the nicest people in the world strung Jesus up on the cross."

Mary Anne murmured: "What does that mean?"

"I mean, Nitz is a nice guy, but he has certain preconceptions and ideas. And he wants certain things like everybody else does. He isn't outside, looking down. He has deep feelings toward you, deep personal feelings."

"Good," she said. "I'm glad to hear it."

He was aware that talking was a mistake. She was in no shape to listen, to be rational, to decide. But he couldn't help himself. "I'm sorry," he began.

"About what?"

"That we had that run-in."

"Yes." She nodded. She gazed out the window.

As they drove along the dark street he said suddenly: "Are you really sure you want to do this?"

"Do what? Yes, I want to. I'm sure."

"You heard what he said. And you trust him. What about your roommate? Can she find somebody else? Will she be able to handle the rent on your old place?"

"Don't worry about her," Mary Anne said with a gesture of dismissal. "She's got plenty of loot."

"This all happened so fast. There wasn't time to plan."

She shrugged. "So?"

"You should have more time, Mary." Nitz had forced him to say it. "You should be absolutely certain what you're getting into. He has a point. I don't want you to be—well, involved in something.

"Don't be silly. I love the apartment. I intend to get prints and mats to fill it up. You can drive me around and help me pick everything out. And clothes . . ." Her eyes shone as ideas and schemes passed through her mind. "I want to get clothes I can wear, so when we go to another—"

"Maybe that was a mistake, too," he said. "Maybe I shouldn't have taken you up there." Although it was a little late to think of that.

"Oh—" She shoved against him. "You're talking like a moron."

"Thanks," he said.

Mary Anne leaned around, cutting off his view of the street ahead. "Are you mad at me?"

"No," he said, "but get back so I can see."

"See what?" She waved her hands in front of his face. "Phooey—run over somebody. Wreck us—see if I care." In a burst of taunting nihilism she grabbed the steering wheel and spun it back and forth. The heavy car wandered from side to side, until Schilling pried her hand loose.

Slowing the car, he demanded: "Do you want to walk?"

"Don't threaten me."

Goaded by fatigue, he said: "Somebody ought to paddle you. With a leather strap."

"You sound like my parents."

"They're right."

"Drop dead," she said, unruffled, but subdued. "Would you hurt me? You wouldn't do that, would you?"

"No," he said, driving carefully.

"Maybe you would . . . it's possible. All kinds of things are possible. Nothing and everything." She slid down on the seat and meditated. "Do you feel like stopping and having something to eat?"

"Not really."

"Neither do I. I don't know what I want—what do I want?"

"Nobody can tell you that."

"Do you believe in anything?"

"Of course," he said.

"Why?"

They had reached her new apartment. Upstairs on the second floor, lights blazed out into the darkness. The newly painted ceilings could be seen, glittering and sparkling, still moist.

Looking up, Mary Anne shivered. "It's so barren. No curtains, no anything."

"I'll help you get your things unpacked," he said. "Whatever you need for tonight."

"That means we're not going to do any more painting."

"Go to bed and get some sleep. You'll feel better tomorrow."

"I can't stay here," she said, with a mixture of loathing and fear. "Not half-finished, this way."

"But your things—"

"No," she said. "It's absolutely out. Please, Joseph; honest to God, I can't stand it like this. You understand what I mean, don't you?"

"Certainly."

"You don't."

"I do," he said, "but it's awkward. Your stuff is up there—clothes, everything. Where else can you stay? You can't go back to your old place."

"No," she agreed.

"Do you want to go to a hotel?"

"No, not a hotel." She pondered. "Jesus, what a mess. We shouldn't have started painting. We should have just moved the stuff." Wearily she hunched over and covered her face with the palms of her hands. "It's my own fault."

"Do you want to stay at my place?" he asked. It was something he would not normally have suggested; the idea was created by fatigue and the need of rest, and this blank wall at which they had arrived. He could not cope with it; he was too tired. It would have to wait until tomorrow.

"Could I? Would it bring on a lot of trouble?"

"Not that I know of." He started up the car.

"You're sure it's okay?"

"I'll take you over there and then come back here for your things."

"You're sweet," she said dully, leaning against him.

He drove her to his own apartment, parked the car, and led the girl inside.

Sighing, Mary Anne dropped into a deep chair and sat staring at the rug. "It's peaceful here."

"I'm sorry we didn't finish your place."

"That's okay. We'll finish it tomorrow night." She had nothing to say as Schilling removed his coat and then came over to receive her red jacket.

"What would cheer you up?" he asked.

"Nothing."

"Something to eat?"

Irritably, she shook her head. "No, nothing to eat. Christ, I'm just tired."

"Then it's time for bed."

"You're going back there now?"

"It won't take long. What are the essential items?" He searched for a pencil and paper, then gave up. "I can remember, if you tell me."

"Pajamas," she murmured. "Toothbrush, soap . . . oh, the hell with it. I'll go over with you." Rising to her feet, she started toward the door. Schilling stopped her; she stood leaning against him, saying nothing, doing nothing, simply resting there.

"Come along," he said. His arm around her, he led her into the bedroom and showed her his big double bed. "Climb in and go to sleep. I'll be back in half an hour. What I forget I can pick up for you tomorrow morning, before work."

"Yes," she agreed. "That's so." Mechanically, she began to unfasten her belt. Schilling paused at the door, concerned. She was stepping out of her shoes; without a word she grasped hold of her paint-streaked T-shirt and tugged it over her head. At that point despair overwhelmed her; she stood mutely in the center of the bedroom in her bra and jeans, making no progress in any direction.

"Mary Anne," he began.

"Oh, *what?*" she demanded. "Leave me alone, will you?"

Tossing her T-shirt on the bed, she unbuttoned her jeans and dragged them off. Then, paying no attention to the man at the door, she finished undressing, padded naked to the bed, and climbed in.

"Turn out the light, please," she said.

He did so. There was no comment from the darkness. He lingered, not wanting to leave. "I'll lock you in," he said finally.

From the darkness stirring sounds were audible. She turned over, adjusted the covers, tried to make herself comfortable. "Whatever you want," her voice came.

Schilling crossed the darkened room to the bed. "Can I sit?" he asked.

"Go ahead."

He did so, on the very edge of the bed. "I feel guilty. About not finishing." And more, too. Much more.

"It's my own fault," she murmured, staring up at the ceiling.

"We'll collect some help, maybe not Nitz. And finish up, perhaps around the middle of the week." When she didn't respond, he went on: "You can stay here until then. How's that?"

Presently she nodded. "Fine."

He drew a little away. In the bed beside him, Mary Anne seemed already to have drifted into sleep. He watched, but he couldn't be sure.

"I'm not asleep," she stated.

"Go ahead."

"I will. This is a nice bed. It's wide."

"Very wide."

"Do you notice how the rug looks like water? It looks as if the bed's floating. Maybe it's because of the light . . . I had to work with it shining in my face. I'm dizzy." She yawned. "Go on and get my things."

He left the room on tiptoe. Closing the front door of the apartment, he tried the knob to be certain it was locked, and then strode off down the front steps.

The lights still burned in Mary Anne's new apartment. The air, as he entered, was heavy and unpleasant with the reek of paint. As quickly as possible, he collected her possessions, snapped off the heat and lights, and backed out.

When he unlocked the front door of his own place there was no response from the darkened bedroom. He laid down his armload and removed his coat. Hesitating, he announced:

"I've got your stuff."

There was no answer. Probably she was asleep. Or, on the other hand, there was an alternate possibility. Locating a flashlight, he stalked into the bedroom. She was gone, and so was her discarded clothing. His bed, rumpled and recently occupied, was still warm.

In the living room he found a note lying on top of his record cabinet.

"I'm sorry," the note read; it was a carefully prepared pencil scrawl, composed of blunt, direct letters in Mary Anne's hand. "I'll see you tomorrow in the store. I've thought it over, including the business with Paul, and I've decided it's better if I stay with my family tonight. I don't want to create any kind of situation. Until we're really sure, anyhow. You know what I mean. Don't be mad at me. Sleep tight. Love, Mary."

He crumpled the note and shoved it in his pocket. Well, better it should happen now than later. He felt a measure of relief, but it was flat and unconvincing.

"Oh, Christ," he said. "Christ!" He had failed; he had let them drag her away.

Anguished, he went back into his bedroom and began smoothing out the empty bed.

19

By the refrigerator, Mrs. Rose Reynolds poised and leaned forward, arms folded, watching her daughter pour herself a bowl of Post Toasties. Mary Anne dribbled milk into the bowl. As the cornflakes sank into a mass, she stirred her coffee and buttered a piece of dry toast.

"Dear," Mrs. Reynolds said. "Let's have it."

"Let's have what?" She spooned up her breakfast. "I can't sit around here talking; I have to be down at the record shop by nine."

The woman said steadily: "Tell me who you're sleeping with."

"What makes you think that? Why do you say that?"

"Just so it isn't a jig. I couldn't stand that."

"It isn't."

Mrs. Reynolds pursed her lips. "Then you are sleeping with somebody. Did he throw you out? Is that why you came home?" Her voice dimmed to a monotone. "Your life's your own, of course. You moved out of here to be with him; then he got tired of you. May I ask you something? When did you start? You were living under this roof when you started. I say that because I've noticed you feel yourself, poking around inside your pants. That's been several years at least."

"Shout away," Mary Anne said. She had finished breakfast and now she carried her dishes to the sink.

"I'd like to discuss it with you," Mrs. Reynolds said. "People, good friends of mine, tell me there's a singer at a bar you've been with. I don't recall the particular name of the bar—it's not important. The singer is colored, isn't he? People have a way of finding out; it's surprising. I was reading in the paper about that jig who killed the white man, the one they arrested. I'm surprised they let him out on bail. They must have a good deal of influence in California, especially down in Los Angeles." Her arms folded, she followed after Mary Anne. "When you and I were discussing marital relations earlier this year, I mentioned to you the difficulty of an unmarried woman obtaining a diaphragm. However, through friends a girl is sometimes able to—" She ceased talking.

In his leather jacket and work trousers, a lunch pail under his arm, Ed Reynolds appeared in the doorway; he was on his way to the plant. "How's my girl?" he said. "Where have you been the last few months, and let's have a straight answer."

"I have an apartment—you know that." She retreated from her father, turning her back to him.

"Where'd you come from last night?"

"They say she's been bedding down with a colored fellow," Mrs. Reynolds said. "You ask her. I can't get a respectful answer; maybe you can."

"Has she started to swell? Have you looked at her?"

"I didn't have the opportunity last night."

"Keep away from me," Mary Anne said, leaving the kitchen and hurrying into what had been her bedroom. "I have to get to work!" she shouted apprehensively as her mother scuttled after her. Starting to close the door, Mary Anne wailed: "You keep your goddamn hands off me!"

"Better let me," her mother said. "Or he will; you don't want him to, so for your own good let me." She pushed the door open. "When was the last time?"

"The last time what?" Pretending to ignore her, Mary Anne searched through her closet, getting out a dark red suit. From the dresser she took her old purse; the forty dollars was still there, where she had stuffed it. They hadn't found it.

"Your period," Mrs. Reynolds said. "Or can't you remember?"

"No, I don't remember. Last month sometime." Rapidly, nervously, Mary Anne shed her jeans and T-shirt, the clothes she had worn when she appeared at her family's house the night before. As she began getting into a clean slip, Rose Reynolds leaped from the door and ran toward her.

"Let go of me!" Mary Anne screeched, clawing and scratching at her mother. Ed Reynolds appeared in the doorway and fixedly witnessed.

Catching the girl around the waist, Rose Reynolds pulled her underpants down and dug her hand into the girl's hard belly. Mary Anne, shrieking, struggled to tear her mother's hand away. Finally satisfied, Mrs. Reynolds released her and strode back to the doorway.

"Get out of here!" Mary Anne screamed, grabbing up a shoe and hurling it. Her face collapsed in furious tears. "Get *out!*" She ran, shoved her mother and father out of the room, and slammed the door.

Sobbing, fumbling with her clothing, she managed to dress. She could hear them outside the closed door, conferring about her.

"Shut up!" she wailed, wiping at her face with the back of her hand; and, as she hurried, planning out what she was going to do.

At nine o'clock she put in her appearance at the Lazy Wren. Taft Eaton, somber in his dirty apron and work trousers, was sweeping the sidewalk. When he saw her he pretended first to ignore her. "What do you want?" he demanded finally. "You always mean trouble."

"You can do me a favor," Mary Anne said.

"What kind of favor?"

"I want to rent a room."

"I'm not in the rooming business."

"You know all the property around here. Where's a vacant place? Just a room—something cheap."

"This is colored around here."

"I know. It's cheaper." And, in her state of mind, she needed the comforting presence of Negroes.

"What's the matter with what you got?"

"None of your business. Come on—I don't have all day. I'm not going to tramp around looking; I don't have time."

Eaton considered. "No kitchen. And you know it's colored. Yeah, that's right; you like to hang around with colored. What for? What sort of kicks do you get out of it?"

Mary Anne sighed. "Do we have to go into that?"

"On account of you, Carleton's in trouble with the law."

"It's not my fault."

"You're his girl. Anyhow, you were, once. Now it's that big blonde. What'd he do, get the taste?"

Patiently, Mary Anne waited.

Eaton picked up his broom and began tugging bits of fluff from it. "There're a lot of rooming houses around here. I know one place; it's not so hot, though. One of the fry cooks lives there."

"Fine. Give me the address."

"Go ask him; he's inside. No," Eaton said, changing his mind as the girl started toward the door. "I'd be just as happy if you kept out of my place." He wrote a note, tore it from the imitation-leather pad, and presented it to her. "It's a dump; you won't stay there. Full of drunks and sewer rats. You ever seen those big sewer rats? They swim in from the bay." He indicated with his hands. "As big as dogs."

"Thanks," Mary Anne said, pocketing the note.

"What's the matter?" Eaton said as the girl started off. "Don't you have somebody to pay your bills? A nice girl like you?"

He shook his head and resumed sweeping.

The building, she discovered, was as Eaton had described. Narrow and tall, it was wedged between two stores: a surgical supply house and a television repair shop. A flight of unpainted steps led up to the front porch. There she found a chair and an overturned wine bottle.

She rang the bell and waited.

A tiny, dried-up old colored woman with sharp black eyes and a long, beaked nose opened the door and inspected her. "Yes," she shrilled, "what did you want?"

"A room," Mary Anne said. "Taft Eaton said maybe you had one."

The name meant nothing to the old woman. "A room? No, we don't have any room."

"Isn't this a rooming house?"

"Yes," the old woman said, nodding and barring the door with her skinny arm. She wore a gray, shapeless dress and bobby socks. Behind her was the dim interior of a hallway: a dank and gloomy cavity that contained a table and mirror, a potted plant, the origin of a staircase. "But they're all full."

"Great," Mary Anne said. "What do I do now?"

The old woman started to close the door, then stopped, reflected, and said: "How soon did you have to have it?"

"Right away. Today."

"Usually we rent only to colored."

"That makes no difference to me."

"You don't have many boyfriends, do you? This is a quiet house; I try to keep it decent."

"No boyfriends," Mary Anne said.

"Do you drink?"

"No."

"Are you positive?"

"I'm positive," Mary Anne said, tapping her heel against the porch and gazing over the woman's head. "And I read the Bible every night before I go to bed."

"What church do you belong to?"

"The First Presbyterian." She picked it at random.

The old woman pondered. "I try to keep this a quiet home, without a lot of noise and goings-on. There are eleven people living here and they're all decent, respectable people. All radios are expected to be off by ten o'clock in the evening. No baths are to be taken after nine."

"Swell," Mary Anne sighed.

"I have one vacant room. I'm not certain if I can rent it to you or not . . . I'll show it to you, though. Do you care to step inside and see it?"

"Sure," Mary Anne said, stepping past the old woman and into the hall. "Let's have a look."

At nine-thirty she arrived at the redwood apartment that Joseph Schilling had acquired for her.

With her key she unlocked the door, but she did not go inside. The smell of new paint drifted around her, a bright, sickening smell. Cold morning sunlight filled the apartment; bands of pale illumination spread over the crumpled, paint-smeared newspapers scattered across the floor. The apartment was utterly lonely. Her possessions, still in pasteboard cartons, were stacked in the center of each room. Cartons, newspapers, sodden rollers still oozing from the night before . . .

Going downstairs to the companion apartment, she rapped sharply on the door. When the owner—a middle-aged man, balding—appeared, she asked: "Can I use your phone? I'm from upstairs."

She called the Yellow Cab people and then went outdoors to wait.

While she was supervising the loading of the cab, the landlady showed up. The meter ticked merrily as she and the driver carried the pasteboard cartons downstairs and piled them in the luggage compartment; both of them were perspiring and gasping, glad to get the job finished.

"Good grief," the landlady said. "What does this mean?"

Mary Anne halted. "I'm moving."

"So I see. Well, what's the story? I think I have a right to be informed."

"I've changed my mind; I'm not renting it." It seemed obvious.

"I suppose you want your deposit back."

"No," Mary Anne said. "I'm realistic."

"What about all that trash upstairs? All those newspapers and paint; and it's half-painted. I can't rent it in that condition. Are you going to finish?" She followed after Mary Anne as the girl took an armload of clothes from the cab driver and stuffed it among the cartons. "Miss, you can't leave under these circumstances; it isn't done. You have a responsibility to leave a place in the same condition you rented it."

"What are you complaining about?" The woman annoyed her. "You're getting a free fifty bucks."

"I've got a good mind to call your father," the landlady said.

"My what?" Then she understood, and at first it seemed funny. After that it didn't seem so funny, but she had already begun to laugh. "Did he tell you that? Yes, my father. Father Joseph, the best father I could hope for. The best goddamn old father in the world." The landlady was astonished at her outburst. "Go jump in the creek," Mary Anne said. "Rent your apartment—get busy."

Sliding into the front of the cab, she slammed the door. The driver, having loaded the last carton in the back, got in behind the wheel and started up the motor.

"You ought to be ashamed of yourself," the landlady said.

Mary Anne didn't answer. As the cab pulled away from the curb she leaned back and lit a cigarette; she had too much on her mind to pay attention to the landlady's complaints.

When the cab driver saw the room she was moving into, he shook his head and said: "Girlie, you're nuts."

"I am, am I?" She put down her armload and started back out of the room into the dusty, water-stained hall.

"You sure are." He plodded alongside her, down the hall and down the stairs to the sidewalk. "That was a swell apartment you left—all those redwood panels. And in a classy neighborhood."

"You go rent it, then."

"Are you really going to live here?" He picked up two cartons and began lugging them up the steps. "This job is going to cost you plenty, girlie. What's on the meter is only the down payment."

"Fine," Mary Anne said, struggling after him. "Lay it on as heavy as you can."

"It's the custom. We're not in the moving business, you know. This comes under the heading of a favor."

"Nobody's in any business," Mary Anne said. From her doorway, the tiny dried-up old colored woman—her name was Mrs. Lessley—watched with suspicion. "I guess I'm lucky; you're so kind."

When the last carton had been carried upstairs she paid him. It wasn't as tough as she had expected; the meter read a dollar seventy and the tip—when he finally named it—was two dollars more. Three seventy wasn't so much to get herself moved. And, of course, the twenty dollars for the room: a month's rent in advance.

Maybe the driver was right. With growing horror she surveyed her room; it was clean, dark, and smelled of mold. There was one small window over the iron, high-posted bed and one larger window on the far wall over the dresser. The carpet was frayed. A mended rocking chair occupied one corner. There was a tiny closet, a sort of upright drawer constructed of plywood by some amateur handyman long since gone.

The smaller window overlooked a path that led to the garbage cans and back porch of the building. The larger window overlooked the street; she was facing a neon sign:

DOCTOR CAMDEN CREDIT DENTIST

On the wall of the room was a cheap framed religious print showing the young Jesus with lambs. She took it down and stuck it away in a drawer; she had enough to bear.

Perhaps she was crazy, as the driver said. But at least she had her own place, paid for with her own money. She had found the place herself—not counting Eaton—and, very soon, she would be painting and furnishing it by herself, with paints and objects she herself selected. And she would have time to think.

It was ten o'clock. He would have to be told. She had left; she had given up the apartment. And, anyhow, he would find out. So she had no choice.

While she was thinking, wondering how to tell him, the door opened and Carleton Tweany peeked cautiously in. Horrified, she said: "How did you find this place?"

"Eaton gave us the address." He entered, and Beth Coombs followed him. "And I *know* this house; quite a few people have lived here at one time or another." He wore his best double-breasted suit; his cheeks were scrupulously shaved; his hair was combed and oiled; and the odor of cologne billowed from him. Beth, as usual, wore her heavy coat and carried her bag.

"Hi," she said, smiling her dazzling smile.

Mary Anne nodded curtly. Going to the bed, she opened her suitcase and began to unpack.

"Looks like you're busy," Tweany said.

With quick interest, Beth prowled around the room, inspecting the still-packed cartons. "Who's helping you?"

"Nobody," she said. "And I have to leave; I have to be at work."

Beth perched on the edge of the bed; it gave protestingly and she arose again at once. "We had some trouble finding you . . . you've moved around so much."

Abandoning her suitcase, Mary Anne picked up her coat and started toward the door. A lot she cared how the hell much trouble they had, either of them.

"Wait a minute, Mary," Tweany said, blocking her way.

"What's this all about?" Her mind scurried in fright. "Did you just happen by?"

"We stopped at the store," Beth said, "thinking maybe you were there. But Joe said you didn't come in today."

"I'm going there," she said. "I'm on my way there now. I had some things to do."

Beth said: "Then we stopped by that—apartment Joe fixed up for you; you weren't there. We stopped by your old place, the room you had with that waitress. The room Carleton found for you."

"Phyllis," Mary Anne murmured.

"She had no idea where you were. It was Carleton's idea to ask Eaton; I never would have thought of it."

"We want to talk to you about the inquest," Tweany said. He looked solemn and doleful, and his face grew long at the mention of grave matters.

She had totally forgotten about it. "Jesus," she said. "Of course."

"You got served with a subpoena, didn't you?" Beth asked. "You have to testify. If you got served with a subpoena, you have to show up."

She had indeed been served. The paper was somewhere in one of the pasteboard cartons; she had accepted it and put it out of her mind. It simply was not her concern. This was why they had tracked her down; they were worried about their own skins.

"When is it?" She tried to recall; the inquest was sometime soon, in a few days.

"It's Wednesday," Tweany said, scowling.

"Well," she said, "you might as well sit down. You figure out where." Turning away from the door, she removed her coat. She had time for this, at least; it was trivial. She, herself, sank down on a cane-bottomed chair. Beth and Tweany, after a brief exchange of glances, settled themselves on the bed, neither quite touching the other but very close together.

"What do you think of my pad?" Mary Anne asked.

"Terrible," Tweany said.

"Yes, I agree."

"Why aren't you living with Phyllis?" Tweany inquired. "What happened to that?"

"I got tired of Oregon apples."

Beth said: "It seemed to me that setup of Joe's was halfway decent. We only saw it for a second, of course. You were painting; you hadn't even finished. The door was unlocked . . . you must have just left."

"This morning," Mary Anne said.

"So." Beth compressed her lips. "I see."

"You see what?"

"That's what I thought it was. You were right the first time."

Warily, Mary Anne said, "What time?"

"When you didn't take the job. You were afraid something would happen, weren't you?"

She nodded.

"I could have told you," Beth said, gazing around the room.

"Then why didn't you?" she demanded with venom. "I tried to pry it out of you—all you did was spout about his wonderful record collection and his vivid personality."

To Tweany, Beth said: "Be a sweet—go down and get us some beer."

Disgusted, Tweany rose to his feet. "We came here to discuss the inquest."

Beth located a five-dollar bill in her purse and pushed it to him. "Go on, and don't mumble. There's a grocery store on the corner."

Sullen and grumbling, Tweany walked out of the room and down the hall. The measured vibration of his footsteps subsided.

For a protracted interval, Beth and Mary Anne sat facing each other. Finally Beth lit a cigarette, leaned back, and asked: "Did you ever find a bra you could wear?"

"No," Mary Anne said. "But it's my fault. I'm too thin."

"Don't be silly. In another couple of years you won't feel that way."

"Really?"

"Of course not. I felt the same way—everybody does. You get over it; you'll put on more weight than you care to drag around—like me."

"You look okay," Mary Anne said.

"I looked better in '48."

"Was that when it happened?"

"It was in Washington, DC. In the dead of winter. I was twenty-four years old, not much older than you. So you're not the first."

"He told me," Mary Anne said. "About the cabin on the canal."

Across from her, the heavy blonde stiffened. "Did he?"

"Why did you go with him? Did you love him?"

"No," Beth said.

"Then I don't understand it."

"I was laid," Beth said. "Like you. So let's face it: we have something in common."

"Thanks," Mary Anne said.

"You want to know the circumstances? We can compare notes."

"Go ahead," she said.

"Maybe you'll learn something." Beth put out her cigarette. "I don't know what he used with you. The job, probably. But in those days, Joe didn't have a record shop; he was in the publishing end."

"Allison and Hirsch."

"He told you that, too? In those days I—but you heard one of them. My songs."

" 'Where We Sat Down,' " Mary Anne said with aversion.

"Well, there's not a lot more to tell. I wanted them published. One day Joe showed up at the apartment. I was painting a chair in the kitchen—I remember that. He stood around and we had a couple of drinks and talked. We talked about art, music, that sort of thing."

"Get to the point."

"He had looked over my songs. But he couldn't publish them. Not enough water had gone under the bridge, he said."

"What did he mean?"

"At first I couldn't imagine. Then I saw how he was looking at me. Do you understand what I mean?"

"Yes," Mary Anne said.

"Well, that was it. He said something about not doing it there in the apartment; he had a cabin he liked to use, a few miles out of town. So nothing could interfere."

"He was using his job to get girls?"

"Joe Schilling," Beth said, "is a very kindly, very thoughtful man. I like him. But I'm realistic. He has a weakness: he wants his women."

Thoughtfully, Mary Anne said: "So you went to bed with him to get your songs published."

Beth flushed. "I—suppose you could put it that way. But I—"

"Danny was a photographer, wasn't he? I remember that night . . . you were jumping around naked and he was snapping pictures of you. I never worked it out; it didn't make sense. You used to pose for him, didn't you?"

"I was a professional model," Beth said, her cheeks blazing. "I explained it to you; I was an artist."

Suddenly Mary Anne said: "It serves Tweany right."

"What do you mean?"

"I just realized what you are." Matter-of-factly, she said, "You're a whore."

Beth stood up. Her face was pale, and little lines, like cracks, spread between her eyes and radiated from her mouth. "And what do you suppose you are? Going to bed with him to keep your job—isn't that being a whore?"

"No," she said. "That's not what happened." It had not been that at all.

"And now you've suddenly become fastidious," Beth said

rapidly. "Why? Because he's older than you? Be realistic—you're being kept in grand style, continental style. You have a lover who knows how to do it right. It sounds ideal; you're lucky."

Deep in thought, Mary Anne scarcely heard her. "Good God, and you like all that junk—all those 'White Christmas' tunes. What a joke. What a joke on Tweany."

"What is it?" Beth said. "How about letting me in on it? I think I deserve to be let in on it."

"Jesus," Mary Anne said. "It's true; it's really true. 'Where We Sat Down.' 'Sleigh Ride at Christmas.' My God, you're a *sentimental* whore."

"I see," Beth said. "Well, perhaps from your standpoint, from a cynical adolescent's standpoint—" She ceased, as the door opened and the great brooding figure of Carleton B. Tweany appeared. He carried three cans of Golden Glow beer and a can opener. "So soon?" she said briskly.

"They're warm," Tweany muttered.

"I'm feeling a little ill," Beth said, picking up her purse and moving toward the door. "Nothing serious, just a sick headache. Come along, Carleton. Please take me home."

"But we—" he began.

Beth opened the door and went out into the hall. Without looking back, she said:

"This is certainly the dirtiest building I have ever been in." Then she was gone, and, after a moment of hesitation, Tweany put down the beer cans and followed after her. The door closed, and Mary Anne was alone.

She looked around for her coat. She waited until she was sure Beth and Tweany had gone, and then she dropped the door key into her purse, slammed the door, and started down the hall.

On the front porch sat two obese colored women; they were reading movie magazines and drinking wine. Mary Anne edged past them, descended the steps to the sidewalk, and joined the midmorning crowd.

* * *

Music flowed around her, the outpourings of a symphony orchestra. She halted in the entrance, and then she walked two slow steps, studying her feet and seeing, at the same time, the pattern of the floor. She saw the suddenness of the counter, and it surprised her; she opened her mouth in an exclamation of bewilderment. Had she come that far into the store? Lifting her head, then, she saw Joseph Schilling stationed behind the counter. He was discussing records with a young man who seemed to be a student. At the front of the store, Max Figuera was sweeping the floor with a push broom, and she had walked past him.

"Hello," she said.

"Well," Max said, eyeing her grumpily. "Look who showed up."

"I'm sorry," she said.

Turning, Max said across the store to Schilling: "Look who decided to drop in for a few minutes and say hello."

Schilling glanced instantly up. He put down the record he was holding and said: "I was beginning to worry."

"I'm late," she said. "I'm sorry."

"Not too late, though." He returned to his customer.

Removing her coat, she carried it carefully downstairs. When she returned, the young man had left, and Joseph Schilling was alone at the counter. Max was outside sweeping off the sidewalk.

"I'm glad to see you," Schilling said. He was sorting records, a new Victor shipment. "Are you back for good?"

"Naturally," she answered, going behind the counter. "I'm sorry you had to call Max to come down."

"No harm done."

"You haven't had your morning coffee, have you?"

"No." His face was lined and drawn; he seemed especially ponderous today. When he bent down to rummage in a carton, he lowered himself with care.

"Are you stiff?" she asked.

"Like a steel plank."

"My fault, again," she said. "I'll check the shipment; you go back and get your coffee."

Schilling said: "I was getting the idea you weren't going to show up at all."

"Didn't I tell you I'd be in?"

"You did." He concentrated on the records. "But I wasn't positive."

"Go drink your coffee," she said. Suddenly she said: "Why is it up to me?"

He stared at her with emotion; his eyes were intense and he cleared his throat to speak.

"Go drink your coffee," she repeated, wanting him to stop confronting her. He had forced her to leave; or, at least, he had not made it possible for her to stay. She felt frightened, and now she went away from him toward the front of the store. A customer had entered and was examining a display rack.

Behind her, Joseph Schilling changed his mind and did not speak. He moved in the direction of his office. She could hear him going. So she didn't have to tell him now; she could tell him later. Or perhaps not at all.

"Yes, ma'am," she said, turning quickly to the customer. "What can I do for you?"

20

That evening after work Joseph Schilling took her to dinner at La Poblana. It was the restaurant to which they had gone that first day. It had become their special spot.

Candles spotted the gloom as they followed the waiter to their particular table. The tables were low and covered by red-checkered tablecloths. The walls—Spanish in style—were adobe; the ceiling was low, and at one end of the room was a rococo railing overgrown with elderly ivy. Beyond the railing three musicians in Spanish costume were playing dinner music.

The waiter seated Mary Anne, laid the menu open before Schilling, and departed. A low haze of cigarette and candle smoke hung over the room; the murmur of voices mixed with it, smudging out the orchestra.

"It's peaceful here," Mary Anne said.

Joseph Schilling listened to her voice, and now, as he held the menu, he looked across the table at her and tried to be sure what she was feeling. "Yes," he agreed, because the restaurant was peaceful. People came here to eat and relax and talk with one another; the light was dim and there was a low quietude, as if everything, the people, the tables, were melting and flickering with the candles, flowing together into passivity. He rested. He felt the cessation of pressure, and he joined the people around him.

But the girl was not relaxed; she said she was peaceful, but she sat like a little ivory rod, her hands on the table before her: white hands, folded, cold with the light of the candle. She was not calm; she was a hard, chipped, highly polished device that seemed to have no particular feelings; she was withdrawn, as if she had shut off everything but her wariness. She heard everything, watched him without even looking at him; but that was all.

"Want me to order?" he said. If he meant to help her, he would have to proceed sentence by sentence. He could take no risks, and he could not let himself make a mistake. He required of himself a great deal.

"Please," Mary Anne said. "You know what's good." Her voice was hollow.

"Are you hungry?" he asked.

He saw her summon a spurious heartiness. "I'd like something new. Something I've never had before."

"Something new." Elaborately he studied the menu, read all the words and all the prices.

"Something unusual: a treat."

"How about *dolma?*"

Mary Anne considered at length, as if the matter was of vast importance. And—perhaps—it was. "What's that?" she asked.

"*Dolma* is a mixture of rice and beef cooked in grape leaves . . . rolled up like tortillas."

"That sounds wonderful. I'd like that."

He ordered. "What do you want to drink?" he asked her as the waiter stood ready with his pad. He was the same waiter they had had the first night, a light-complexioned young Mexican with sideburns down to his jaw. "Some wine? Their port is excellent, as I remember."

"Just coffee."

He ordered the same for himself, and the waiter left. Sighing, he unfastened his cuffs. Mary Anne watched fixedly as he loosened his necktie. "Beth and Tweany came by looking for you," he said. "Did they find you?"

"Yes." She nodded.

He was disturbed to hear it. He had steered them off in a vague tangent, not knowing himself where she was. "Was it important?" he asked. "They looked dire."

The girl's lips moved. "The inquest."

"Oh, yes."

Mary Anne said: "What'll we do? What's going to happen to us?"

"Nothing is going to happen to us," he said, and he thought how carefully he measured his assurance. And how tangible the girl's suffering was. "The roof isn't going to fall. The ground isn't going to open up and swallow us." He paused and watched her. "Did they say anything?"

She nodded.

"They did?" He would have liked to get at them. "Is there anybody else you expect to hear from? What about your family?"

"My family—doesn't know."

"But they'd have something to say."

Mary Anne said, "Can't you think of something? You have the brains—you ought to know what to do. Are we just going to sit here and—" She gestured. "Joseph, for Christ's sake, *do* something!"

The waiter appeared then, bringing first bowls of tossed green salad and then their dinners proper. The interruption was good, and he poked and concentrated on the *dolma.* He made an issue of it. "Are these grape leaves?"

"Sorry, sir," the waiter said. "No grape leaves during the winter."

"Cabbage?"

"Yes, sir. The real thing starts coming in about April, early May." The waiter served him and Mary Anne their coffee. "Will there be anything else, sir?"

"Not right now," Schilling said.

The waiter departed, leaving the two of them alone.

"I don't mind," Mary Anne said. She ate mechanically. "This is exactly what I wanted."

"What sort of person is this Dave Gordon?" he said. "You never really told me much about him. This morning I was thinking over what you said. Max was in about the same business; he used to operate a car-rental agency, and he had a gas pump and he did a few repairs. Little odds and ends. He used to sit in his office—I'd see him on my way to work. He never seemed to do anything, just sit there in his office." He sliced a *dolma* in half. "He seemed to enjoy it. In a sense, Max retired when he was fifteen."

She seemed to hear him, and to be following what he was saying. That, at least, was encouraging. But she said nothing. He waited, then went on, speaking conversationally, without emphasis.

"In many ways I'm like that, too. I came here to retire; I wanted a quiet, stable town where I could open my record shop. For me this sleepy atmosphere is exactly right; I can open the store when I want, chat with customers, waste time. There's not really much to do or see. If I wanted to see anything, I suppose I'd have to leave."

"Where would you go?" Mary Anne asked.

"That's hard to say." Showing her his concern, he pondered; he sorted over cities, places, other lands. "Probably New York or San Francisco. I wouldn't go to Los Angeles; in spite of its size, it's really a small town. Of course, it's got informality—you can walk down the street in shorts."

"I've heard that," she said.

"And the climate is nice down there. That talk about smog is mostly propaganda. It's warm; it's spacious; the public transportation system is terrible. If you moved down there you'd have to buy a car." He sipped his coffee. "Have you ever thought of buying a car?"

"No," she said.

"Can you drive?"

"No. I never thought about it."

"Somebody told me cars are two or three hundred dollars cheaper down there. They're high, up here."

She seemed to rise briefly to the surface. "How long does it take to learn to drive?"

Schilling computed. "It varies with the person. If I were you, I'd go to a regular driving school. Two or three weeks. You can get a license then, and practice on your own. There's a lot of satisfaction in owning your own car. You're not dependent on anybody; you can get up and go when and wherever you want. Late at night . . . when the streets are deserted. Sometimes when I can't sleep, I get up and go driving. And when you drive well, it's a source of genuine personal satisfaction. Any skill like that, once you acquire it, you don't lose it."

"Cars cost a lot of money, don't they?"

"Some do. You should—if you get one, or ever think of getting one—try looking at light coupés. Say, 1951 to 1953. A Ford or a Chevrolet. A little two-door Olds would be nice; you could get the hydramatic shift. It can be plenty of fun."

"I'd have to save up," she said presently.

"What you might do is this," Schilling said. He had stopped eating and so had she. "Your biggest decision will be whether you want to marry and raise a family, or go into some profession that makes use of your highest abilities—medicine, law, one of the big commercial arts such as advertising, fashion, or even television."

"I hate clothes," she said. "I couldn't ever see dress designing." Then she said: "I was interested in medicine. I took a course in nursing in school."

"What else have you been interested in?"

"I thought I might—you'll laugh."

"No," he said.

"For a little while I thought of being a nun."

He didn't laugh. He felt deeply troubled. "Did you? Do you still feel that way?"

"A little."

"Don't withdraw," he said. "You should be active; you should be with people, doing something. Not off somewhere, isolated, in contemplation."

She nodded.

"What about art? Have you ever taken any aptitude tests?"

Mary Anne said, "They gave us tests in the twelfth grade. I had ability in—" She counted on her fingers. "I was good in manual skills: typing, and sewing, and working with objects."

"Object manipulation," he said.

"I showed ability at clerical things, like filing and handling forms, using office equipment. I didn't have much artistic ability, like painting or drawing or writing. On the IQ test I did pretty good. In sociology we had to do a paper on what we wanted to be. I chose social welfare work. I did a lot of research on it in the library. I'd like to help people . . . slums and alcoholism and crime. Race relations—I made a speech in assembly on race relations. It went over good."

"If you were in a big city," Schilling said, "you could get training in some field. You can't really get that here. You have a college, but it isn't much. Stanford, up at Palo Alto, would be another matter. Or even San Francisco City College. Or the university at Berkeley."

"Stanford costs a lot. I looked it up once, when I was about to graduate from high school. But—" Her voice clouded and diminished—"I never got anything out of school."

"You wouldn't be going to school," he said. "You'd be getting training in a particular line. It would be something to use, not just facts to know. It would be your job, your life's work."

"How would I live?"

Schilling said: "You could work in the evening. Or you could take your courses in the evening and work during the day. In a city like San Francisco, you'd have opportunity to do both. Or, here's a suggestion. You might be able to get a scholarship. What kind of grades did you get in school?"

"Mostly B's."

From his coat pocket Schilling brought his black leather notebook and fountain pen. He began to make clear, large lines on the paper. "Let's look at this in order. First," he made a note, "you should leave this town."

"Yes." She was watching the pen write; leaning forward, she followed the black lines. But still she showed no emotion, no expression; he couldn't tell how she felt. The tightness was still there; she had not let go. Perhaps, he thought, she never would.

"You'll have to live somewhere. Now, you could move in with a bunch of girls, or one girl, or at the Y, or at a boardinghouse. But I think you'd be happier if you lived by yourself, so you had a place to withdraw to. You should have some sort of a retreat, a place to hide." He put down his pen. "You need that. You have to have a way out. Isn't that so?"

"Yes," she said.

He went on writing. "You might look for a place in North Beach, around Telegraph Hill. Or you might go out toward the Marina. Or even around Fillmore. That's the colored section; bars and shops, lots of noise. Or, if you have enough money, you could rent a swank apartment in one of the new suburbs, like Stonestown. I've never seen it, but they say it's right out of the future."

"I've seen it," she said. "Some insurance company built it, the whole town. It's near the ocean."

"Now the job." He sipped his coffee. "I've been doing a lot of thinking about that. As I see it, you have two good choices. Where have you worked? Go over that again for me."

Mary Anne said: "I worked for a loan company, as a receptionist. And then I worked at a furniture factory."

"Doing what?"

"Stenographer and typist. I hated that."

"And then the phone company?"

"Yes," she said. "And then for you."

"Don't get a job in a small office. Don't get in with six other girls and a messenger. Do one of two things. Either go to work for a private professional man, a doctor or a lawyer or an architect, somebody with a modern office where there's nobody else around you, where you can be in charge. One of those small modern places, with glass and bricks and recessed lighting, a place that's clean and bright."

"What's the other?"

"Or get in with a big outfit—Shell Oil, or the Kaiser Foundation. The Bank of America, even. An organization so large that you'll have an impersonal system and room to advance. And with really specialized jobs. An outfit so big that—"

Mary Anne said: "Maybe I could work for a record store in San Francisco. Like Sherman Clay."

"Yes. You could." And he felt, then, that he had achieved something, that perhaps, after all, he could bring her permanently to the surface and help her.

If he helped her, if he meant to unravel her retreat into despair, he would have to do it now. She was watching him, looking at his notes, listening to what he had to say. He had reached her. Her eyes were not blank with fear; she was rational, attentive, a young woman following his planning.

"I am planning it out for you," he said.

"Thank you."

"Does that bother you?"

"No," she said.

"Do you want anything more to eat? Your food is cold; how about the coffee?"

Mary Anne said: "This morning I was late . . . you know what I did?"

"What did you do?"

"I rented a room. I moved my stuff from the apartment. I told the woman to go jump in the creek."

He was not really surprised. But it was not easy to hear. And he must have showed it, because Mary Anne said:

"I'll pay you the money back—the fifty dollars rent. I'm sorry, Joseph. I meant to tell you right away."

"How'd you move your stuff?"

"I called a cab. There's nothing left in the apartment; just paint and newspapers."

"Yes," he said. "The paint."

"Some is in cans; some is on the walls." The quickness entered her voice. "What do you suppose? What else?"

"Is the room nice?"

"No."

"I'm sorry," he said uneasily. "Why isn't it?"

"It's in a lousy neighborhood. I have a view of—neon signs and garbage cans. But it's just fine; it's just what I want. Twenty dollars a month, something I can pay for."

Schilling turned to a fresh page in his notebook. "What's the address?"

"I forget." Suddenly she was staring at him with the same old hard blankness.

"You must have it written down somewhere."

"Maybe so. Maybe not. I recognize it when I see it."

"Did Beth and Tweany find you there?"

"Yes."

Then, he reasoned, it was in the colored section. She had probably found it through somebody at the Wren. The owner, most likely. "How do you recognize it?"

"No," she said.

"No what?"

"I'm not going to tell you where it is."

He had made a mistake. He had pushed her too far. "Okay," he said agreeably, closing his notebook. "That's all right with me."

"And I'm leaving," she said.

"The store?"

"I'm quitting."

Rationally, he nodded. "All right. Whatever you want." He had accepted it already; it was reality and it had to be faced. "Now, what about money?"

"I have enough," she said.

"Whatever you need," Schilling said, "I'll give it to you.

Over a period of months, preferably. I'll give you enough to go where you want and get started."

She studied him wildly.

"I'll try to get you the kind of job you want," he went on. "But there I'm not worth much. I haven't been out here in years, and my contacts are bad. I know the record wholesalers in the city, though; I might be able to do something there. You could talk to Sid Hethel. Maybe he can do you a good turn. Anyhow, you should drop in to see him if you're going up there."

"I'm going somewhere else," she said.

"Back East?"

"No." She was breathing rapidly. "Don't ask me."

In spite of his care, he had brought her around to this. So he had done nothing. He could not help her after all. He could only try to manage himself so that no further harm was brought to her.

This was the moment, he realized, when the great masterstroke was needed, the solution that would clear up everything. But he did not have it. He sat only a foot from her, close enough to touch her, and he could not do a thing. All his knowledge, all his years, the understanding and wisdom he had built up in many countries, all of it was useless. This one, thin, frightened, small-town girl could not be reached.

"It's up to you," he said.

"What is?"

"I'm afraid I can't help you. I'm sorry."

"I don't want anybody to help me," she said. "I just want people to leave me alone."

"Mary Anne—" he said. Her hands rested on the table, white against the checkered tablecloth. "I love you," he said. He reached out to touch her . . .

. . . but she drew away. The man's hand, as if it were intrinsically alive, was creeping, fumbling at her. She watched, fascinated. The hand located her, and still the old man rambled on, talked and mumbled even as he took hold of her.

As his fingers closed over her flesh, Mary Anne kicked him,

kicked his ankle with the sharp toe of her shoe, and at the same moment scrambled back and up. Springing to her feet, she leaped away from the table. Her coffee cup spun and splashed over its rim, turning on its side and spurting fluid down her skirt, onto her leg.

Across from her, Joseph Schilling gave a little snuffling cry of pain; he reached down and felt for his damaged ankle. On his face was an expression of acute pain.

She stood out of reach for a moment, panting, and then she turned and walked away from the table. There was nothing in her mind, no thoughts, no tensions, only the awareness of the candles, the shape of the waiter, the watching patrons. She seemed to be in a hazy, noiseless medium that was all around her. The patrons, the curious bystanders, were transformed into fish-faces, grotesque and expanded until they filled the room. And she was cold, very cold. A numb and frigid quiet crept into her mind and lodged there; with a great effort she shook her head and saw around her, saw where she had come.

She was by a solitary chair in the corner of the restaurant, a straight-backed chair, varnished and shiny, set apart, isolated. There she seated herself, and folded her hands in her lap. She saw the entire restaurant. She was a spectator to it. And there, far off, distorted and shrunken, a wizened shape crouched at the table, was Joseph Schilling. He did not follow.

Joseph Schilling remained at the table. He did not follow her, and now he tried not to look toward her. The restaurant had returned to normal; the patrons were eating, and the waiter was circulating around. The kitchen doors swung open and shut; busboys pushed their carts out, and the clatter of dishes issued noisily.

At the entrance of the restaurant, by the cashier's desk, a young couple was preparing to leave. The man was putting on his topcoat, and his wife was before the mirror, straightening her hat. Their two children, a boy and a girl, both about nine years old, were wandering down the stairs to the parking lot.

Getting to his feet, Joseph Schilling walked over to the young couple. "Pardon me," he said. His voice sounded gruff, hoarse. "Are you driving back to town?"

The husband eyed him uncertainly. "Yes, we are."

"I wonder if you'd mind doing me a favor," he said. "See that girl sitting there in the corner?" He did not point; he made no motion. He did not even look. The husband had seen her, and he now turned slightly. "I wonder if you'd mind taking her back to town with you. I'd appreciate it."

The wife had now come over. "That girl?" she said. "You want us to take her back with us? Is she all right? She's not sick, is she?"

"No," Schilling said. "She'll be all right. Would that be too much trouble?"

"I guess not," the husband said, exchanging glances with his wife. "What do you say?"

The wife, without answering, went over to Mary Anne and, bending down, talked to her. Schilling stood with the husband, neither of them speaking. Presently Mary Anne arose and went with the man's wife out of the restaurant.

"Thanks," Schilling said.

"Not at all," the man said, and departed after his family, puzzled but compliant.

After paying the check, Joseph Schilling walked across the deserted parking lot to his Dodge. As he started it up, he looked for the young couple and their children and Mary Anne, but there was no sign of them.

Presently he drove alone back to town.

21

The young family let her off in the downtown business section, and from there she walked through the evening darkness to her own room. On the front porch the empty wine bottles of the colored women remained, a heap of glitter and smoothness near her feet as she pushed open the front door.

The hall, narrow and dank, unwound ahead of her as she walked toward her door; she fumbled in her purse, found her key, and stopped at her own door.

Somewhere in a nearby room, a radio thundered out a jump record. Outside, along the dark street, a sweeper made its complicated route among the stores and houses. She put her key in the lock, turned it, and entered.

Shapes outlined themselves in the light from the hall: the pasteboard cartons of her possessions. They had never been unpacked. She closed the door and the weak light cut off; the room dwindled into itself and became a solid surface.

She leaned against the door for a long, long time. Then, removing her coat, she walked to the bed and sat down on its edge. Springs groaned, but she could not see them; she could only hear. She pushed the covers aside, kicked off her shoes, and crept into bed. Pulling the covers over her she lay on her back, her arms at her sides, and closed her eyes.

The room was still. Below, in the street, the sweeper had gone on. The floor vibrated from the sounds of other people, other rooms, but even that was a motion rather than a sound. She could no longer see and now she could no longer hear. She lay on her back and thought of different things, good things, pleasant things, clean and friendly and peaceful things.

In her darkness nothing moved. Time passed, and the darkness departed. Sunlight streamed through the frayed curtains, into the room. Mary Anne lay on her back, her arms at her sides, and heard the sounds of cars and people outside the window. Toilets were flushed; noise vibrated among the other rooms.

She lay, staring up at the patterns of sunlight on the ceiling. She thought of many different things.

At nine o'clock in the morning Joseph Schilling opened up the record shop, found the push broom in the closet, and began sweeping the sidewalk. At nine-thirty, as he was filing records away, Max Figuera appeared in his soiled coat and trousers.

"She didn't show up?" Max said, picking his teeth with a match. "I didn't think she would."

Schilling went on working. "She won't be coming back. From now on, I'd like you to come in every day. Until Christmas, at least. Then maybe I'll go back to handling it alone."

By the counter Max paused, leaning, an expression of wisdom on his face, a knowing dryness that dropped from him like fragments of skin and cloth, bits of himself deposited wisely as he went along. "I told you so," he said.

"Did you."

"When you first looked at that girl, the one with the big knockers. The one drinking the milkshake; remember?"

"That's true," Schilling agreed, working.

"How much did she take you for?"

Schilling grunted.

Max said: "You ought to know better. You always think you can take these little babes, but they always wind up taking you.

They will; they're smart. Small-town girls, they're the worst of all. They sell it high. They know how to cash in on it. Did you get anything for your money?"

"In the back," Schilling said, "there's a Columbia shipment I haven't had time to open. Open it and check it against the invoice."

"Okay." Max roamed through the store. He chuckled, a wet snicker. "You did get *something,* didn't you? Did she pay off at *all?*"

Schilling walked to the front of the store and looked out at the people, at the stores across the street. Then, when he heard Max rooting in the shipment, he returned to his own work.

At one-thirty, while Max was out at lunch, a dark-haired boy wearing a yellow uniform entered the store. Schilling waited on a fussy gentleman at the counter, sent him into a booth, and then turned to the boy.

"Is Miss Reynolds here?" the boy asked.

Schilling said: "You're Dave Gordon?"

The boy grinned self-consciously. "I'm her fiancé."

"She's not here," Schilling said. "She doesn't work for me anymore."

"Did she quit?" The boy became agitated. "She did that a couple times before. You know where she lives? I don't even know that anymore."

"I don't know where she lives," Schilling said.

Dave Gordon loitered uncertainly. "Where do you suppose I can find out?"

"I have no idea," Schilling said. "May I suggest something?"

"Sure."

"Leave her alone."

Dave Gordon went out, bewildered, and Schilling resumed his work.

He did not expect that Dave Gordon would find her; the boy would search for a while and then go back to his gasoline station.

But there were others who might. Some of them had found her already.

That evening, after work, he remained in the store by himself, preparing a Decca Christmas order. The dark street was quiet; few cars moved by, and almost no pedestrians. He worked at the counter with a single light on, listening to one of the phonographs playing new classical releases.

At seven-thirty a sharp rap startled him; he looked up and saw Dave Gordon outlined in the doorway. The boy made a sign that he wanted to come in; he had changed from his uniform to a stiff, double-breasted suit.

Putting down his pencil, Schilling walked over and unlocked the door. "What do you want?" he asked.

"Her family doesn't know where she is either," Dave Gordon said.

"I can't help you," Schilling said. "She only worked here about a week." He started to close the door.

"We went down to that bar," Dave Gordon said. "But it isn't open yet. We're going to try later. Maybe they know."

"Who is 'we'?" Schilling asked, stopping.

"Her father's with me. He doesn't have a car of his own. I'm driving him around in the truck."

Schilling looked out and saw a yellow service truck parked at the curb a few spaces down. In the cabin of the truck was a small man, sitting quietly.

"Let's have a look at him," Schilling said. "Tell him to come over."

Dave Gordon left, stood talking at the truck for a time, and then he and Edward Reynolds returned together.

"Sorry to bother you," Ed Reynolds murmured. He was a slender, lightly built man, and Schilling saw some of the girl's lines in his face. There was a nervous tremor in his arms and hands, an involuntary spasm that might have been a suppressed abundance of energy. He was not a bad-looking man, Schilling realized. But his voice was thin, shrill and unpleasant.

"You're looking for your daughter?" Schilling said.

"That's right. Dave here says she worked for you." He blinked rapidly. "I think something's happened to her."

"Such as?"

"Well." The man gestured and blinked again. He twisted on one foot, his hands opening and closing, a shudder of movement that reached his face and put a series of muscles into activity. "See, she was hanging around with colored people down at this bar. I think there was one, murdered a white man. It was in the newspaper." His voice trailed off. "Maybe you noticed it."

This was her tormentor. Schilling saw a small man, in his middle fifties, a workingman hunched with fatigue from his day at the plant. The man, like most human beings, smelled of age and perspiration. His leather jacket was stained and crinkled and torn. He needed a shave. His glasses were too small for him, and probably the lenses were obsolete. Around one finger was a ragged strip of tape where he had cut or hurt himself. There was nothing evil or sadistic in the man. He was as Schilling had expected.

"Go on home," Schilling said, "and mind your own business. All you can give her is more trouble. She has enough of that." He closed the door and locked it.

After a conference with Mr. Reynolds, Dave Gordon again rapped on the glass. Schilling had returned to the counter. He went back and opened the door. Dave Gordon looked embarrassed and the girl's father was flushed and humble.

"Get out," Schilling said. "Get out." He slammed the door and pulled down the shade. The tapping began again almost at once. Schilling yelled through the glass: "Get out or I'll have you both arrested."

One of them mumbled something; he couldn't hear it.

"Get out!" he shouted. He unlocked the door and said: "She isn't even in town. She left. I gave her her money and she left."

"See," Dave Gordon said to the girl's father. "She went up to San Francisco. She always wanted to; I told you."

"We don't want to bother you," Ed Reynolds said doggedly.

"We just want to find her. You know where in San Francisco she went?"

"She didn't go to San Francisco," Schilling said, half-closing the door. Then he went over to the counter and resumed his work. He did not look up; he concentrated on the Decca order sheet. In the darkness Dave Gordon and Ed Reynolds came softly into the store toward him. They stopped at the counter and waited, neither of them speaking. He went on with his work.

He could feel them there, waiting for him to tell them where she was. They would remain for a while, and then they would go to the Wren, and there they would find out where she was. And then they would go to her room, the room in which she looked out at neon signs. And that would be it.

"Leave her alone," he said.

There was no answer.

Schilling put down his pencil. He opened a drawer and took out a folded piece of notepaper, which he tossed to the two of them.

"Thanks," Ed Reynolds said. They shuffled away from the counter. "We appreciate it, mister."

After they had gone, Schilling relocked the door and returned to the counter. They had carried off the scribbled address of a San Francisco record wholesaler, an outfit on Sixth Street in the Mission District. That was the best he could do for her. By ten o'clock they would be back, and then they would go to the Lazy Wren.

There was nothing else he could do for her. He could not go to her, and he could not keep others away from her. In her twenty-dollar-a-month room, not more than a mile away and perhaps as close as a few blocks, she sat as she had sat in the restaurant: her hands in her lap, her feet together, her head slightly down and forward. He could help her only by not hurting her; he could keep himself from doing her further damage, and when he had done that he had done everything.

If she were let alone she would recover. If she had always been let alone she would not need to recover. She had been trained to be afraid; she had not invented her fear by herself, had not generated it or encouraged it or asked it to grow. Probably she did not know where it came from. And certainly she did not know how to get rid of it. She needed help, but it was not as simple as that; the desire to help her was no longer enough. Once, perhaps, it would have been. But too much time had passed, too much harm had been done. She could not believe even those who were on her side. For her, nobody was on her side. Gradually she had been cut off and isolated; she had been maneuvered into a corner, and she sat there now, her hands in her lap. She had no other choice. There was no other place for her to go.

He wondered what it would have meant if her grandfather had not died, or if she had had another father, lived in a bigger town, known somebody she could trust. What sort of person would she have been? He could not believe that she would be much different. The fear, possibly, would be more deeply buried; layers of complacency would hide it, and nobody would realize it was there. He did not feel like blaming her father. He did not imagine that Carleton Tweany was responsible for letting her down, or that Dave Gordon was somehow culpable for being young and not very bright or very perceptive. The guilt—if there was any guilt—spread out and diffused itself over everybody and everything. Across the street a man had parked with his lights on to examine his rear left tire; perhaps he was the person to be considered responsible: he was as good as anybody. He, also, was a participant in the world; if he had, at some early time, made some particular gesture he had not made, or refrained from some gesture—then perhaps Mary Anne would be healthy and confident, and there would be no problem.

Perhaps, at some point in time, at some spot in the world, a moment of responsibility existed. But he doubted it. Nobody had made Mary Anne go wrong, because she had not gone wrong; she was as right as anybody else and far more right than some. But that was of no use. He could know she was right, and she could sense it in her compulsive fashion; but still no way remained by which she could live. It was not a moral issue. It was a practical issue. Someday, in a hundred years, her world might exist. It did not exist now. He thought that he saw the new outlines of it. She was not completely alone, and she had not invented it in a single-handed effort. Her world was partially shared, imperfectly communicated. The persons in it had insufficient contact; they could not communicate with one another, at least not yet. Her contacts were brief and fragmentary—a child here, a Negro there, an isolated thought that brought some response and then faded out. The fact that he felt it, even a little, proved that she was not sick, was not merely misconceived. And he was much older. He could not possibly have come closer. He loved her and others loved her, but that was of no use. What she needed was success.

Across the street the unidentified individual was kicking his tire and bending to see. Schilling watched as the man circled the car, bent once more, and then, getting behind the wheel, roared noisily off. Had a tire been low? Had he run over a bottle, a beer can? Had something of inestimable worth fallen out and been lost? The man was gone, and he would never know. Whatever the man had done, whatever he had, in secret, hatched and developed, would remain unknown.

Schilling opened the telephone book and found the number of the Lazy Wren. He dialed and listened.

"Hello," a man's voice, a Negro voice, came in his ear. "Lazy Wren Club."

He asked to talk to Paul Nitz. Eventually Nitz was at the phone.

"Who was that who answered?" Schilling asked.

"Taft Eaton. He owns the place. Who's this?" Nitz sounded dulled. "I have to go play a set."

"Ask him where Mary Anne Reynolds is," Schilling said. "He found her a place."

"What place?"

"Ask him," Schilling said. He hung up. When he felt better, he returned to his work.

Beyond the locked door, individuals passed. He heard the sound of their shoes against the pavement but he did not look up. He put new records on in the listening booth; he sharpened his pencil; he sealed up the Decca order sheet in an envelope and started on the Capitol order sheet.

The darkness hung over her, modified by the scatter of light from the hall. When she turned her head she saw that the hall door was open. She had not locked it; there seemed to be no point. In the dim light a figure was outlined, a man's figure.

"It didn't take you long," she said.

The man entered the room. But it was not Joseph Schilling.

"Oh," she said, startled, as the opaque form materialized close beside the bed. "It's you. Did—Tweany tell you?"

"No," Paul Nitz said, and sat down on the bed beside her. After a moment he reached out and stroked her hair back from her forehead. "I found out at the Wren, from Eaton. This is sure a ratty-looking dump."

"When did you find out?"

"Just now. I just went down there, to start work for the evening."

"I'm not in very good shape," she said.

"You were running," Nitz said. "And you ran right into yourself. You weren't even looking where you were going . . . you were just going, trying to get away. That's all."

"Nuts to you," she said feebly.

"But I'm right."

"Okay, you're right."

Nitz grinned. "I'm glad I got to you."

"So am I. It's about time."

"I wanted you to leave, that night at your apartment. I was sick of that painting."

"Me too," she said. After a moment she asked: "Do me a favor?"

"Anything you want."

"You could go get me my cigarettes."

"Where are they?" He stood up.

"In my purse, on the dresser. If it's not too much trouble."

"How far's the dresser?"

"You can see it. There's only this one room—is that too far?"

A period passed in which she lay listening to the noise of Paul Nitz fumbling around in the dark. Then he was back.

"Thanks," she said as he lit a cigarette for her and placed it between her lips. "Well, it's been hectic. A hectic week."

"How do you feel?"

"Not too good," she said. "But I think I'll be okay. It'll take a while."

"Lie there and rest."

"Yes," she said gratefully.

"I'll turn on some heat." He found the small gas heater and lit it. Blue flames became visible; the fire hissed and sizzled in the darkness of the room.

"I can't see him again," Mary Anne said.

"All right," Nitz said. "You don't have to worry. I'll take care of you until you're back on your feet, and then you can take off, wherever you want."

"Thanks. I appreciate it."

He shrugged. "You took care of me once."

"When?" She had no memory of it.

"That night when I passed out and hit my head on the toilet. And you sat down with me on the couch and held me in your lap." He smiled a little, awkwardly.

"Yes," she said, remembering. "In some ways we had a lot of fun, that night. Lemming . . . I wonder what became of him. That was such a strange night."

"I took some time off from the Wren," Nitz said. "I don't have to go back for almost two weeks. A sort of premature Christmas vacation."

"With pay?"

"Well, partially."

"You shouldn't have to do that."

"Now we can go places."

Mary Anne considered. "Would you really take me places?"

"Sure. Wherever you want."

"Because," she said earnestly, "there're a lot of places I want to see. We can do a lot of things . . . could we go up to San Francisco?"

"When you feel like it."

"We can ride on the ferry. Can we do that?"

"Absolutely. There's one that goes to Oakland."

With fervor she said: "I want to visit some of those little restaurants out in North Beach. Have you ever been there?"

"Plenty of times. I'll take you to the Hangover Club to hear Kid Ory."

"That would be wonderful. And we can go out to Playland . . . to the funhouse. We can go down the slides. Would you like that?"

"Sure," he agreed.

"Jesus." She reached up and hugged him. "You're a kid."

"So are you," Nitz answered.

"I am," she said. And then she thought of Joseph Schilling. And, presently, snarling with pain and despair, she clutched the man beside her, crying: "What the hell am I going to do? Answer me, Paul! How can I live like this?"

"You can't," he said.

"It was bad enough before. I knew something was wrong—but now it's worse. I wish I hadn't gone in there; Christ, if only I hadn't gone in there that day." But it wasn't true, because she was glad she had found the store. "It's still there," she said brokenly. "The store. Joseph Schilling. They're both there. In a way."

In a way, but it was a dead shell. There was nothing inside. She lay in the darkness, her arm around Nitz's neck, cigarette between her fingers, sobbing. It had come and gone, and left her by herself. But she didn't want to be by herself.

"I can't stand it!" she shouted. She hurled her cigarette across the room; it struck the far wall and dropped to the rug, a little flicker of red light. "I'm not going to die here in this rat hole."

Nitz went over and put out the cigarette. "No," he said, coming back. He gathered her up in his arms, and the bedcovers also, and carried her to the door. "Here we go," he said, holding her against him. He carried her down the hall and down the stairs; he carried her past the closed-up doors and their blaring sounds, past Mrs. Lessley the landlady, who peered out, suspicious and wary-eyed and hostile. He carried her down the front steps and along the night sidewalk, among the people wandering here and there in droves and in couples among the stores and gas stations and drive-ins and hotels and bars and drugstores. He carried her through the slums, through the business district, past neon signs and cafés and the office of the *Leader,* past the modern little shops of Pacific Park. Holding her tightly against him, he carried her to his own room.

22

Old men sat in the park, old men in rows covering the benches with their coats and newspapers.

Across the grass a scatter of yellow leaves broke under the feet of people. Two children, boys in jeans, tramped with brown paper bags—their lunches—toward the rim of the park. The old men read their *L'Italia* and accepted the autumn sun. Beyond the park the Catholic church was tall, and it cast its shadow. A handful of pigeons strode through the gravel around the drinking fountain, seeking remnants of food. The San Francisco sky was a thin, brittle blue. Turning on her bench, Mary Anne saw the slope of Telegraph Hill and the tower at its top: Coit Tower, like a pre-Christian column.

A bus, green and large, went along Columbus Avenue and was lost behind offices. On Mary Anne's lap her baby stirred, reached out his arms. She drew him back. He had no need for a bus.

He had no need of anything: he was plump and wrapped in warm clothes, clean and cared-for. He dozed. Against his mother he rested and heard the clang of the city. Above and around him, Mary Anne was his protection.

On the park bench with her baby she was young and fresh. She wore a long white smock and low-heeled slippers, and her brown hair, still short, tangled over her ears and fringed her forehead. Earrings, copper and hooped, glinted. Her ankles, pale, bare, were lean above her slippers. Once she took a cigarette from her pocket and lit it with her lighter.

The day was peaceful. Overhead a gull wheeled. Now and then the gull croaked like the sound of dry ropes and wood. Presently a kindly middle-aged lady in a black coat came along the path and seated herself on the bench facing Mary Anne.

Mary Anne picked up a paperbound book that she had brought with her, that Paul wanted her to read. She examined the cover, turned it over, and then she put it down. She did not feel like reading or doing anything at all; she was content to sit. It was three o'clock in the afternoon, and in an hour Paul would appear. She met him here; she liked to meet him in the park.

On the opposite bench the kindly middle-aged lady leaned forward, and, with a smile, said: "What a healthy little fellow."

Mary Anne raised the baby up against her. "This is my son."

"What is his name?"

"Paul. He's eleven months old."

"What a nice name," the kindly middle-aged lady said. She waved at the baby and pantomimed faces.

"His father's name is Paul," Mary Anne said. Looking down, she examined the baby's collar, smoothed the cotton fabric. "I have seven other children. This is the youngest. The oldest is thirteen."

"Good heavens," the kindly middle-aged lady said, amazed.

"I'm just kidding," Mary Anne said. But someday it would be true; she would have a whole houseful of sons, big sons, strong and noisy sons. "He can't talk yet. He likes to listen to music. His father is a musician."

The kindly middle-aged lady nodded sagely.

"His father," Mary Anne said, "is a student in the afternoon, and in the evening he plays piano at the Club Presto on Union Street. Bop piano. There're five men in the combo."

"Music," the kindly middle-aged lady said. "I believe I

haven't heard any music in the last few years, not since the war, that can compare to Richard Tauber."

"That's square," Mary Anne said, playing with the baby's hand. "Isn't it, Paul?"

"And Jeanette MacDonald," the kindly middle-aged lady said nostalgically. "I'll never forget her and Nelson Eddy in *Maytime*. That was such a lovely movie. I cried at the ending; I still cry at it, when I think about it."

"Go cry somewhere else," Mary Anne said, joggling her son up and down on her knee.

The kindly middle-aged lady gathered up her purse and departed. Mary Anne smiled down at Paul, and he gurgled and frothed.

Beyond the park the rise of houses glinted in the afternoon sun. Cars, dark specks, crept up the narrow streets, up the hill between the houses. At Mary Anne's feet a pigeon wandered, pecking at random.

"See the big bird?" Mary Anne said softly to her son. "Nice pigeon. Dinner for one. How about a pigeon pie? Come here, pigeon. Feed the poor."

She nudged at the pigeon with her toe and it flapped away. Almost at once it was back, again traveling in an aimless circle. Mary Anne wondered what it found to eat, and what it was thinking. She wondered where it lived and who took care of it, if anybody.

"Are you a lady?" she asked the pigeon. "Or a man?"

She sat on the park bench with her son, holding him against her and watching the pigeons and the old men and the children. She was very happy. She watched people appear and go; she saw the leaves fall from the autumn trees and the grass glow with dampness. She saw the whole cycle of life: she saw the children grow old and become bent little men reading *L'Italia* and she saw them reborn in the arms of women. And she and her son remained unchanged, outside the birth and decay that went on around her.

They could not be touched. They were safe. She saw the sun go out and return, and she was not frightened.

She wondered where she had got this peacefulness. It had come with her baby; but where had he come from? She did not completely understand him. He was a mystery, a separation of herself, and he was her husband held tight in her arms. Perhaps he had come to her on the wind. The warm spring wind had plucked at her and brought her this, had filled her up with permanent life. Had carried off the emptiness.

Mary Anne and her son watched the world change around them, watched everything that had ever happened and would ever happen. And after that they got up and went to the end of the park. There they waited, because the hour was up and it was time to wait.

People hurried along Columbus Avenue, and Mary Anne shaded her eyes with her hand to see if he was coming. She held the baby across her shoulder, and the people moved by her on both sides. Presently she saw a gaunt, ambling shape making its way along, hands in its pockets, coat flapping, hair long and umcombed.

"There he is," she said to her son. "You're facing the wrong way." She turned him around to see. "See?"

"You sure look good," Paul Nitz said, arriving shyly.

"You don't; you look like a bum." She kissed him. "Let's go eat. Did you shop?"

"We can shop on the way home," he said.

"Don't you have any money?"

As they walked he searched his coat pockets, bringing up ticket stubs, paper clips, pencils, folded notes. "I guess I gave it to you." He squinted in the glare of the sidewalk. "To one of you, anyhow."

Lagging behind him, Mary Anne strolled along, hugging her son and looking into store windows, as Paul Nitz searched the rest of his pockets. Once she yawned. Once she stopped to peer at a display of imported Scottish pipes and then a shelf of harmonicas. Once she caught up with her husband and leaned against him while the three of them waited for the streetlight to change.

"Tired?" he asked.

"Sleepy. Would you look good smoking a pipe?"

"I'd look like the wrath of God," he answered.

The light changed and, with the other people, they crossed.